To John -
The love of my life

ACKNOWLEDGMENTS

Many people, with or without knowing, have helped this story come to fruition. Several people have helped in special part, and I would like to take a moment to express my gratitude. John Spencer, Erin Rychalsky, Bonnie Ursprung, and Amanda Whitwell, between your willingness to share your opinions and tolerance of my random questions, from the bottom of my heart, thank you. This book wouldn't be what it is without you.

This story wouldn't have happened at all had it not been for my dedicated readers of The Boomerang Effect, who have come to me and said, "What happened to (insert name here)? I want to know!" Thank you for your persistence. For every one reader who asks the question, fifty others are quietly nodding in support. Your tireless questions have brought this sequel into existence.

As always, any errors or omissions are mine alone; even knowing the facts doesn't always change the way I write. I willfully throw rules out the window, and live with the consequences of creative license. With that in mind, I give you *Ripples of the Boomerang*. Enjoy!

PROLOGUE

"I'm coming!" I tried to yell, but my voice wouldn't work, nothing came out. Maybe it was because I was floating above the ground, outside of myself, watching over my own shoulder, unable to help even myself.

It shouldn't be this hard to get to her, what's wrong with my legs? I looked down. There was nothing there, yet she, I, my body self, couldn't get my legs to go any faster—it felt like waist-deep water was rushing, shoving, tumbling by, and pushing me back as it passed. The harder I tried, the more solid it became.

"Katy, I'm coming!"

I/we turned the corner and across the street, there in the dark, dank alley, was Katy. She was screaming, and I/we could finally see why—they were attacking her, holding her down, beating her, hitting her, kicking her, throwing her around like a rag doll. 'They' were two male figures and their bodies were shifting and growing, pulsing, with every blow.

My body self held out her hand, my ghost self held out both. "Hang on, Katy, I'm trying!"

Our eyes met, mine and Katy's. The raw terror in hers struck a new fear in my soul and my need to help her instantly increased tenfold.

The horror continued for what seemed like days, my not being able to move quickly, not able to get to her, to make them stop, to help.

The passers-by weren't stopping. They weren't helping, they weren't hearing. I/we yelled at them, tried to get their attention. When they did finally look, I saw it was the cop, Webster, and the lawyer, Hanson. They weren't helping; they weren't going to help anyone, ever. They hurt her last time the same way they were hurting her again, by not doing anything.

They turned their heads toward me, opened their mouths wide, wider. With an audible crack their jaws unhinged and maniacal laughter rolled out, black and sinewy, shifting and writhing, undulating in a death dance. Their heads grew and grew, their mouths bigger and wider, until my/our view of Katy, as well as everything else, was blocked.

Every streetlight exploded at once, raining down shards of angry glass and Katy's screams were cut off abruptly. Silence and darkness wrapped around us like hot tar. I couldn't hear, I couldn't see. I had no way of knowing if it was just me or if, on the other side of the tar, the horror continued for Katy.

"Stop! I need to get to her!"

~~*~*~*

Tom had spent the last ten nights at the hospital. The chair they'd moved into her room for him was uncomfortable, but better than nothing. He was dozing off in the chair, his hand resting on her arm, when he felt it. His eyes flew open and he bolted upright. She twitched again.

"Nurse. NURSE," Tom bellowed even as he pounded the "call" button repeatedly. He didn't want to take his hand or his eyes off her; he wanted her to know he was right there waiting for her.

There wasn't any conclusive medical data as to whether coma patients could see or hear while they were under, but Tom wasn't taking any chances. This much he'd learned through extensive research over the last several years. He wanted to be right there if she could hear, or feel, what was happening outside of her body.

"NURSE…"

What felt like hours was really only seconds.

Tom rubbed her arms with his hands. "Come on, Sweetie, you can do it. I'm right here. Come back."

Gabrielle, the night nurse, ran in and went straight to the patient. She'd been on the job for seven years and knew how to do it and do it well.

Without looking at her, he said, "She moved her arm twice. She's waking up, get the doctor!"

"Stand back, please." Her tone of voice was kind but firm, and left no room for argument. As she began her examination, a second nurse rushed in.

"Nancy, would you please page Dr. Alister and ask him to come in," Gabrielle said quietly.

The second nurse left quickly.

Tom wanted to touch her again. *I know it would help, she needs to know I'm here.* Without waiting for permission he slipped around the back side of the bed and wrapped her hand in his, holding on and rubbing hers gently between his. He didn't know how much more he could take, and if Andy was going to come out, he would be damned sure to do everything he could to help her.

~~*~*~*

Andy's subconscious was shoving at her, pushing her toward … no, not toward, away from the light. It wasn't time. *What isn't it time for?* She didn't understand, but she went anyway. The moment before she walked through that door she looked back over her shoulder. *No…could it be? KATY!* The last thing she remembered before falling through the floor on the other side of the door was Katy watching her, waving, and shaking her head. Was she saying she was sad to see Andy go, or was it her voice saying it wasn't time?

The falling turned into floating. She floated above her own body, saw Tom and a nurse by her side. Commotion and tension filled the room. An invisible tether tugged and pulled at her. She fought it and tried to turn back, looked to see if Katy was still there, needed to ask her when she was coming home. Tom would want to know that, too.

The pull increased. She was too weak to ignore it; either that, or she was too close to her body. The force, like the moon's control over the tides, dragged her against her will.

He held her hand, talked to her. The nurse checked the machines... no, she pushed a hypodermic needle into the IV. A clear liquid flowed through the tube, into her body.

Andy snapped back into her body, felt her soul and body reconnect, forced back into living. Confused, she didn't know whether she wanted to be here or back there with Katy. If she could have talked to her, brought her back, made her understand she was needed here.

The light was there again, only this time on the other side of her eyelids. She didn't want to open her eyes, knew without a doubt that whatever was waiting would hurt...

CHAPTER ONE

Andy was different, somehow, after waking from the coma: Withdrawn, sullen, and at times, downright surly. Her natural inner beauty was tamped down, held captive by her current condition. She was still beautiful to him, with her past-the-shoulder brown hair and cute button nose. But her eyes, so expressive before the accident, were now dull and lacked the vitality that once overflowed. Tom wasn't sure what to do to help her; he only knew he had to keep trying. It's all that was left.

"Do you want to talk about it?" The only light in the room was the glow from the alarm clock. Three thirty-three a.m. The concern in Tom's voice brought her back from the edge quicker than anything else could.

Her breathing was still ragged, but her heart rate was slowing down. The fear slid off her and slunk back into the dark night to lie in wait for the next time.

"It was a Katy nightmare again. I could hear her screaming, but I couldn't get to her. I was watching from above myself, and my body wasn't working, it was like trying to walk through water or pudding or something. I pushed on and finally got to where I could see her, and they were beating her, and beating her, and I couldn't stop them. Then the cop that was on her case and that lawyer that was supposed to put those guys in prison, Officer Webster and what's his name, that bastard attorney, Bruce Hanson, were walking

by and they looked at me and their heads came apart and they
laughed and the tar came…"

Katy, Tom's sister, while walking home from after-school band
practice six and a half years ago, had been attacked in an alley by
two classmates. When an older couple out for a stroll happened by
and saw the two males leave the alley in a hurry, they looked in to
see what had been going on and saw her there. They'd called the
police and told them to send an ambulance. Afterward, they'd
worked with a sketch artist to render illustrations of those men, and
from those drawings the police were able to identify the persons as
Darnell Taylor and Jerome Johnson. Katy was already in a coma by
the time she'd arrived at the hospital, and had remained in a coma
ever since.

The bitch of it for Andy was the guilt. She and Katy were best
friends. They were both in band and at that same practice. Their
moms took turns picking both of the girls up, and it was Andy's
mom's turn to get them. The plan had been for Katy to ride home
with Andy when her mom got there. Practice let out a few minutes
early. It was snowing, and Katy loved the snow. She'd decided to
walk home instead. Andy told her to wait, but Katy waved and went
anyway. Andy felt that if she'd have tried harder to get Katy to stay
and wait for her mom, she'd be with them today instead of lying in
that hospital bed in a coma, her life on hold.

Tom continued to hold her. "Those men are all dead now. None
of them can hurt Katy anymore, and they can't hurt you either."

"I'm sorry I woke you. I wish I could control it. I know they're
dead, but they're still monsters in my nightmares." The truth was,
the reason they were dead was because of Andy. The computer virus
she'd created had done its job well.

Tom didn't know about the virus, or about the flash drive Andy
had kept it on or that she'd lost the flash drive sometime between
leaving the house and waking up in the hospital. She'd been in her
wedding dress and on her way to the church to marry him when

she'd been struck by a car and left for dead.

Almost every night since she'd come out of the coma the nightmares had plagued her. She couldn't be sure if it was a by-product of the time she'd spent comatose after the accident, or if seeing Katy right before she woke up had something to do with it. She hadn't told Tom yet about the coming-out memory…was still trying to decide if it had really happened at all or if it was a combination of medical treatment and wishful thinking. It sure felt real, though. She missed her best friend so much, it was great to see her; if only she'd had more time to talk to Katy before she'd tumbled and woken up, she could have asked her what was happening to her, why she was still in the in-between, if there was a reason she stayed there. She could have figured out what she could do or say to convince her to wake up and come back. The sooner, the better; she was missed and very much loved, and the in-between isn't a permanent answer to anything.

CHAPTER TWO

Karen studied her reflection in the mirror. She'd read somewhere once that keeping her hair the same length, color and style gave the television viewers a sense of stability, so that's what she did. Hers was shoulder length, brown, and straight as a board. Luckily her hair didn't have curl to start with—a welcome genetic gift from her mother—or that would require a higher level of maintenance. The slight crook in her nose, not genetic but man-made, was her daily reminder to be careful, be aware, and be prepared.

Adding lipstick to her full lips was a mandatory finishing touch, as well; though if it were up to her she'd forego it entirely. If you weren't careful it got on your teeth, smeared all over the cup when you tried to drink your coffee, and just tasted nasty.

Unlike before "the incident"—as she referred to the night she'd shot the person who had tried to rob her in the alley—she gazed into her own eyes last. The word that came to mind was "haunted." That look was something she was trying to shake, but hadn't quite gotten rid of yet. Karen wondered idly if her eyes looked the same now to her viewers as they had before, or if it were only obvious to her that they had changed.

There were so many questions left unanswered. She'd thought they would come naturally over time, as her subconscious determined she was ready to handle the details. It had been seventeen months now since her week spent in the coma, and all she remembered was walking into that alley, intending to cut through and save herself some time, hearing a voice behind her that sent the icy fingers of dread skittering up her spine, getting the worst headache she'd ever had in her life, and then waking up in the hospital. No matter how hard she tried, she couldn't remember anything else.

Karen pushed the thought from her mind. She didn't have the luxury of dwelling on things she had no control over, not now. She flashed her award-winning smile, checked her teeth for lipstick, tugged the hem of her blazer down and turned the light off as she left the bathroom. It was time to get her butt to work.

~~*~*~*

"Karen Fielding," she said absently when she picked up the ringing phone.

"Hi there, I missed you this morning."

The sexy voice sent a punch of heat straight through her. It still embarrassed her that her cheeks flushed every time Ben called her at work, and she hoped no one was paying any attention. Her desk was in a large open room full of desks, where all the reporters sat to get their copy ready for the news. A good television reporter could write copy under pressure while tuning out the constant background chatter at the same time. That didn't mean they weren't listening to what was going on around them. Being nosy was part of the job. She was close-mouthed about her private life, and that made the other reporters want to know that much more.

There weren't many people in the room at the moment, luckily, and none close enough to eavesdrop. Leaning forward in her chair, hovering with a pencil over her note pad, she tilted her head down so that her hair would hide her face. If anyone looked over, she would appear to be hard at work.

"Hi, yourself. I had an early meeting. Right after it wrapped up, Bob sent me out to cover the conference that had just been called by the Chief of Police."

Bob Barnett was the Station Manager. He was getting closer to retirement every day; though by the way he acted you couldn't tell. He ran the station and everyone in it with an iron grip. He was tough but fair, and Karen admired his dedication and drive. He'd acknowledged the job she did for him as well as the station by putting her on the cop beat after she proved herself with the Michael Carion story the day he'd tried to escape from the enclosed walkway between the courthouse and the jail a year and a half ago.

That story broke a few days before her incident. Hmmm. That *was* right around the same time, wasn't it? Karen tapped her pencil against her desk blotter, lost in thought.

"Are you still there?" Ben asked.

"Ah, yes, sorry, got sidetracked for a minute there. That happens more and more these days."

Ben's smile was evident in his voice. "One of the many things I love about you. So, what time do you think you'll be here tonight? I've got some steaks to throw on the grill, and potatoes to bake. We can even have a salad if you want."

"As far as I know, I don't have anything that will keep me late. Let's plan on six o'clock, but don't start the steaks before I get there. You know how crazy this place gets if something breaks."

"I'll look forward to seeing you then. Let me know if something gets in the way." He was so easygoing; one of the things *she* loved about *him*.

"Will do. See you tonight."

"Can't wait."

Karen hung up the phone and noticed she'd been doodling hearts on her note pad. Ripping out the page, she folded it over and started to throw it away. Thinking twice, she tucked it in her pocket. It wouldn't do to have a co-worker, *any* co-worker, find that. She'd never live it down.

~~*~*~*

Karen could smell the charcoal burning as she walked up onto the porch. He'd already started the grill. Knowing he wouldn't leave it unattended, she changed direction and followed the wraparound porch to the back where she knew he'd be watching the flames. She was right. He was standing there, king of the backyard barbeque, in a pair of khaki knee-length shorts and a dark blue t-shirt, holding a water bottle to squirt the flames with in case they got out of hand.

They'd been introduced the winter before last by her camera man, Keith. Ben and Keith had gone to school together and Ben had talked Keith into the introduction. Karen hadn't been too keen on the idea at first; dating was outside her comfort zone.

She didn't like most men, didn't trust even more than that, and hated the thought of letting one get close enough to her to hurt her again. Self-consciously she reached up and touched her nose.

But Ben had been sweet and kind and, most of all, persistent. Surprising even herself, she'd relented and agreed to one date. It was the night of that date "the incident" happened.

When she came out of the coma, Ben had been right there by her bedside. He'd taken care of her after she'd been released, and she found herself caring for him before she could stop herself. They'd been dating ever since.

He turned from the grill and saw her standing there watching him. He pulled his sunglasses up, perched them on top of his head and smiled. His baby blue eyes twinkled as he reached his hand out to her, inviting her to join him. "Hey, you…"

Her heart skipped a beat, and she returned his smile as she walked over to him. "Hey yourself…"

He wrapped his arm around her and gave her a kiss. "I'm glad you're here. I was just trying to decide if we should have corn on the cob or asparagus with our steaks. What do you think?"

She put a finger to her mouth, miming deep thought. "I think, and this is only my opinion, that a steak and baked potato wouldn't be complete without corn on the cob." Reaching up she brushed his bangs out of his eyes. "You need a haircut."

"I know, I keep meaning to stop for one. It's not high on my to-do list."

The flames shot up from the grill and he gave them a little squirt. The charcoal sizzled, letting loose a plume of white smoke.

"You know, if you'd clean that grate before you put it back over the charcoal there wouldn't be any flames to worry about." She muttered, watching the smoke rise and curl.

"I *am* cleaning the grate, the man's way. With fire."

Karen shook her head and smiled. "What can I do to help?"

"This grill looks almost ready. Can you bring the plate of steaks out for me?" He winked at her and as she turned to go in the house, swatted her on the rear. "Thanks, babe."

She opened the sliding glass door and stepped into the kitchen. Pale yellow walls kept the room bright and happy, offsetting the dark wood of the antique dining room table and chairs standing near the bay window to her left, overlooking the backyard. To her right was the sink, directly below another window that looked out on the same view. Past that, on the far wall was the door leading to the garage, next to that the pantry, and on the wall backing the living room stood the refrigerator and stove. Her favorite part was the stone island in the middle. She'd never seen a rock that big, let alone functional in the middle of a room.

Karen opened the fridge and reached for the platter. He'd already known she would choose corn; there were two ears prepped and ready on the plate with the steaks. Chilling in the door was a bottle of Pinot Grigio. He'd thought of everything. She was smiling as she closed the door and turned. She bobbled the plate and almost dumped the contents on Ben, who had apparently followed her in.

"Oh! You startled me. You're so quie—"

He caught the plate, took it and set it on the counter and cut her off with a kiss. He pressed his body to hers, fitting them together like a puzzle. He pinned her between himself and the counter and, tilting his head, deepened the kiss. His hands roamed over her back before he tangled them in her hair and held her.

Heat shot through her. Nothing existed except them, him, his hands, his body, his tongue on hers. She wrapped her leg around his, giving herself completely to the moment.

He broke the kiss. Nuzzling her neck, he murmured, "I missed you this morning. Just wanted you to know what you missed, too." Giving her butt a squeeze, he backed away and flashed a smile, picked up the steak plate and headed back outside.

She took a minute to catch her breath. She'd never felt like this about anyone before, and it scared the hell out of her. Being in control was important to her, and he could take that away from her so easily. *Okay, alright, so you give it to him. So what?* She thought. *You don't have to be in control every single minute of every day, not when you've got someone who is willing to take care of you when you're out of control.*

The question she struggled with was whether she trusted him unconditionally. Trust like that left you open. It led to getting hurt. She wanted to trust him, wanted to believe in the fairy tale...

She straightened up. *When did he unhook my bra?*

~~*~*~*

The sun was still up, but he'd lit candles on the table anyway. She thought it was sweet that he remembered the little things she enjoyed, like candles at dinner.

Conversation was non-existent until dinner was finished. The silence was comfortable; neither felt the need to fill it with words while they ate. When they'd finished, Karen took the plates to the sink. "That was good. I'm full as a tick."

"Best compliment I've had all day." He picked up his wine and sipped while he watched her scrape the scraps into the garbage disposal and rinse off the dishes. She'd been quieter than usual while they prepared their meal, and she seemed to be somewhere else again.

"Everything okay?"

She continued loading the dishwasher. "Sure, fine."

"Karen."

"I've just had something serious on my brain all day that I haven't been able to shake."

"Want to tell me about it?"

She finished stacking the dishes in the dishwasher before she answered. "Now's as good a time as any, I guess." As she turned back toward him he stood and picked up her glass, met her halfway and handed it to her.

"Let's sit on the deck." Leading the way, she opened the door and chose the chairs instead of their normal seat on the porch swing. Needing a little space, not wanting to be too close to him while she arranged her thoughts and figured out how to say what she found she really did want to talk to him about.

On the inside his gut clenched just a little bit. In his experience women didn't have something serious to talk about that required distance from him unless it was bad news. On the outside he stayed calm, hoping he seemed to understand she needed space. He sat in the other chair, leaving it where it was instead of pulling it closer, though it went against everything he wanted to do.

She didn't see the squirrel run up the tree or the blue jay flit from branch to branch of the cedar tree as she stared off across the ten acres that was his backyard. Instead, she saw the pieces her memory retained of the incident surrounded by an overwhelming blank space with no memory.

"I thought..."

He drank his wine and waited, knowing she would get there quicker if he didn't question her. He didn't want to hear, feared she was about to say… her voice broke through his train of thought.

"I thought I'd remember things long before now. I've tried trying to remember, tried not thinking about it, tried talking to a therapist. Nothing has worked to fill in the blanks. I've got this huge hole in my memory, and I don't know how to get it back. I can handle whatever should be there, it happened, and somewhere in my brain is the memory. I just can't access it."

He felt a weight lift off of his chest. Relieved, he reached in his pocket and ran his thumb over the ring he'd begun to carry with him. A slight frown creased his face. *With the first thought being something bad was coming when she needed to talk even after she said everything was fine, I'm obviously not ready. Better put the ring back in the safe for now. No need to rush, there's plenty of time. What the hell is wrong with me? I'm such a dumbass… it's not always about me. This is Karen, not the psycho ex.*

Ben returned to the present, and to Karen. He thought out loud. "Okay. Have you tried putting pen to paper, writing down what you do remember?"

She nodded. "Yes, I have. I've written it in a list as well as a narrative." Perhaps she should rewrite everything she could remember, from the third-person point of view. Maybe that would help, writing as if she were reporting it. She could try that.

"You could always research the kid you shot. Maybe knowing more about him would back you through the door into your own memory."

The only way they'd ever referred to the man in the alley who'd beaten her down and tried to rob her was as "the kid." From the first time she'd spoken of what had happened, the only way she could talk about him was through depersonalization. Ben went along with it; he figured she was still traumatized by the whole event and her subconscious needed time. He'd be the first to admit that he was curious as to what she'd find out and what memories that might trigger.

Karen looked at him for the first time since they'd moved outside. "Research the kid." She turned her head, looked back out over the yard. *Why didn't I think of that?*

She was quiet for a long minute, thinking it through. "Yes, I'll do that. Surely knowing something about him will help me understand why he did what he did, and maybe I'll be able to understand what really happened out there."

Having made that decision she felt instantly better. Formulating a plan of action put her back in control, right where she liked to be. Scooting her chair closer to his, she reached for his hand and intertwined their fingers.

It felt fantastic to him. The woman he loved, reaching for his hand. With one more mental kick, he decided to keep the ring close by, in case the perfect moment presented itself.

CHAPTER THREE

Jumping the tracks, the train bore down on them, following her as she followed Katy, running down the dirt road, gaining momentum as Katy cut off and she followed into the woods, the train, smashing trees like toothpicks, close enough that she could feel the heat from the engine licking at her scalp, her back, her legs...

Andy jerked awake, her heart racing. She was drenched in sweat, a scream strangling in her throat.

Tom's bedside lamp was on, glowing softly behind him. The shadows fell across his face, though she could see well him enough to register the worry creasing his brow.

"Andy, honey, wake up," Tom gently rubbed her arms, brushed the tears from her cheeks. "There you are, you're okay, I've got you now." He wrapped his arms around her and held her while her body shook.

Tom stroked her hair, kissed her head, murmured reassuring words while she cried herself out.

Blinking the tears away, the last shreds of the nightmare let go of her mind. She looked around and took in her surroundings to convince herself she was really awake and in her own bed. Directly across the room were the ivory lace curtains her mother had given her, hanging across the window and keeping the dark at bay; the tan overstuffed chair that held the cream- and red-striped throw pillows for the bed; the tiny end table with the framed picture of Tom's parents.

Keep scanning, she told herself, *nightmares are tricky.* Then there was the door to the hallway, open, the way they always left it. The bathroom door was next, also open, with the night light just inside. The closet, door closed. Or was it almost closed? Sometimes Andy's mind played tricks on her. She squinted her eyes. No, the door was really closed. She took a deep breath, blew it out.

"Oh, God, Tom, it was horrible. This time it was a train, I couldn't get off the tracks, and when I finally did, it followed us, faster and faster, until..." Andy shuddered.

Tom held her and rubbed her arms and back.

She hadn't realized until now that her hand was fisted in his t-shirt he habitually wore to bed. Unclenching her fingers, she smoothed his shirt.

The accident wasn't only in her nightmare; it was in her waking life. Six weeks ago she'd been on her way to marry Tom, walking from her car to the church, when a car struck her. Among other injuries, a vertebra in her spine had been cracked causing swelling in her chest. The swelling blocked her breathing and the doctors had to intubate. They'd put her in a medically-induced coma until the swelling went down enough for her to breathe on her own again.

When she'd come out of the coma, she was told that her spine would heal on its own. She'd tried to sit up, and that's when she realized she couldn't feel her legs.

The doctors ran tests. They couldn't find any reason why she couldn't walk; there was nothing physically wrong with her.

Not only had the accident taken her ability to walk, it had taken the only copy of the virus from her. The flash drive on which it resided had been in her clutch, and wasn't among her belongings given back to her when she'd checked out of the hospital. She still didn't know where the flash drive was and she needed to find it. That kind of thing in the wrong hands....

"Why don't we get your chair and you can clean up a little while

I change the sheets."

For the first time, Andy looked down and realized the bed and her pillow were soaked with sweat. She scooted herself to a better sitting position, pulling her useless legs after her.

"That would probably be good."

Tom got up and padded across the carpeted floor to Andy's side of the bed, wheeling her chair from the other side of her night stand to the bed. He picked her up and gently set her down in the chair.

"Thank you for taking such good care of me." Andy's half-smile quivered, tears filling her eyes.

He squatted down, took her hand, and looked her in the eyes. "You're welcome. I love you, Andy. This is temporary. You know, when they had to put you in that coma and hooked you up to those breathing machines, I was terrified. They assured me that you would come out of it when they brought you back, that it would only be until the swelling went down on your spine so that you could breathe on your own again. The swelling went down, they unhooked the machines. They tried to bring you back, only you didn't come right back. The next three days, until you woke up, were terrifying. Every minute from finding out at the church that you were hit, to your waking up, was a nightmare for me. I know that this," he tapped the arm of the chair, "is a nightmare for you. We'll get through this together."

The doctor had said that the thoracic spine, where the crack was, has nothing to do with leg function. Tom didn't understand the reason her body wasn't letting her feel her legs. It was frustrating for him; he could only imagine how frustrating it was for her.

Andy sighed. "This *is* a nightmare for me, every day. Not being able to remember is a nightmare. The nights bring nightmares. Then here you are, making it as okay as it can be by being so strong for both of us. I *know* the doctor said I should be able to walk again, that I should be able to walk now, but I'm not feeling *anything* in my legs. Nothing. That's another nightmare on top of everything else."

"We have to trust that the doctor is right. We just need to give it some time."

"Time. I know. Knowing doesn't make it any easier, though." Andy wiped the tears out of her eyes. "I'm going to get cleaned up. Be back in a minute." She wheeled herself into the bathroom.

She turned the faucet on and watched the water level rise in the bathtub.

I've got to remember what happened that day if I'm ever going to find my flash drive. Okay. I was waiting for the limo. The company called to say he wouldn't make it in time, the car had broken down. What happened next? I drove myself to the church. I must have. Tom said my car was there. Can't remember driving...

Andy tried hard to remember more, but it just wasn't there. Frustrated, she peeled off her nightgown and lifted herself out of the wheel chair, braced herself on the edge of the bathtub, then slid down into the water.

It was in my purse. It should have still been in my purse when I woke up at the hospital. But it wasn't. There should have been lipstick, a safety pin, clear nail polish, and the flash drive. Who would take a safety pin? The only explanation is the latch must have come open... did I see it come open, or am I making up memories to fill the blank spaces? No, I can't do that, I need to see the real memories.

Andy tried to stop thinking about it and concentrated on getting through the chore of a bath. Maybe if she thought about things that were happening right now, and ignored the blank spaces, the memories would come back quicker than her trying to force them.

~~*~*~*

Tom stripped the bed and brought fresh sheets and a dry pillow from the linen closet. She thought he was strong. He wasn't so sure at this point. With his sister in a coma, his parents killed in a car accident that Katy still didn't know about, and now Andy in a wheelchair… how much more could he take?

He looked at the clock: three fifty-eight a.m. Groaning inwardly, he resigned himself to the fact that he wouldn't be able to fall asleep again tonight. It was going to be a long day. Scrubbing his hands over his face, he sat down on the end of the bed and waited for Andy.

Light pouring out through the bathroom doorway crossed the carpet and up the bed next to him. Water splashed, then the slight swooshing sound as the towel slid off the rack. Still, he waited, too tired to jump in and help unless she needed it.

She'd always been self-sufficient, and this was no different. Andy would argue with herself, as well as the wheelchair, until she forced things to work for her or until she couldn't do a single thing more to help herself. Maybe that was stubborn. Whatever it was, it had Tom waiting where he was.

Shadows crossed the light, creating patterns on the carpet. From the looks of things, she was managing to get back into the wheelchair on her own. *Good,* Tom thought, as guilt immediately washed over him for even thinking that. *Shit. I'm just tired,* he explained to himself. He didn't need to; he already knew. Deep down he was bone weary. Making excuses to himself didn't help. It made him feel worse.

CHAPTER FOUR

"Come on, you can do it!" The perky voice only served to piss her off.

The sweat from her brow trailed down the sides of her face from the exertion. "I'm *trying*, get out of my face!" she growled through clenched teeth.

Grabbing the arms of her wheelchair, Andy grunted and used every ounce of energy she had. Her arms quivering, she lifted herself an inch, then two, then two more. Almost up. She reached for the parallel bars with her left hand while bracing herself up with her right.

"Aaaahhhh," she cried, as her right arm gave way and dumped her unceremoniously back into the wheelchair. Ineffectively pounding her fists on her legs, she let out a stream of curse words that would have made a drunken sailor flee.

"There, now, you shouldn't be mad, you're doing better than last time." There was that perky voice again. Thin, young, perfectly straight white teeth, strawberry blonde ponytail bouncing and swishing. It wasn't her fault, it was the accident that had put her here. Still, Andy glared at her until the smile fell off of her face.

Reminds me of Tigger every time I see her, with that bounce and terminally happy disposition, Andy thought hatefully. *If I could get out of this chair right now I'd put HER in one.*

"We've been at this for a freakin' hour, how long do you think my arms are going to last before they dump me on the ground instead of back in this damn chair?" Andy shoved her bangs out of her eyes as another bead of sweat trickled down her temple.

"You really did make progress today." Tigger punctuated her words with exaggerated nods and hand flutters. "The doctor says you'll probably get the use of your legs back, and this could help. He's a really good doctor, I know he's right. It's totally temporary, so we'll keep trying. But we're all through for today, so let's get you back out to the front, k?"

"All this is doing is irritating the fire out of me." Her arms were like wet noodles, there was no way she could wheel herself out, but out of sheer stubbornness she tried anyway. The chair didn't move an inch. "You want to help me over here, or do you get off on watching people fail?"

Tigger bounced behind her chair and out of sight. "No problem, I've got you."

Andy pulled the towel out of the side pocket on her chair and wiped the sweat from her face and neck, visualizing snapping it at Tigger and leaving a welt.

As they wheeled through the double doors into the waiting room, Tom looked over. His hazel eyes zeroed in on Andy. Dropping the newspaper on the end table, he stood, his six foot two frame and one hundred ninety pounds giving him mouth-watering appeal. The shaggy dishwater blond hair looked right on him.

"There she is, Miss America." His dimpled smile went a long way toward making her feel better, for just a second.

A ghost of a smile crossed Andy's face and then was gone. "Hi. Can we get out of here, please? I think they're trying to kill me."

"Hi, Tom, she did great today, we're really making progress." Tigger smiled and batted her eyelashes at Tom.

Andy whipped her head around, cut her a look and snarled. "Back off, sister, he's not talking to you."

Tigger blinked a few times rapidly as she took a step back. "Uh, okay, I guess we'll see you Wednesday, then? Bye bye!" She waved, turned, and bounced back through the double doors, hitting the button to close them behind her.

Tom's eyes never wavered from Andy's. He smiled to himself. *If anyone could help Andy get the use of her legs back, it would be that girl and the mental image of choking the happy right out of her.* He winked at Andy. "So, making progress, are you? Cartwheels? Hundred meter dash? Trying out for the Olympics back there?" Circling around, he took the handles and pushed Andy outside to the waiting truck. Lifting her up, he set her gently in the seat and closed the door. He folded the chair and loaded it into the truck bed.

Climbing into the driver's seat he started it up. Putting his arm across the back of the seat, he rubbed her shoulder tenderly. "How do you feel about visiting Katy today? I told her this morning that we might come by, if you were up for it after your appointment." He looked at her and waited. Sometimes it took a minute for her to answer; he didn't know if it was a side effect of the accident, or if she was just considering her answer before she said anything.

"I don't know. Hospitals are so depressing, and I haven't been out of there for very long myself." She looked down at her hands, toying with the engagement ring on her finger.

"Oh, come on, it will be good for you. Before the accident you visited her every week. You've got to be missing that, spending time talking to her. I think it would do both of you good to have a chat."

She let out a deep sigh. "It's just that..."

"What is it?" Reaching up, he touched her neck, stroked her cheek. "You can tell me anything, Honey."

Her mouth moved but no sound came out. A single tear slid down her face.

Tom wiped it away.

"It's just that I can't help but think if it hadn't snowed, if she'd ridden home with mom and me that day from school, she wouldn't have gotten attacked, she wouldn't be in a coma, and somehow I wouldn't be in a wheelchair. Those guys that did that to her and left her in that alley, they may be dead but it doesn't feel like that made anything right. She's still there, and I'm still here like this." She slapped at her legs.

"I feel the same way about the injustice of it all. They're dead. The cop who didn't do his job, who didn't find any evidence, is dead. The lawyer that was supposed to represent her interests is dead. The problem is that she's still there, in that hospital, in that coma. All we can do is what we've been doing—helping her stay current with the television tuned to news stations and talking to her about everything that's going on in the world, reading the newspaper aloud...all so she's ready to re-enter this life if—when—she comes out of her coma. I'm not sure I see how her situation plays any part in the accident that caused your temporary need for a wheelchair, though. Help me understand what you mean."

She couldn't; she hadn't told him what she'd done and she couldn't tell him she thought karma was paying her back for the deaths she'd been instrumental in causing.

"I don't know. Maybe she would have been waiting with me at the house, helping me get ready to marry you, and would have driven me to the church. Then I wouldn't have been in the way when that car... that car..." She choked back a sob.

Tom scooted closer to her on the bench seat and put his arm around her, drawing her close. "I'm sure she would have been there with you, getting ready for the wedding. I don't like it that she wasn't, either. I don't like it that *I* wasn't. I don't like that the limo broke down and couldn't pick you up, I don't like that I was inside the church waiting for you instead of picking you up to bring you to the church, and I hate it that whoever was behind the wheel of that car drove away and left you in the street. But for now, until they catch that person, we have to go on from where we are and make things as right as we can. We can't think about what wasn't, we have to think about what will be. We're still going to get married. I'd marry you today if you'd let me."

The ghost of a smile returned. "Not until I can walk down the aisle."

"I know, that's your choice and I'm willing to wait. Until then we need to do what we can for you and what we can for Katy. So what do you say, let's go see her, huh?"

Andy reached into the glove box and pulled out a pack of tissues, wiped her face, and then leaned her head on his shoulder. "Okay. Let's go see Katy," she said softly.

Tom kissed the top of her head and squeezed her gently. "That's my girl."

"One more thing." Andy's voice sounded tentative, which was entirely unlike her, even to her own ears.

"Anything."

"See this?" She twirled her ring all the way around on her finger. "I'm worried I'm going to lose it. It spins around and gets in the way when I'm trying to do PT. Will you put it in the jewelry box, just until I've gained some weight back and it fits again?"

His stomach dropped. "Just until then?"

The question left unspoken—were they still engaged—was thick in the air.

"Yes. Just until then. I still want to marry you. I don't want to lose my ring. Please?"

"Okay. Just until then." Tom slipped the ring off Andy's finger, feeling what she felt as he did. "I see what you mean. I've got it."

"Thank you." She sniffled.

"Everything will work out, I promise." Tom kissed her again, wiping away her tears.

"I know." She didn't sound sure at all.

~~*~*~*

"Katydid, I brought company." Tom spoke to Katy as if she were sitting awake in her bed. He maneuvered the wheelchair around the bed to the far side where Andy could see Katy and the door at the same time. Since the accident she'd been goosey about not being able to see what was behind her.

"Hi, Katy." Andy was surprised to find that she was actually happy to see Katy even though she knew the conversation would be one-sided. They'd been best friends for most of their lives and it felt natural to spend time with her, regardless of her condition. Besides, she had things she felt she needed to tell her this time.

Tom engaged the brake on the wheel. "I'm going to leave you two alone for a few minutes while I track down Dr. Alister. You okay, Andy?"

She looked at him and smiled. "I'm fine. Go ahead, Katy and I have a lot to talk about."

He brushed his hand down Katy's arm and then gave Andy's shoulder a squeeze. "Holler if you need me."

As Tom left the room, Andy leaned forward and put her hand over Katy's. "I'm sorry it's been so long since I've stopped by. I'm sure Tom told you about the accident, and..." she flashed back, fragments of a memory that hadn't fully returned making their way into her consciousness without making any sense. She shoved them back down. No sense looking at them and making herself crazy until her memory unlocked more details and gave her something to go on. Clearing her throat, she continued. "...And then the time I spent in the hospital. Since then I've been working hard at physical therapy, trying to will my legs to work again, but even sheer force isn't helping much. I can lift myself out of this damn chair but once I do the legs still don't work. At this rate, my biceps are going to be hugely disproportionate. Sure makes me wish I'd have gotten a gym membership instead of blowing it off in favor of that trip to San Diego. Too late for that now, though, isn't it?"

Andy sighed and shook her head. "Tom mentioned the wedding again, but I don't want to do that until I can walk down the aisle. I'd still like you to be my maid of honor, so the sooner you can come on back and get out of that coma the better. Speaking of comas, when I came out of mine, or right before anyway, I swear I heard you talking to me and when I saw you standing there... I wanted to stay, but it was too late. I'd already started tumbling. I'm not sure if that was a dream, the meds, or if we were in the same place. I'm calling that the 'in-between' because that's what it was and I don't know exactly what else to call it. Was that really you there? I need you back here, and Tom needs you back too. Please come back."

When Tom left Andy with Katy, he headed for the nurse's station. The nurse currently manning the station was standing behind the rounded countertop, head bowed down as she flipped pages in a chart. "Hey, Julie, how's it going?"

She looked up and smiled. Julie had been a nurse on this floor since before Katy was admitted and knew Tom from high school. "Hey, Tom, it's going. I didn't see you come in. How's Andy doing?"

"She's doing better, physically. No movement or indications in her legs yet that anything's changing. We're staying positive though."

"You're the most positive person I know." Julie smiled. "What can I help you with?"

Tom leaned on the counter. "I was hoping Dr. Alister was around. Has he been through today?"

"He's already made his rounds but I can page him if you like. He's probably still in the building."

Tom nodded. "That'd be great. Thanks."

Julie picked up the phone and dialed. She gave the page and replaced the receiver in its cradle. "He's usually pretty quick about coming up when he's here. Oh, by the way, thought you'd like to know...turns out Dr. Stoltz, Katy's old doctor, has a sister. Well, a half-sister, but she's the closest blood relative they've been able to find. Right now she says she doesn't want to take him off of life support until she goes through his personal effects and sees if he's got a Living Will. That's all I know."

"I'll bet he does, he seemed to have an opinion on whether or not anyone else should be kept alive; I'd guess he has one on himself as well. Has there been any change?"

Dr. Alister rounded the corner and headed for the desk. Julie saw him and shook her head at Tom. "Dr. Alister, Tom was looking for you."

Tom lifted his hand in a half-wave at Julie. "Thanks, catch you later."

Turning to the doctor, he said, "Hi, Doc. Haven't had a chance to catch up with you lately, between Andy's physical therapy appointments and the contractor who installed a wheel chair ramp at the house, then work, I've been off of my normal routine. Do you have a minute to talk about Katy?"

"Sure. I know you've got a lot on your plate right now. I'm happy to take time." They started off down the hall, heading toward his office.

Dr. Alister unlocked his office door and motioned Tom inside, closing the door behind them. "What's on your mind, Tom?" he said, making himself comfortable in his desk chair.

"I've been reading some interesting articles and wanted to pass them by you before I put any faith in what I've read. There are some people who believe stimulation procedures can help bring coma patients back out. We already leave the TV on, and I've played her favorite music as well. What do you know about smell stimulation therapy?"

Leaning forward, Dr. Alister flipped through a stack of papers on the corner of his desk. "Funny you should mention that, I've just read an article myself on that very thing. It appears there's been limited success noted, enough so that they've begun writing articles about it and holding trials to more accurately note the reactions of patients to different smells." Pulling a medical magazine from the middle of the stack, he turned to a marked page. "Here, let me get a copy of this for you."

He hit the intercom button on his phone. "Annise, can you come in here for a minute, please?"

"Yes, Doctor." A tinny voice replied. Seconds later the connecting door opened and a very tall, very slender middle-aged woman stepped through. *Not pretty, that's not what I would call her. Striking is more like it.* As though reading his thoughts, she looked at him as if looking through him, her grey eyes as pale as her skin.

"Annise, this is Tom Oliver, Katy's brother. Tom, Annise Garner, my assistant."

Tom stood and shook her hand. "Pleased to meet you, Annise. Beautiful name."

She blinked rapidly several times, clearly flustered, and managed to stutter a quick "Thank you, it's nice to meet you, too." She stared at Tom for a few beats longer before returning her attention to the doctor.

"Would you make a photocopy of this article for Tom and bring both back in here, please?" Dr. Alister held out the magazine. She snapped it from his hand as quick as a hummingbird, whirled around and almost fled, startling Tom.

"Wow, is she okay?" Tom asked, a crease marring his brow.

"She's fine." Dr. Alister chuckled.

Tom returned to the subject. "Alright. Well, as far as the smell stimulation therapy goes, I get the impression you're not opposed to my trying it with Katy. Would that be a fair assessment?"

"Yes, in fact, I'm all in favor of it. Does she have a perfume she liked to wear, or a particular flower she liked best?"

"Her favorite food is lasagna. Would it be too much to ask to bring a plate in and have it reheated in the microwave?"

"I don't think that would be a problem. I'd prefer you bring it around mealtime, perhaps dinner one night, so that the rest of the floor smells like food already and a home-cooked meal will be less likely to distress the other patients."

"Sure. I hadn't thought about the other patients having a problem with it. Andy and I can bring it around dinner time. Would Saturday be good? I'll be off work and Andy won't have physical therapy so we can spend the day at home cooking."

Annise knocked lightly and came back into the room, magazine and several stapled pages in hand. "Here you go, doctor."

"Thank you." Dr. Alister took the stack and Annise practically ran back out without so much as a glance in Tom's direction.

"Are you sure she's okay?" Tom scratched his head. "She seems... almost scared."

"She'll be alright. She's more comfortable with paperwork than with people."

"Well then."

Dr. Alister handed the stapled pages across the desk. "Here you go, give this a read and we can talk more about it after Saturday's experiment. I'd like to be here when you bring the lasagna, see for myself if there's a visible reaction."

"That would be great. I'd like you to be there, as well. See you then." Tom shook Dr. Alister's hand and left the office, closing the door behind him. *It will be great if this works to bring Katy out of it,* Tom thought as he wound his way back through the maze of the hospital toward Katy's room.

CHAPTER FIVE

"Good morning, Katy, what's happening in your world today?" Tom tossed the newspaper down on the chair as he rounded the bed. "Is it too bright out there, is that why your blinds are closed?" As he pulled the string to flip the blinds open, a nurse came out of the bathroom.

"Hi, Tom."

"Oh hi, Tish. I didn't realize anyone was in here with Katy."

"I'm just checking supplies." Her bright pink scrubs dotted with kittens dressed up as doctors were almost too much for his eyes.

"Any idea who keeps closing these blinds? I'd sure like them left open for her, she's loved watching the sun come up for as long as I can remember."

"No, but I'll put a note in her chart if you want." Tish smiled seductively at him and tilted her head, her brown hair pulled back in a pony tail swishing as she walked toward him.

The undercurrent of attraction coming off of Tish in waves was lost on Tom. "That would be good, thanks." He turned his back to her and pulled the visitor's chair near the bed, into his usual spot, picked up the newspaper and got comfortable.

"Which part do you want to read first today?" Tom snapped the paper open to a random page. "My choice? Well, then, the classifieds it is."

He was obviously done talking to her; Tish took the dismissal and lack of interest as personally as if he'd slapped her in the face. She'd worked up to making a play for him over the last few weeks, spending countless hours daydreaming about what it would be like to be held in his arms, kissed, undressed, made love to by Tom, and the reality was like ice water being poured over her.

The hurt flashed in her eyes and tears began to well as she turned toward the door. The lump in her throat prevented her from saying anything else as she half-ran from the room.

"Let's see. There's a house on Eucalyptus Street for sale. *'Four bedroom, two bath, study that's big enough for a pool table, in-ground swimming pool and hot tub, circle drive. Open House on Sunday from 2-6. $120,900.'* And another on Sycamore, *'Two-story, open floor plan, master bedroom/bath spans entire loft floor, two bedrooms/one bath, mudroom, living room, dining room and newly remodeled kitchen with walk-in pantry, granite countertops and large center island located on the first floor, priced to sell, contact Reanna at Barister Realty.'* What do you think, either one of those worth looking at, or should we keep looking tomorrow? That's all for today in the For Sale column."

Tom scanned through the various columns for something interesting to read to Katy. Usually there wasn't much, so he played up the ones that were. "There's a trailer park on Seventh Street that has an ad. *'Mobile homes for rent, 2 and 3 bedroom available. Empty lots ready and waiting for your owned home.'* That one kinda sounds like they're waiting for a house to drop." Tom laughed at the visual, then sobered at the thought of a tornado. "Sorry, I know, that really isn't funny. You would have laughed if you'd seen the cartoon mobile home I imagined, twirling like a ballerina and then setting down nicely, in line with the rest of the trailers, with the grandma still in the rocking chair on the porch, blanket over her lap, not even disturbed enough by the event to stop knitting."

Tornadoes were all too common in Oklahoma, and after the losses over the last few years caused by Mother Nature's temper tantrums, even the thought of a joke about a tornado wasn't funny for long before reality took over.

"Moving on… oh, look at this, *'Chihuahoodles for sale, ready for adoption on 7/11, two males, one female unspoken for. Call Charlie at…'* Those Chi-hoo-ah-hoodles must be popular, they're in the paper pretty often."

Tom tried to keep his tone of voice light. It was important to transmit happiness to Katy if there was a chance she would come back on her own. *Who wants to come back to a place that isn't happy?*

"That's all for the classifieds. Are you ready for the Police Blotter? I am, too. Let's see what stupidity the criminals are up to today. *'Andrew Braxter, 36, found dead of a gunshot wound to the chest in Crixbury Creek, face down in two inches of water. Leta Braxter, 34, found dead on a nearby bank from an apparent self-inflicted gunshot wound.'* That's too bad. Here's another one. *Carlotta Espinoza, 19, was unconscious on a walking trail near Nineteenth and Hill where she was found by joggers early this morning. Espinoza is currently in ICU at Mid-State Hospital. If you have any information, please contact the Aspen Grove Police Department.'* Huh. Obviously they don't have any idea what happened to her; I hope they find whoever did that."

He looked at his watch and closed the newspaper. "I'm afraid that's all the time we have this morning. I know it was a short visit, I'm sorry. Andy should be done with her physical therapy and after I drop her at home it's off to work for me. Be good, Katydid. I'll see you tomorrow."

Tom smoothed Katy's blanket around her. She didn't seem to be aging, which was good; it would be easier on her when she woke up if many of the things she remembered were the same, including her looks. He turned her television on to a news station, tucked the newspaper under his arm and headed out.

~~*~*~*

When he pulled up to the front entrance, he saw through the glass doors that Andy was in the waiting room. He took a minute to just look at her; she appeared to be off in her own world, staring at nothing, her mouth turned down in a frown and wrinkles creasing her forehead. Absently she brushed her bangs out of her eyes. His frown mirrored hers for a moment. He hated to see her like this, but there was nothing more that he could do than he was already doing. Pasting a smile on his face he hopped out of the truck and went in.

"Hi! Done already?"

She turned at the sound of his voice, the frown and wrinkles left behind. She smiled weakly. "Yeah. She tried to kill me again today, but I made it out alive."

"Well, I'm glad for that. Let's bust you out of this place before she comes back to try again." Tom wheeled her chair toward the door. "What's on your agenda for today?"

"Mom's coming by and taking me shopping. We need groceries and so does she."

Andy gripped the arms of her chair and half-lifted herself out. Tom picked her up in his arms and set her in the truck before stowing the wheelchair in the bed of the pickup.

Tom jogged around the back and climbed in behind the wheel.

"Here's something interesting, speaking of groceries. I don't think I told you, I spoke with Dr. Alister about something I found while researching. Have you heard of smell therapy?"

"Mmmm, no, I don't think so." She secured her seatbelt and

waited while Tom did the same.

"It's a relatively new treatment that's been used on a limited number of coma patients. I found something obscure on the internet about it, and asked the good doctor. He had just read an article in one of the medical magazines about it, and had his secretary copy it for us. It's in the glove box, if you want to read it."

"Give me the high points. Moving vehicles and reading don't mix for me."

"Oh, right. Anyway, making a favorite dish and putting it in close proximity to the patient has brought positive reactions in the one case they relied heavily on in this research. Nothing else had ever worked, but she woke up within forty-eight hours of the pancakes and maple syrup being brought to her room."

"That's interesting." Brushing her bangs out of her eyes, she pursed her lips in contemplation. "So, you're thinking we can do this for Katy, and see if it helps. What kind of smell are you…"

They turned their heads and looked at each other. At the same time, as if in stereo, said, "Lasagna."

Laughter filled the cab of the truck. "Yes, that's perfect. She would love lasagna. I'll get the ingredients at the store today. When do you want to do this?"

"Dr. Alister said Saturday would be fine, and we'll time it so the other patients on the floor have been served their dinner and the smell won't be nearly as likely to upset anyone. He wants to be there, too, to see if it has any effect on her."

"Do we dare get our hopes up?"

"I don't know. I would like to think so, but I think we should reserve our excitement for when she wakes up."

"You're probably right. We can hope, though. Okay, what else do you want from the store?"

"Will you also pick up some charcoal? I thought we'd do some grilling this week."

Andy nodded. "It's on the list. I'm way ahead of you there."

Some of the roads between Oklahoma City and Aspen Grove weren't kept up. Potholes and upheavals from tree roots were dotted all around, random in some areas and more concentrated in others. Tom missed a big pothole only to hit a smaller one; Andy yelped involuntarily.

"What happened, are you okay?" Tom slowed the truck, pulling it over to the side of the road.

"Ow, yes, I'm okay. It was just a twinge in my...." She realized what she was saying at the same time Tom did.

"In your...." He put the truck in park and turned off the key. Twisting to face her, he watched her intently. "Where, Andy?"

She held her breath and made an internal examination. "In my left hip, back here by my spine." She turned as far as she could and marked the spot with her index finger.

"Can you feel your finger touching your back?" Tom asked hopefully.

Her elation deflated. "No. I know what I felt, but I can't feel it anymore."

Tom slid across the bench seat and held her tight. "But you felt it, and that's great. Your feeling is coming back."

She slid her arms around him and let the hope in. "Oh my God, then it might not be much longer..." Her sobs choked out any other words she thought she'd say. Gripping Tom tightly she let herself believe as the tears flowed uncontrollably.

He rocked her and let his own tears fall. Something good to believe in—it was about time things started turning around for him. He needed something good to happen in his life. So many bad things had happened in the last few years, it was almost too much to believe that things might, finally, start going right for him.

He couldn't help but think back to that day. He'd thought then that something good was happening, it was certainly time for something good... *for the wedding, but everyone was so quiet, the undercurrent palpable. Waiting was the worst part, wondering if she was going to change her mind at the last minute, leave him at the altar. Ten minutes past time, still no word. He checked his watch before stepping out of the groom room. Andy's mom was pacing in the hallway, her cell phone to her ear. He heard a piece of the message she left as she turned back toward him... 'where are you, I'm worr...'' was when she saw him standing there. She turned her back again, finished her sentence and closed her phone. He didn't need to hear any more than that to know why the wedding wasn't happening right now. She hadn't shown up at the church. He went out onto the steps to look for her, fear niggling his brain. The street was lined with the cars of guests seated inside the church. There was no limousine in sight. He looked left, then right, and it was then that he'd seen the man running toward the church, out of shape and out of breath, raising one hand in signal to Tom, the other pressing his cell phone to his ear. The man waved, then pointed down the block, still talking. Denial bloomed as Tom shook his head. As if underscoring the man's meaning, sirens grew louder in the distance; a police car and then an ambulance screeched to a halt a couple of blocks down. The denial burst into full-blown fear, exploding inside him...*

He slid back over behind the wheel. There wasn't much traffic; Tom merged back onto the road, driving on autopilot.

The rest of the trip was quiet, each of them in their own world. They pulled in the drive and Tom came around to help Andy out of the truck, and pushed her up the ramp and into the house. She turned her chair around as they both spoke at once. "I'll call the doct—"

"You might want to—"

They both smiled and Andy nodded, pointing at her head and then his, and back again. "We're right there again. I'll call and talk to the doctor, see if he wants to see me."

Tom leaned over and kissed her. "Call me if he wants to see you today, and I'll come home to take you. Otherwise, I'll see you tonight and we'll plan from there. Love you."

"Love you too."

He made the drive in good time, though still five minutes late, parked in the lot and jogged up the steps. The historic building had felt like his second home for years; the unmistakable smell of old books and inked paper enveloped him, relaxing him in a way few other things did. Right now he felt good—cautious about hoping for too much, but definitely feeling good. It was about time something started going right.

Andy wheeled herself to her current favorite spot in their living room, in front of the plate glass window. The sun felt good on her face, warm and comforting. She would take all the comfort she could get; things were so far out of her control right now, anything that helped her not go crazy was welcome. The twinge in her back had caught her off-guard. Was it above where the 'paralyzed' started, or below? At this point it almost felt like the paralyzed portion started lower than it had before. Probably just her imagination; wishful thinking at its finest. Still, she'd call about an appointment and talk to her mom about it. Glancing up at the clock on the mantel, she realized the office wouldn't open for another hour.

Picking up the newspaper from her lap, Andy flipped pages until she found the Police Blotter.

Andrew Braxter, 36, found dead of a gunshot wound to the chest in Crixbury Creek, face down in two inches of water. Leta Braxter, 34, found dead of an apparent self-inflicted gunshot wound on a nearby bank.

Murders/suicides? The ratio of those in this town was very low. You had a better chance of reading about a lotto winner who lived near you than a murder/suicide. Andy's heart rate quickened.

I need to figure out what happened to my flash drive. What if someone found it and either figured out what the code meant or, worse, sent it to a friend? What would happen if the video was watched without a specific target defined in it?

She didn't know. She'd never thought about an eventuality like this before—what if 'no variable' translated to 'random'? *Surely not...*

Movement outside the window caught her attention. Her mom had pulled into the drive and was walking toward the front door. She waved when she saw Andy looking out at her. Andy robotically returned the gesture.

What the hell am I going to do? I've got to find that flash drive. What if it's my fault the Braxters are dead?

During the last two hours of his shift Tom usually helped the interns re-shelve the returned books. As he came down the stairs from the second floor toward the main lobby to do just that, he could see moms were arriving with their children for the weekly reading group. He glanced over and saw that the pit was already almost full; that was unusual for a weekday afternoon. He glanced at his watch and was even more surprised to see it was only three-fifteen p.m.; the reading wasn't scheduled to start for another forty-five minutes. Apparently today's guest reader was a popular one. The poster said G. E. Beyers was traveling through and would be reading *Pumkiniah the Brave* to the children. Without children of his own he didn't know the name, though he seemed to be in the minority from the number of people still coming in.

"Hi, Tom, how are you?" At the sound of his name he turned to see Nina Lopez. They'd graduated high school in the same class. She and her high school sweetheart had married the summer they'd graduated. Nina was currently being followed close behind by two children, a boy and a girl.

"I'm good, Nina, how are you? Looks like you're here for the reading." He looked at the kids. "Hi, guys, what's shakin'?" They looked at him without answering.

"Thomas, Rosie, you were asked a question." She raised one eyebrow at them.

In unison they obeyed. "Hello."

Nina shook her head as she turned back to Tom. "Some days it's like pulling teeth. Other times I can't get them to stop talking."

Smiling, he winked at the kids. "Are you guys here to listen to an author read her book to you?"

Little heads nodded in unison.

"Well, enjoy yourselves. It was nice to meet you." Tom turned his attention to their mother. "There aren't many seats left, good thing you got here early. It was nice to see you again. Say hi to Larry for me."

CHAPTER SIX

Andy waited at the front window. As her mom backed out of the drive, they waved at each other.

Turning the chair around, she rolled toward the kitchen to put away the few groceries left on the counter that she'd told her mom she could handle. Thoughts of her accident returned. An unbidden memory flashed before her eyes.

She'd found a parking space in a residential neighborhood only two blocks from the church. Pulling in, she parked her car and picked up her clutch, dropping her keys inside. As she opened the car door, her veil fluttered on the seat next to her. Picking it up, she stepped out of the car, lifting the train of her wedding gown to keep it from trailing on the ground.

The mild temperature and light breeze felt perfect to her as she walked along the sidewalk, her heels clicking in time to the beating of her heart. Today was the day she would marry her best friend and everything was going to be perfect. She'd never felt more beautiful.

The flashback ended, leaving Andy sweating and aching for more. The memories came back to her slowly but surely; she wished they wouldn't take so much time.

A sharp twinge of pain in her low back made her leg twitch involuntarily. Her entire body tensed, her hands gripping hard enough on the arms of the chair to turn her knuckles white. The pain was definitely lower than where she'd had feeling before today.

As soon as it passed, she reached into the side pocket of her wheelchair and felt around until she found her phone. She definitely needed to schedule an appointment with her physician—the sooner, the better.

~~*~*~*

"They can't see me before then." Andy's voice belied the frustration she felt over the lack of consideration the doctor's receptionist showed for her condition.

Tom rolled his neck. Then, since she was on the other end of the phone and not right in front of him where she could see, he allowed himself a head shake. He sighed. "I'll call the doctor myself and get the appointment moved up. Surely if the staff would have asked him..."

Andy heard his sigh. That was all it took for her blood pressure to skyrocket. She cut him off. "Do you not think I made that suggestion? I *told* her to tell him about the pain. She put me on hold and left me there for almost five minutes. When she came back on the line, she said he couldn't see me before the appointment she'd already scheduled."

She knew it was more than the appointment that had her aggravated. It was everything: the wheelchair, the memory fragments, the missing flash drive, the lack of knowledge on where it was or who had it, not to mention the secrets she'd kept—and was still keeping—from Tom. Everything combined to shorten her temper and her attention span. She knew she was taking it out on Tom, but it was as if she were outside her own body looking in and unable to stop herself.

Tom was nearing the end of his rope. He'd been doing everything for everybody for so long that it almost seemed more than he could take. He dug deep; he just had to hang on a little longer...

Instead of snapping at her to call the doctor back and be forceful and responsible for her own situation, to stand up to that receptionist and demand to talk to the doctor herself, Tom used every last bit of restraint. "If that's all they have..."

Before he could finish his sentence, the phone went dead in his hand. Andy had hung up mid-conversation.

Something switched off inside. He felt it go, followed by the last of the energy as it drained out of his body. The immense pressure and weight of everything he carried on his shoulders pressed down on him, crushing him physically as well as mentally. There had to be a point where things would get better, would turn his way. *Had* to be.

He'd never felt so alone.

CHAPTER SEVEN

"I can't, I have to set the table," Andy screamed above the cruckling roar of the fire, the heat undulating closer to her with each passing second. Every plate she set disappeared as she rounded the table to set the next, showing up back on the stack in her hand. Katy called to her from the hallway, her words drowned out by the incessant noise. Shut up fire I can't hear Katy! Andy ran faster and faster, around and around the table, trying to get the plates set. The witch was coming, she'll be so mad if the table isn't ready...Katy, where are you? Andy felt the flames licking at her legs and back as it followed her, all the while hypnotizing her from across the table with its seductive sway, shooting up between her and the doorway, blocking Katy from her view.

The sound of the witch's footsteps broke Andy from her trance; she took off again, racing faster around the table, around and around, setting plates and setting plates and setting plates...

"I'm trying, don't let her come in here!" Andy looked at where Katy had been moments ago and all she saw was fire...fire that was coming for her, too.

Tom awoke slowly to moaning and thrashing beside him.

"Andy, honey...Andrea..." Reaching over, he rubbed her arm. "Sweetie, wake up."

Andy flung her arm out, catching Tom by surprise. Her hand cracked him square in the bridge of his nose, bringing tears to his eyes.

The stress that had been building slowly but surely over the last few years finally got the better of him. Quick as a whip he reached out and pinned her arms to her sides, and swung his body up and across to straddle hers.

"Wake *up*," he cried furiously. "*Andy.*"

She didn't respond, continuing to thrash around under him, mumbling incoherently.

Before he realized it, he'd slapped her across the face.

Her eyes flew open, looking around wildly for the threat.

Instantly he let her arms go, and almost as quickly regretted it. Her left hand swung up, landing a solid blow near his temple.

Rolling off her, he continued rolling until he was off the bed and out of striking range. "I'm sorry, Andy, honey, are you alright? I didn't mean to hurt you."

Her eyes focused slowly as she came out of her nightmare. She blinked twice, hard, before her eyes narrowed, pinning him where he stood.

"You hit me," she exclaimed. "Why would you *do* that?"

"I don't know." His voice was resigned. "It was a reaction. I wasn't thinking." The weariness in his voice was something he couldn't control. "You hit me first, bringing me out of a dead sleep. I haven't had a good nights' sleep in months, maybe years, and my body reacted. By the time I realized what I was doing, you were struggling to get loose under me. I'm sorry..."

Tom hadn't looked at her since he'd first seen the terror on her face. The look she'd given him was like ice water to his soul.

Andy's voice was even colder than ice water. "You. Hit. Me."

She didn't appear to have heard anything he'd said. It became apparent that, once again, it was all about her.

"Yes. And I said I was sorry." He looked at Andy, really saw her for the first time since she'd woken up. "Did you not hear what I just said?"

His voice was resigned and incredulous at the same time. Something inside him had broken, and he wasn't quite sure what it was or how to fix it. At this point in time, right this minute, he wasn't sure he wanted to fix whatever it was.

Andy heard something in his tone of voice that she didn't understand, recognize, or know how to react to. She stared at him.

Tom took her silence as stonewalling. Before he knew what he was going to do, he grabbed his pillow and a blanket from the hope chest at the foot of their bed and strode out of the bedroom toward the den. He didn't look back.

☥~☥~☥~☥~☥

Tom woke early, unsure as to why he was in their den until the fight from the middle of the night came back loud and clear. Frustration followed his every move as he folded the blanket and stacked it with the pillow on the end of the couch.

Moving quietly, he went about his morning routine. Only today, he used the downstairs bathroom. He didn't trust himself to have a productive conversation with Andy yet this morning. After he'd showered, shaved, and dressed, Tom made coffee for both of them. Before he left the house, he scribbled a note and carried it with him to check on her. She was snoring softly, no evidence of a nightmare in progress. He moved the wheelchair close enough to the bed where she could reach it when she woke, and placed the note where his pillow would normally be.

As he looked down at her one more time, tears shimmered in his eyes. Shoulders slumped like a broken man, he turned to go.

~~*~*~*

Sunlight painted a warm glow across her skin as it streamed into the room.

Andy woke slowly. The lack of noise in the house was unusual. Normally by the time she woke up, Tom was getting ready to go to work.

She reached across the bed, looking for him. He wasn't there. In his place was a piece of paper. There was a moment of confusion before she remembered they'd fought in the middle of the night.

Her first reaction was indignation, followed by sorrow, and then righteousness. How was it that he felt justified in yelling at her, and *striking* her, after everything she'd been through?

Almost immediately Andy felt disgusted by her thoughts. How did she think she deserved more pity than he did? She'd been like this for weeks; he'd been dealing with these feelings for *years.*

Pushing herself into a sitting position, she picked up the sheet of paper and read what Tom had to say.

> *Dear Andy,*
>
> *I'm sorry about last night. I snapped and I shouldn't have. I've reached the end of my rope, I can't do this anymore. Something has to change. Please, schedule a session with a therapist; I can't handle anything more than I'm dealing with now.*
>
> *If you need anything today, call your mom. I'm going to the hospital to see Katy, and then I'm going to work.*
>
> *I love you,*
>
> *Tom*

Her hands dropped to her lap, still clutching the note. What gave him the right to think that his situation excused what he had done to her, and then he had the nerve to say *she* needed to see a therapist? *Could he really be so self-involved, to think I'm the one who needs to talk to a professional when HE's the one who hit ME?*

She crumpled up the paper and shrieked like a banshee in frustration. *HOW DARE HE...how could...*

...He was waiting for her at the church. Her shoes weren't as comfortable for walking as they were when she'd been standing in them at the store. No big deal, if this was the worst thing that happened on her wedding day, she would be alright.

The gentle breeze lifted her hair from her face, giving the sun full access. She tipped her head back, closed her eyes, and breathed deeply. Today she would marry her friend. Life is good. Not good, fantastic!

A small laugh bubbled up and out of her chest. Holding the train of her dress up, Andy stepped off the curb to avoid the cracked sidewalk. No sense getting her heel caught in between the chunks of concrete. The shoes could be uncomfortable, but they didn't need to be scraped up as well.

The birds chirping were a nice touch, as was the smell of gardenia that floated in the air. Stepping lightly, Andy moved between the bumpers of two parked cars and started across the street. The church was a block and a half away; idly she wondered if carrying her shoes was a better idea than wearing them. She'd be in them for another few hours, through the ceremony and then the reception. If she'd have thought about it at the time she would have packed a set of flats as well. Too late now, she thought. Oh well, I'll live.

The flashback ended as abruptly as it had appeared. Every muscle in her body was tense, while her heart rate tripled for several seconds as she realized what she'd just seen—a fragment of memory from that day. Stars exploded before her eyes and tears shimmered across her vision.

A warmth spread throughout her body, an almost tingling sensation climbed up her spine and back down again, working its way past her hips, down the backs of her thighs, and ending in her toes. The feeling was not painful, but certainly uncomfortable enough to make her stay still and just feel. It slipped away again almost as if it had not been there at all, like she'd imagined the entire episode. Andy tried to move her legs, to no avail. A sob broke free. She sat there on the bed, alone in a too-quiet house, feeling abandoned and adrift. He should have been here with her for this; he could have made sense of it. She knew she'd driven him away but didn't know how to fix it, had no idea how to make him come back. None of it was his fault. This whole situation was hers alone. She cried like there was no tomorrow. She didn't know if there would be a tomorrow for them, and that thought alone made her cry harder.

After the last tear had been shed, she pulled herself together and reached for her chair. It hadn't been this close to the bed last night; he must have put it closer so she wouldn't be stuck in bed when she awoke. A glimmer of hope took hold. She could make this right. She had to—he was the love of her life and she'd screwed things up.

But, how? Andy had no idea what to do to fix it. Her mom would, though. She slid herself down into the wheelchair and reached for her cell phone.

"Hi, Mom. Are you busy?"

"Hi, honey. No, not at all." Denise knew that tone in her daughter's voice.

"I need some advice. I've really screwed things up with Tom." Andy explained what had happened, how they'd fought, and about the way she'd been acting lately, only worried about herself and not about Tom at all.

"Sounds to me like you two need to sit down and talk about things."

"I don't know how, Mom. How do I tell Tom I'm sorry I've been a bitch?"

"The same way you've just told me. He loves you, Andy. You love him, too, right?"

"More than anything."

"Then tell him that. He deserves to be treated the way you want to be treated by him. He knows this has been hard on you, but have you thought about how hard this has been on him, as well? Not only is he taking care of you, he's doing everything he can for Katy, and unlike you, he doesn't have his parents around anymore to lean on. Tom has so much on his shoulders, he's bound to crack under the pressure. Talk to him. You love him, you are his support system. He probably needs you more than you realize, and you have to make this right, honey, if you want to make a life with him. Communication is everything."

Several seconds went by before she answered. "You're right. You're always right, and I'm so glad you're here for me to talk to, Mom. I can't imagine what it would be like to have to go through this without you. I hadn't thought about everything from Tom's point of view. I've got to make this right."

"That's good, then. When he gets home tonight, sit down and talk with him. The sooner you clear the air, the better."

"I'll do that. Thank you, Mom. I'll talk to you later. Love you."

"You're welcome, honey. I love you too."

After they hung up, Andy rolled into the bathroom and drew a bath. *How am I going to start this conversation with him? His note was so... sad. Broken. He needs to know I'm here for him, that I'm not the self-centered moron anymore. God, how thoughtless of me. What's wrong with me, acting this way?*

She finished her bath and got herself dressed. As she made her way to the kitchen, she smelled the coffee. He'd made enough for both of them and left the pot on for her. The glimmer of hope grew.

The rest of her morning went by in a blur; the afternoon followed in the same view, as well as the evening. She spent from seven o'clock in the evening on in front of the window, watching for him to pull in the drive.

By the time ten o'clock pm came and went without his arrival or even a phone call, Andy rolled her chair down the hallway and put herself to bed. Another two hours of tossing and turning didn't bring him home. When she awoke next, daylight was filtering through the windows and around the edge of the bedroom curtains.

CHAPTER EIGHT

The nurses' voices in the hallway outside the room woke Tom. Pushing himself upright from the armchair where he'd slept, he rubbed his eyes and yawned. The light coming through the window shocked him; it couldn't be daylight, he'd only closed his eyes to rest them for a minute.

One look at his watch told him differently. It was almost eight thirty in the morning. He'd slept here all night. Panic took over—he'd left home yesterday before Andy had awakened, and he'd not called or gone home since. This wasn't his intention. He'd only wanted to check on Katy before going home late, in hopes that Andy would have cooled off by the time he got there and would be in a better frame of mind than when he'd left their bed to sleep in the den.

Stopping long enough to tuck the covers in around Katy, Tom whispered to her. "I'll be back to see you soon, Katydid. When I come, I'll have a surprise for you. Be ready, okay? See you later."

He slid his feet into his shoes and strode out quickly. He might make it home before Andy woke. That would be best—and easiest—for everyone. Not that he'd done anything wrong by sleeping in Katy's room. It was just that he didn't want Andy to think he didn't come home because he didn't want to. He'd intended to go home, and he would have if he hadn't fallen asleep. He had to admit it was a good night's sleep, even though it was in a hospital chair; he'd not slept that deeply since before Andy's accident.

The drive took twenty minutes. As he pulled in to the drive, he saw Andy sitting in front of the window, watching him. *Damn it.*

Getting out of the truck, he took quick strides to the door. She met him there.

"Where have you been?"

Crap, that's not the way I wanted to start this conversation. "I've been at the hospital. After work yesterday I stopped to see Katy, and next thing I knew it was this morning. I fell asleep on that chair in her room. I'm sorry..." Tom squatted down by her chair. "I didn't mean to be gone all night. Are you alright?"

"Don't apologize. I'm the one who needs to do that. We need to talk."

Andy looked like she'd been crying. Her face was puffy, and her eyes were red-rimmed. Dropping his weight to his knees, he leaned forward. Both arms out, Andy leaned forward and they hugged tightly.

Andy closed her eyes and held on tightly. She held love in her arms, and wanted—needed—to make things right. Tom meant everything to her. "I've been awful, and it's not you, it's my lack of ability to deal with this, this...situation. I've never been incapacitated before and it's very hard. I have a newfound respect for anyone who is wheelchair-bound and still polite." Holding him close as he shook his head and began to pull back, she continued. "No, I need to say this and looking into your eyes while I do is not possible. Let me finish."

His arms tightened around her again in response.

"When I went to bed and you weren't here, I was scared. Then, when I woke up and you still weren't home, I was terrified that I'd lost you. I knew it was my own fault, and I told myself if you would only come back, I would do what I'm doing now and fall on my sword, begging you to take me back. You are the most amazing man, and I'm an idiot for not telling you so and thanking you for all you're doing for me. You've got a lot on your plate these days, even more with me being like this. I'm going to try even harder, do everything I can to make your life easier. Until I get out of this chair, it won't be much, but I can stop griping and blaming you for things that aren't your fault. That's a start, right?" Without giving him time to respond, she continued. "I apologize from the bottom of my heart for the way I've acted lately. I promise, I'll work harder at controlling my frustration and channeling my anger into getting better. Forgive me, please, and I'll make it up to you. I promise."

Tom rubbed her back and held her. *This* was the woman he fell in love with. His heart swelled. "I love you, Andy. Thank you. I'll take all the help I can get, and if that's only verbal cheerleading for now, that's great. I know you'll get better, and when the feeling in your legs comes back—and it will, don't you think it won't for even a second—we'll share the load again."

Hearing his words and the tone of his voice, Andy's stress lessened considerably. She melted into his embrace, relaxing for the first time in days.

"I do have one request, though."

"Anything."

"About the cheerleading..."

It was her turn to try to pull back, and his not to let her. "Yes?"

"When you do get out of this chair, how about we get you a cheerleading outfit? I'm sure I've still got my football jersey around here somewhere...we could play 'our high school just won the championship' and see what happens."

Her laughter burst out, releasing even more tension, as he'd hoped it would. "I don't know about that..."

"I didn't think so, but you can't blame a guy for trying." He pulled back enough to look into her eyes. His hands slid up to cup her face before he kissed her tenderly.

"So. What's on your agenda today?" Tom asked.

"Tonight we're supposed to take lasagna to the hospital for the smell therapy. I can make it this afternoon so it's cooled off enough to take when we're ready to go, if you'll pull the ingredients down from the shelf. I can't reach the noodles or the jar of sauce. That's all I've got planned. What about you?"

"Sure, that sounds good. I'll get those down for you now, and then I'm going to change the oil in the truck."

"Okay." He stood and turned toward the kitchen. Andy watched him walk away, and enjoyed the view.

That was a step in the right direction, Tom thought. He still needed her to hear what he had to say, but it would hold. While he worked on the truck, he could work out how to tell her.

CHAPTER NINE

Karen walked up the chipped cement steps and reached for the handle on the heavy wooden door. Before she could grasp it, the door pushed open and a young, harried-looking mother came out, stern look on her face, firmly gripping the hand of a toe-headed boy who looked to be six or seven years old. She pulled him along, telling him how lucky he was that the police didn't put him in jail this time, how stealing is a crime and he'd better believe that officer when he said next time he would be looking out through the bars from the inside of that jail cell. His eyes were wide with fear and shimmering with tears ready to spill down his already tear-streaked face.

Karen kept her face serious until they'd passed, the mom glancing back over her shoulder once they had, and gave Karen a conspiratorial look. Karen smiled and winked, then added a 'thumbs up,' pleased to see a parent who took an active role and taught her child right from wrong. *Good job, mom, scare him straight early.*

Her hands were uncharacteristically clammy; she wiped them on her suit pants as she walked up to the counter. She had been to the police station a few times in the last year to talk with different detectives about other cases; she hadn't yet approached the topic of her incident with anyone here.

Without a look up from his paperwork, the officer who manned the desk managed to sound disinterested and gruff at the same time.

"Help you?"

Karen's eyes twinkled, and a smile played at the corner of her lips. She put forth her best reporter voice. "I'm here to report a theft."

The officer's hand reached out and picked up the phone's handset. "Something was stolen? Where?"

Before he had a chance to dial to the back, Karen broke into a grin. "Here. Your personality. Not sure when, but that boy who just left looked like he had a good one."

The officer froze for a split second, his hand over the phone's numbers. Slowly he cradled the receiver before he looked up, eyes narrowed to slits. "What did you—"

Karen broke into an uncharacteristic belly laugh. "Ted, I'm kidding. When did you transfer out here?"

His face lost all of its sternness and broke into a huge smile. "You had me for a minute there, kiddo," he grinned as he came out from around the counter and towered over her, then swooped her up into a bear hug. "How have you been?"

Ted, Officer Dunphy to most people, stood six foot five and went a solid two hundred eighty pounds. His military buzz cut lent itself well to his dark brooding eyes and square jaw to give the impression of someone you didn't want to mess with—and you really didn't want to mess with him. He was the officer who had responded to her first frantic call many moons ago when someone had broken into her apartment. She'd been new in town, didn't know anyone, and was so shaken up he'd broken protocol and taken her to his house to stay with his wife that night while he worked the rest of his shift. The two women had stayed up talking and bonded that night, and by the time he'd arrived back home the next morning Karen was asleep on the couch and Maria knew why Karen had freaked out. Maria told him about the stalker who had terrorized Karen before she moved to Aspen Grove. She was worried he'd found her.

Karen stayed with Ted and Maria for a couple days until the apartment manager had the door replaced and fitted with better locks. Ted had kept an eye on her until he'd transferred to Tulsa. They hadn't seen each other in a good while.

Karen hugged him back, hard. "I've been good. How are you? How's Maria? The kids are good, right? When did you transfer back in?"

He set her back on her feet. "They're good, all good. Maria's great, and the kids are growing like weeds. I've been back a week or so." He looked her over and stared intently into her eyes. "You look good, except your eyes."

He called out to one of the guys at the back desks. "Hey, Johnny, man the counter for a few, huh?" A hand shot up and waved in response.

"Let's go back here, talk about it." He walked her back to an unoccupied room, followed her in, and closed the door behind them. Both the door and wall that faced the inside of the station were made of glass. They could see everything that was going on, but no one could hear their conversation.

She sat in one of the worn out metal chairs and blew out a breath. "Before you say anything, it's not the stalker. He stuck around for a bit but has been quiet lately. Maybe he lost interest, I don't know. I wasn't much fun for a while there." She scooted around, tried to get comfortable on the worn-out cushion, crossed then re-crossed her legs. "There was an incident seventeen months ago. I was cutting through an alley and was attacked by a thug. Things went south and I shot him. I was in a coma for a week, though the doctors don't know why. There are some details I can't remember, and I really need to talk to the officer that responded to the scene, see if he remembers anything else. Maybe take a look at the report."

Ted narrowed his eyes at her for the second time in two minutes. "Why didn't you call me?"

"Because you would have come back to Aspen Grove, and there wasn't any reason for that. The attacker was dead, I killed him myself, and I came out of the coma, physically fine, with most of my memory intact. What good would it have done?"

Ted felt a paternal tug. "After all those cookouts and hanging out at our house, you didn't feel the need to call and let us know you were okay? That something had happened?"

"So you'd worry. Yeah, that's what I wanted. More people fussing over me."

"*More* people? Hmmm, you've met someone." He leaned back in his chair and laced his fingers behind his head. "Tell me, Miss Smartypants, who is this person that worries about you."

She looked at the floor. "I didn't want to tell you because I didn't know how serious it would be, and then as time has gone on its gotten more and more...I don't know what it is. I just know that Ben is a good man. We'd just had our first date the night of the incident, and he stuck with me at the hospital during the coma, and took care of me when I woke up and after I was released. We've been dating ever since." She knew she was rambling, but Ted was the closest thing she had to a friend, other than Ben.

"What's his last name?"

Her eyes snapped to his and her index finger shot up in the air. "Oh, no you don't. You're *not* running him in the system." She looked at him for a long second, then dropped her hand. "No need. I already did."

"Good girl." Ted nodded his approval. "I'm glad you've found someone. You should bring him around for dinner one night. I know Maria would love to see you and it will tickle her to know you've got a special someone."

"I'd like that, too. I'll talk to Ben and we'll get something worked out soon."

"Now, tell me more about the mugging. When did it happen, exactly? I'll pull the report and get the officer's name."

While Ted went to pull the report, Karen checked her email on her phone. Not seeing anything that couldn't wait until she got to the office, she dropped the phone back in her purse and stood up. There wasn't much space in this room, but she could see the detectives' desks through the glass and watched them going about their normal routine. *Not much different from the television station*, she noted.

"Okay, sorry that took so long. Computers were down." Ted strode through the door with a slim stack of papers in his hand. "I've skimmed the report and pulled your mugger's sheet, too." Ted passed the one-page incident report to Karen. "Officer Brighton was the first on scene. He's off duty today, I checked, but he'll be back tomorrow. I've left a message for him to give you a call."

"That's great, thank you."

As she read the report, he read through several pages of arrests. He gave her the highlights. "His name was Darnell Taylor, twenty years old, in and out of the system. Spent some time in juvy between foster homes. He was apparently well-known by several officers from the looks of this. He'd been picked up on everything from drug charges to robbery, and slid on a charge eighteen months ago for lack of Miranda rights. That one was for robbing the Zippy Mart. Was a suspect in another—"

Karen looked up, clearly startled. "Wait. Go back. What happened eighteen months ago?"

"Zippy Mart robbery. Caught in the alley with a paper sack of money and a ski mask. Why?" Ted watched the color drain from her face. "Karen?"

"Darnell Taylor. I'll have to look to be sure, but I think he was the one in the breezeway by the courthouse with Jerome Carion when the fight broke out. I was there with my camera man covering the Carion trial and we arrived late. There wasn't anywhere left for us to set up our shoot, nowhere that wasn't already occupied, so we set up on the side of the courthouse with a view of that walkway. There were two prisoners and some guards, four I think, and when they got near each other there was shouting and one of them attacked the other. I don't know who started the fight, I was focused on the camera. I do remember that was the piece that got me promoted to the crime beat because no other station caught that fight. Keith and I were in the right place at the right time. That was my lucky break. You're telling me *he* was the one that tried to mug me?" Sweat popped out across her brow as the stars clouded her vision.

Ted was around the table in three steps, pushing her head down between her legs. "Don't pass out on me. Breathe." He reached over and opened the door. "Can we get some water in here, please?"

"I'm okay, I'm okay." Sitting up, Karen fanned herself. "Just got hot for a minute there."

"No you didn't, you lost all color, broke a sweat, and started to sway. You were going to pass out on me and I don't do well with that. Not on my watch, young lady."

Another uniform brought a bottle of water in. "Everything alright in here?" His eyes were kind, and he did a double-take at Karen.

"Thanks, Nunez. She'll be fine in a second. Got a little shock."

He nodded, still staring. "Aren't you…" he asked, not quite sure he believed it.

Even as Karen nodded, Ted pinned him with a look. "Keep this up and you'll make detective one day."

Nunez paled a little bit himself and backed out of the doorway.

"That wasn't nice." Karen drained half of the water.

"He's new. He'll learn. Feel better?"

"Yes, thanks."

"Now you want to tell me why you almost passed out?" He sat on the edge of the table, not sure she was fine yet.

"Um, if he was the one in that alley, was the attempted mugging a coincidence or was he following me, waiting for a chance? I'm the reason that fight landed on the six o'clock news. If he knew that, it might not have been an accident that our paths crossed. What if…"

She still felt lightheaded.

"Drink." Ted commanded. She drank.

"Did anyone know you were going to be in that alley that night? Did you tell anyone where you were going or how you were getting there?"

"No. I met Ben for dinner, and afterward I told him I was going home. I didn't want him to worry about me, I had to meet with a confidential source who's skittish and wouldn't have trusted me if I didn't go alone. My source has always been paranoid. So I said goodnight to Ben, got in my car, drove around the block, and parked back at the restaurant. I went through the alley to cut time off the walk. I'd planned to walk all the way around since it was dark, but it was freezing too. I didn't see him, he was just there."

"You got in your car and left. If he'd been watching you, he wouldn't have stuck around, not with it being cold. No reason to, you were gone."

"Then why was he in the alley?"

"That's not the best part of town, and you should have known better than to take the alley in the first place. Having said that, he was probably hanging out, waiting to meet someone and you were an opportunity to score cash."

"You think it was a coincidence." She shook her head, more to clear it than to deny.

"Think about it. He had a record of stealing from people, a drug habit, and no job, so I doubt he had a car. No one except your informant knew you'd be walking down there, and probably didn't know you would be in the alley. Informants don't normally tell people when they're going to meet with reporters. That's how the information and the cash flow dries up. I don't normally believe in coincidences, but I don't see anything that links the two instances together."

She thought about that. "You're probably right. But can I keep this police report and that copy of his sheet? I'd like to do some more research, give myself some closure on this. I'm still trying to remember what happened and I need all the facts I can get."

"I can let you keep the report, but I can't give you his sheet." He laid the pages face down on the table. "Can I get you some more water?"

Karen's brows drew together for an instant, then smoothed back out. "That would be nice, thank you."

"Okay. I'll be right back." Ted got up and walked out.

As soon as he disappeared from sight, she flipped the pages face up, took out her phone and snapped a picture of each page before hastily sliding the stack back together and flipping it back over.

He came back a minute later with another bottle of water. Karen stood up. "On second thought, I feel better. I don't think I need any more water. I should get going."

She gave him a quick hug. "Thank you for everything."

"Call us, we'll set up that dinner." He watched her go. Stepping back into the room he picked up the stack of papers and flipped through them. They were out of order. *Gee, how did that happen?* Taking a big swig of water, he folded and pocketed the pages before strolling back toward the front counter.

The drive to work took Karen fifteen minutes on a good day and closer to twenty on a bad. So far it was looking like a good day. As she pulled in the parking lot and angled toward her assigned space, her cell phone rang. The number on the readout was unfamiliar.

"Karen Fielding."

"Miss Fielding, this is Officer Brighton from the Aspen Grove Police Department. I have a note here asking me to call you." His voice sounded very young. She didn't remember meeting him at all; she'd already been in a coma in that alley when the police had arrived.

"Yes, thank you for getting back with me so quickly." Karen explained what she was looking for and why.

"I can pull that report and leave a copy at the front desk for you, if that would help." Officer Brighton offered.

"I've got a copy of the report; I was wondering if we could sit down and talk, face to face, about what you remember. I know it's a long shot, but I'm still trying to piece together what happened that night, and anything you might remember, no matter how small, could be a big help to me. The hole in my memory is driving me crazy."

After a short pause, Officer Brighton cleared his throat. "Alright. I'm on shift, but can meet you at the Brew 'n Stew around eleven o'clock."

The Brew 'n Stew was a coffee house that locals flocked to for the soups Betty made daily. She was the owner and a whiz in the kitchen. Karen looked at the clock on her dashboard. Seven-thirty a.m. By her calculations, the time it would take to get through the morning meeting and run through her story with the cutting room for the noon edition of the news would be tight, but she thought she'd be able to make it. "Great, I'll see you there. Thank you so much."

~~*~*~*

It was just shy of eleven o'clock when the bell over the door tinkled as Karen walked in to the Brew 'n Stew. The place always reminded her of a 1950's soda fountain: long counter down the middle, red plastic-covered stools lined up like soldiers in front of that, and booths to the right and left covered in the same red plastic. Black and white checkerboard floor tiles fed into the same feeling. The only thing that was missing was a juke box in the corner. Looking around, she didn't see any uniforms, so she took a booth near the back and positioned herself where she could see both doors.

By her watch, it was exactly eleven a.m. sharp when a lone

officer stepped through the door and removed his hat. He ran a hand over his short, sandy blonde hair and looked around. She raised her hand in a wave; he nodded and made his way toward her.

His thin frame took nothing away from his air of authority. The crisp lines of his uniform made her think he was probably detail-oriented. He strode her direction. His right hand rested on the butt of his gun, while sunlight coming in through the front windows flashed off the gold band on his left hand, with which he carried his hat. The wedding ring didn't stop heads from turning, though; the women couldn't help but watch him walk by. Could have been the uniform; more likely it was the combination of that and his baby face that enticed young and old alike.

"Miss Fielding?" His smile made her feel secure, for some strange reason.

"Officer Brighton. Please, call me Karen. Thank you for meeting me." She returned his smile and waved her hand in a gesture offering him to join her.

"Call me Zeke. I wasn't sure you were the same Karen as on the news, but I see now that you are. I was glad when you were moved to the crime beat. I appreciate the way you word your stories, not giving away anything that's being kept under wraps, even if you've managed to get that information out of the police department."

Her smile brightened. "Ah, a fan I see. The way I see it, you 'boys in blue' do a fantastic job in Aspen Grove. I want to do my job without stepping in the middle of yours... makes for a better relationship all the way around, and a better community."

The waitress came by and took their order. After she left, Karen pulled out a note pad and pen from her purse. "You don't mind if I take notes, do you?"

"No, not at all. Though I'm not sure what I can help you with. I took the liberty of refreshing my memory by reading the report, and I believe everything is in there." He folded his hands on the table in front of him, appearing relaxed. His eyes didn't come off of her, yet she got the distinct impression that he was aware of everything going on around them.

"The report is helpful, it has details that I wasn't aware of. What I'm hoping you'll be able to help with is your impressions, maybe something that struck you as out of place but wasn't directly related to what had happened to me, something that wouldn't have gone in the report—something…seemingly insignificant, maybe?" Her eyes were hopeful.

He wanted to help her. Thinking back, he went through everything he remembered from the time he got the call to the time he filed the report, relating everything to her as if he were giving a report. There wasn't anything unusual, nothing she hadn't heard before.

By the time their lunch arrived, she hadn't made one mark on her paper. She exchanged her pen for a fork and picked at her salad and pushed it around on her plate.

Zeke ate his hamburger and fries like a starving man. Probably more like a man who could get called away at any minute and didn't want to waste a perfectly good meal. When he finished, he wiped his mouth and placed his folded napkin over the empty plate.

"Someone had to have seen something. How else am I going to go about finding them? I'm certainly not going to hang out in that area without knowing whose door I'd be knocking on." Almost to herself, Karen talked it through. "There weren't any businesses open that late, the movie theater was already done with its last showing that night. I remember thinking about that before I decided whether it would be better to walk all the way around the block or save a few minutes and cut through the alley."

"If you thought all of that, why did you walk through the alley anyway? You had to have known it wasn't the safest part of town."

"I'd thought about it, sure, and made my decision to go around… and then I got sidetracked thinking about something else. Next thing I knew, I was in the middle of the alley already. Thought it was silly to go back just to go around. Probably wouldn't have helped anyway, the report says I was found at the far end of the alley from where I'd started. He'd have still been there."

"Have you talked to the person who called in the report in the first place? I believe it was a security guard working at the First State Bank and Trust on the corner. He may be able to help you with more."

Officer Brighton pulled out his wallet.

Karen waved him off. "No, no, this one's on me. I appreciate your help."

"That's not necessary." He flipped open his wallet. A photo showed through the plastic protector sheet of a beautiful brunette smiling up at the camera, holding a tiny bundle wrapped in a pink baby blanket.

"No, really, I mean it. Go on, keep us safe out there." She flashed her hundred-watt smile again.

"Thank you then. If there's anything else I can do, let me know." As he walked out, the women followed him with their eyes. Karen shook her head and smiled. The photo in his wallet told the rest of the story…it was obvious he didn't see the other women at all.

Pulling out her phone, she checked the internet for the phone number to the First State Bank and Trust. She dialed and then waded through the electronic choices until she got to one that let her talk to a real person. "Hi, can you tell me what time the night guard comes on duty? I'd like to speak with him. Four-thirty? Thank you."

She looked at her watch. It was now a few minutes before noon. Karen gathered her things and scooted out of the booth. With nothing pressing and no assignments currently on the table, now would be a good time to get started with the research. Her apartment wasn't far from here, and it would be much quieter there than at the newsroom.

~~*~*~*

She squeezed her eyes closed and held them that way for several seconds. Reading on the computer screen as much as she had this afternoon always gave her a headache from the eye strain. Even with her eyes closed, she could feel one coming on. Karen shut down her computer and tossed back a couple of aspirin with a glass of water.

The amount of information she'd been able to come up with on one Darnell Taylor was astounding. A couple different articles reported his having been raised in foster care, and alluded to the homes he'd been in at the time not being in existence any longer. His obituary was only two paragraphs long and didn't contain any information except that he was not survived by any relatives that were known.

Picking up her keys, she locked the door behind her and climbed into her car for the short drive to the bank.

She arrived a few minutes early. After checking in with the security guard currently on duty and letting him know she was waiting for his relief guard, Karen sat in one of the comfortably oversized armchairs in the sitting area.

It didn't take long before she saw the guard on duty stand up and greet his replacement when he arrived. She waited while they talked over a clipboard for a minute. When both men turned and looked at her, she took it as her cue. In one fluid motion she stood and smoothed her skirt, then strode over to where they stood, her heels clicking on the tile, punctuating each step.

"Hi, I'm Karen Fielding." Her outstretched hand directed toward the new arrival. "John was kind enough to let me wait for you in hopes that we could talk for a moment before the bank closes."

"Henry Anderson." He took her hand in his and patted the back of it with his other hand. "It's nice to meet you, Miss Fielding. I've seen you on the news a time or two." His brown eyes twinkled behind his glasses and the smile he gave her rivaled her own. He stood close to her same height and looked like he might outweigh her by twenty pounds or so. She guessed his age at somewhere around sixty, though she couldn't be sure. His dark hair was combed back, giving an uninterrupted view of the lines in his face. They were happy lines, the kind possessed by a man who enjoyed life to the fullest, and she imagined he had stories to go with each and every one of them.

"You got it from here, Henry?" John asked. "Kim's making pot roast tonight."

Henry let go of Karen's hand, turned back and grinned. "Yep, I've got it. You go on, now, and if there's any left, bring me some for tomorrow night's dinner, okay?"

"Will do, though you know there aren't usually any leftovers from pot roast. Miss Fielding." John clapped Henry on the shoulder, nodded to Karen and turned to go. He called over his shoulder, "Speaking of leftovers, there's meatloaf in the fridge for you."

Henry laughed. "Thank you, my friend, and thank Kim too."

John waved over his shoulder in acknowledgment on his way out the door.

"You can't imagine how long I've waited to hear that a beautiful young woman was waiting for me." Henry turned his attention, and his smile, back to Karen. "You've made my day. Now, what is it I can do for you?"

"First of all, I want to thank you. There was a night when you called 9-1-1 about something happening in the alley over there," Karen pointed to where the incident had happened. "I was the woman they took to the hospital."

His smile faded, replaced by concern. "Oh, you are most welcome. It looks as if they arrived in time and you're doing well now. I'm so glad. I had no idea who it was or what had happened, I just saw something and reported it. Couldn't leave my post or I'd have checked on it myself. That was my first instinct. Military training, you know. My job is to guard the bank, though, so here I sat, watching while they tended to you and took you away in the ambulance."

"You did everything I could have asked. I'm glad you were paying attention and I appreciate your calling the police. I'd really like to hear you tell the story from the beginning, if you don't mind."

"Let's sit." Henry motioned her to the chair next to the guard stand and, after she'd settled, claimed his own chair. "That night was cold, I remember that. There was snow on the ground and the heater in this building was on the fritz. Sometimes it worked, sometimes it didn't. Come to think of it, sometimes it worked too well. I remember sitting right here where I am now when I heard it. More like heard 'them' since there was more than one shot. I know a gunshot when I hear it, and that's what I heard. Several of them, four or five best I remember." His eyes were distant, seeing into the past. "I'd gotten through my rounds, just settled back to read a bit when the pop cracks happened. The shots, then the reverberations off the building, heard them both. I jumped up and went over to the window there, and saw a lady, guess that was you, on your knees and a body prone on the ground. Didn't look like that one was moving much, but it looked like you needed help, the way you had your hands on your head. To be honest, I thought you were shot, or maybe that was your husband and someone had shot him and run away."

Henry blinked and came back to the present and looked at her, eyebrows furrowed. "What was it that happened that night down there?"

"You didn't see anything before you heard the gunshots?" Karen avoided answering his question for the time being.

"No, ma'am, I didn't. Wish I would have, might have saved the other one's life too. He was dead then, wasn't he?" Henry looked at her with sadness in his eyes.

She nodded. "The police told me he was dead when they

arrived. Though don't feel sad for me, I ..."

He waited patiently.

"Henry, the reason I'm here to visit with you is twofold. I did want to thank you for calling the police that night. I should have come before now to do that, though I didn't know who called it in. Secondly, I have a hole in my memory where most of the details from that time period should be and I was hoping you could fill in some of the blanks."

"I'm happy to tell you what I know." His eyes were kind.

"I remember walking into the alley from the other end, and I remember waking up from a coma several days later. I've been told by the police that the person who died was not a nice person; from what they can put together he attacked me and I killed him. He had a record and was a frequent guest of the jail. The doctors tell me I should be able to remember what happened when my brain thinks I'm ready to handle it. They can't tell me why I ended up in a coma in the first place or when my memory will return. I'm trying to help it along."

"I'm glad he's dead, then. No one has the right to attack another person who isn't doing any harm. It sounds like he had it coming one way or another anyhow. I didn't see anything when I came back down to the lobby after making my rounds, and I usually look out the windows to make sure. Another lesson learned the hard way in the military. I sure wish I could help you more, Miss Fielding, but I didn't see anything beforehand."

"Please, call me Karen. Thank you for your time and for telling me what you did see. I don't remember kneeling over his body, and I don't remember shooting him, but it was my gun that killed him and nobody else's fingerprints were on it, they tell me, so I must have. In this part of town, had there been someone else around, my gun wouldn't have still been there when the police arrived, either." She stood to go, reaching out her hand again. He took it and patted it the way he had earlier. She patted his hand in response.

Henry checked the clock and walked her to the door. "Take care of yourself, Karen, and keep that gun handy. It probably saved your life that night. It may well do it again, this day and age."

"Thank you, Henry. You take care of yourself, too. Enjoy your meatloaf." He held the door for her and tipped his imaginary hat.

CHAPTER TEN

The most current in a long line of young, blonde, and toned receptionists called out to Karen as she strode past. "Ms. Fielding, Mr. Barnett's looking for you."

Karen changed direction and stopped at the desk. It was unusual for the station manager to come looking for her directly instead of picking up the phone. In fact, she couldn't recall even one instance when any one of the parade of receptionists who'd graced the front desk had stopped her with a personal request from Bob. "Did he say why?"

A look of confusion crossed her face, as if no one had told her she'd have to do more than pass on messages. "Um, no. He looked pretty serious, though." She smiled like she'd done something good.

"Thanks." Karen turned away. *No sense asking more of her than she's capable of,* she thought sarcastically. *Just hire somebody with a brain and be done with it. What's so hard about that?*

The hallway to his office was off the beaten path, and it showed. Even when the rest of the station received a facelift, this area did not. He didn't like change, didn't want change, and wouldn't allow it until he walked out for the last time. The dark paneling dated the look to the 1970's and the threadbare olive-colored carpet was only visible along the edges where the throw rug running down the middle didn't cover. Even the throw rug was worn and in dire need of replacement. What was once a scene from little Italy woven with brilliant reds and golds was now faded. Several feet in the middle were watermarked from the leak in the ceiling that had happened before Karen's time.

Careful not to snag her heel on the loose threads, she tiptoed her way toward his office at the end of the hall. Before she even got near the door she could hear his gravelly voice booming. *Oh, great, he's in a mood.* She contemplated coming back later and started to turn when his phone slammed down. A split second later his door flung open and he stood in the doorway.

"About time." He turned and disappeared back into his office, not once thinking she wouldn't follow.

How does he do that? Is there a camera in the hall or does he have a sixth sense? She asked herself for the umpteenth time and followed him in.

"Close the door." He was an imposing man, standing six foot five and weighing in somewhere around two hundred and fifty pounds; he was used to people doing what he told them to do. She closed the door.

The walls were covered in the same paneling as the hallway, lending the feeling of a man cave instead of an office. Awards and plaques, in chronological order, plastered an entire wall and rounded the corner onto the next. They dated from before she was born and continued through his career. The most recent plaque displayed on the end of the long and distinguished line had a date of last month and was a presentation from the city council for…the writing was too small, she couldn't read it from where she stood. The large window behind his desk looked out over the back parking lot and, beyond that, woods.

"What's going on in crime?" His chair creaked in protest as he settled his large frame into it. The sun peeked out from behind a cloud and reflected off his bald pate; the only hair he had left was all in his bushy moustache and eyebrows. He wore grey suit pants with a tan shirt and blue suspenders. His coat jacket hung on the coat rack in the corner behind the door. She'd never seen him in anything but a suit and suspenders, and couldn't be sure he owned anything else.

She stayed standing behind his guest chairs. "Not much at the moment. No big trials, no murders, not even a jaywalker. People are being nice to each other." It wasn't the answer he wanted but it was the only answer she had.

He leaned back in his chair, causing it to creak and groan.

Picking up his lit cigar from the ashtray, he puffed several times then blew smoke rings. The visual of a dragon came to mind, and she bit the inside of her cheek to keep from smiling.

There was no smoking in the building, but the last guy that made it an issue was flipping burgers and asking, "Would you like fries with that?" She certainly wasn't going to follow in that kid's footsteps by laughing out loud and having to explain the dragon visual.

Karen's expression sobered and her muscles tensed, not sure what was coming but knowing, somehow, that she wasn't going to like it.

When he finally leaned forward, his chair clunked and she thought it was going to give up the ghost. It didn't. "Crime's down, you need a story. Go talk to the widow of the former D.A., the one who died last year..." he narrowed his eyes and looked at the ceiling, searched his memory for a name. "Bruce Hanson. Do a piece, see where she is and what's going on with her. Make it interesting."

Karen didn't know what she'd thought might be coming but this hadn't even crossed her mind. He wanted her to do a fluff piece? She thought she'd gotten away from those. Feeling like the receptionist looked, out of her usual zone, she blinked rapidly several times, processing.

"You want a story on the widow of that attorney, the one who keeled over in his living room?"

His eyes bored holes into her. "Unless somebody whips out an Uzi and goes crazy in the town square. Go."

"Yes, sir." She let herself out, closing the door as quietly as possible behind her lest he take a slamming door as dissention in the ranks. Better a piece on a widow than on the hot dog eating competition.

CHAPTER ELEVEN

Caroline was the first to arrive. Looking at her watch, she saw that she was a few minutes early.

"Welcome. How many in your party, please?" The hostess was slim with dishwater blonde hair, and wore a tailored white button-down shirt and black pencil skirt. The name tag on her shirt read "Bonnie." Her age could have been anywhere from twenty to thirty. It was hard to tell these days.

"There will be four of us."

"Follow me, please." She smiled, flashing a perfect set of teeth and a dimple in her right cheek, then turned and sashayed toward the center of the room.

As Caroline followed, heads turned. They always had. It used to be because she was pretty with her perfectly styled hair and polished manicure, standing five foot four and weighing in at one hundred thirty pounds. Now she suspected it was because she was the widow of Bruce Hanson, former assistant district attorney gone big-wheel private practice, and the mystery that still surrounded his death and her own coma. She'd tried to remember the details, but there were holes in her memory, whether anyone believed that or not.

She did what she'd learned to do over the last year and a half. She held her head high and pretended she didn't see the stares.

"Your server will be right with you. Enjoy."

Caroline chose a seat where she could see the entryway. The décor in this room hadn't changed since she'd moved to Aspen

Grove. Three of the walls were painted a deep dark red; the fourth was floor to ceiling windows with white sheers pulled back and held with thin gold ties. The view through the windows was gorgeous at sunset, the lake reflecting the sun off the water and sailboats gliding by. Each table was covered with a white tablecloth. Gold napkins held by rings the same shade as the walls tied the color scheme together.

Picking up her menu, she looked over the selections while she waited. It had been awhile since they'd chosen Girabaldi's.

"Hi, you're early."

Caroline looked up. Her friend, Amy, was standing there striking a pose in a white summer shift skimming above her knees and belted at the waist. Her eyes sparkled behind her round, rose colored glasses. She was one of those women who didn't seem to age, ever. Her lovely caramel colored skin glowed like a teenager's and her pretty brown bob swayed every time she moved her head.

"Look at you, can you *get* any more tan? What a great dress. Where'd you find it?"

Amy slid into the chair next to Caroline. "I got it online at this place called Edibs, or E-something, I forget the name. Anyway, that website is fantastic. People sell their stuff, and other people bid on it until the auction is over, only Julio—you remember Julio, my pool boy? Well, Julio turned me on to it, and he showed me how to do this thing called 'sniping.' You wait until the last few seconds before you bid, so no one else has time to counter and raise the price, and then you win. Imagine that. I wanted to bid earlier, but he said no, wait, and he made me keep waiting until there were six seconds left, and then he let me put my bid in. Talk about your heart racing, I thought I wasn't going to get it in there in time. Then, you're never going to believe this, I got an email from the lady who had the highest bid before me, and she was pissed. Anyway, if you want, I'll show you how to do it. He said if I want, he can show me how to sell my clothes I don't wear on there, too."

Gina walked up in time to catch the last part of Amy's story. "What site was that? I've got a closet full of clothes I need to get rid of." She pulled out the chair on the other side of Amy and sat down, shaking her long blonde hair back as she did. "Great dress, by the way."

Caroline looked at her watch, more out of habit than anything. "I wonder what's keeping Monica."

"Oh, she won't be here today. She called me yesterday and said she was going on vacation with or without her husband. He cancels at the last minute every time and she's tired of staying home by herself." Amy pressed her lips together to keep the rest of her thought from spilling out. The others shared her sentiment.

"Well, we'll just have to plan lunch for when she gets back, see what's happening then. Being in a marriage with a cheater isn't good for anyone." Caroline had that faraway look in her eyes.

Across the street, Bruce exited the cab and a woman she didn't know followed. The mystery woman kissed him and led him into the hotel.

Gina and Amy exchanged a look.

"What do you know about that?" Gina asked quietly.

Caroline blinked, returned to the present. "About what?"

"About cheating husbands." Amy said, keeping her voice down and leaning closer to avoid eavesdroppers.

The waiter walked up. "Are we ready to order, ladies?"

The moment was gone. "Not quite, we'll need a few more minutes."

As the waiter disappeared, Amy and Gina continued to look at Caroline.

She studied her friends for a few moments. Coming to a decision, she exhaled slowly. "Not here. Why don't we have this conversation at my house this evening? Are you both free around seven-ish?"

They nodded.

"Great. So, what are you going to have? I'm starving." The subject changed for now, Caroline pretended to study the menu and continued to think about what she was going to say to her friends. Until now, she hadn't broken her silence on anything that had happened with Bruce, before the day he died or anything that happened on it.

Caroline studied her eyes in the mirror. Haunted by her past, the shadows lurked deep within, staring back at her, almost mockingly. It was time to try and rid herself of the weight of the secrets—some of them, anyway. Not all. Never all.

She couldn't put this thing to rest alone; she'd been trying unsuccessfully until today. She would talk to her friends and see if they had any ideas on how to fill in the blanks and make the memory whole so she could put it behind her.

The doorbell rang. Caroline left the bathroom and walked down the hall toward the voices.

"Mrs. Hanson will be right in. Follow me, please."

The maid showed her friends to the living room. Caroline followed.

"Thank you, Anastasia. I'll see you tomorrow."

"Yes, Mrs. Hanson. Thank you."

When Caroline returned home from the hospital, she'd kept Anastasia on. Not only because she was an excellent housekeeper; she used her wages to help support her mother. Caroline hadn't, however, continued to make her wear the black and white uniform. That had been all Bruce's idea. She'd always thought it was pompous and unnecessary.

Anastasia had been the one to find Caroline and Bruce the morning after…whatever it was that happened. During the time period that followed her coma and return home, Anastasia had worked extra hours for her. One evening during that time Caroline found out that she'd been taking the bus back and forth, unless she worked too late to catch the last one. When that happened, she'd walked the fifteen miles between Caroline's house and the one she shared with her mother. The morning following that discovery Caroline took Anastasia car shopping. It was the least she could do—had Anastasia not come in that day, the doctor said Caroline probably would have been dead right along with Bruce.

As the front door latch clicked shut behind Anastasia, Caroline turned toward the wet bar and poured three glasses of wine.

"Things were tense before that day," Caroline began. "The story sounds like something out of a book. I should have seen it coming. I'm not even sure where to start."

"Ooh, cloak and dagger." Amy said, sliding on to one of the bar stools, rubbing her hands together.

Gina took the next stool and settled in. "The beginning's always a good place." Gina had always been perceptive, her green eyes giving away the constant turning of the wheels in her mind. The stereotypical blonde act she pulled out when it suited her needs didn't fool her friends at all. She was smart and knew how to work it.

Caroline slid their glasses across the bar to them, and pulled up a seat for herself, facing her friends. She left her glass untouched, instead ticked her nails against the tile counter top. She took a deep breath, blew it out and began. "Okay, it's been awhile now since the accident and the coma. I expected to remember things that happened, figure out what went on between my coming home that day and when I woke up in the hospital. I have yet to remember anything."

Amy toyed with her glass, absently twisting the stem between thumb and forefinger. "We know. It could be awhile yet, or maybe it won't come back at all."

"There are some things I didn't tell you...before. I need some help. I need to figure out what happened. I'm not sleeping, my appetite is off, and I feel like I'm going to go crazy if I don't remember. It needs to be put to rest, once and for all, and I can't do it alone."

Gina reached out and gently put her hand over Caroline's, stopping her from tapping. "We've been waiting for you to bring it up. Listen, we're all friends here, and we want to help."

Tears welled up in her eyes. Caroline had never had true, genuine friends who cared about her and were there for her unconditionally like these two were. The fact that they'd come together over something as superficial as coveting the same piece of jewelry in a store window, and now were such good friends...it boggled the mind.

In every friendship there came a time when the true nature was tested, and it appeared now was that time.

"I appreciate that, and I'm glad. What I have to say has to stay between us."

Amy reached her hand out and put it over the top of Gina's, making a pyramid. "Of course. We wouldn't have it any other way. We're here, whatever you need."

Lifting her glass, Amy said, "To friends, and keeping secrets."

Gina and Caroline lifted their glasses and clinked with Amy's. "To friends." "And secrets."

Caroline picked up a napkin and dabbed the tears from her eyes while she collected herself. She hadn't realized this would be so hard to share, to confide, even with her friends.

"The day before had been when we'd all gone to lunch and Monica was telling us about her vacation. I'd been to Extensions to see Giorgio for my hair and nails appointment and left my car there. It's quicker to walk than to find parking again."

Going over it in her mind again, it was a solid memory until it wasn't. She drained her glass and reached for the bottle to refill.

"After lunch, while I walked back toward my car, I saw Bruce get out of a cab across the street. I started toward him, would have called out if I'd been closer. That's when a woman I didn't know stepped out of the same cab. She kissed him full on the mouth and led him into the hotel."

Even though their glasses weren't empty, Caroline topped them off, as well, unable to look her friends in the eye. If she had, she was afraid she wouldn't have the courage to finish telling her story. She took a deep breath and forced herself to continue.

"I was crushed and heartbroken. I walked without paying any attention to where I was headed. I only knew I needed to think and figure out what to do. The more I walked, the madder I got. Bruce was a high-powered attorney, and I knew I would need proof for a fight when I filed for divorce."

Amy growled low in her throat.

"At some point I went from heartbroken to furious. That's when I stopped, looked around, and saw that I was in a part of town I'd never been in before. Worn out buildings and shady people were dotted all around. I was standing in front of a private investigator's office. The P.I. was standing there in the doorway of his office. He was wearing a suit. I remember thinking it was a little bit out of place, considering his surroundings. He asked if I was lost, and I was, but I wasn't...I was in front of a private investigator's office. Sounds crazy, but I think it was karma answering my question about what to do. So I told him I needed his services and I went in and hired him."

Gina watched her, compassion in her eyes.

Amy hadn't thought this was going to be as serious a conversation as it turned out to be. She looked sad for Caroline. "What happened next?"

"Aston, the P.I., called me the very next day to say he'd gotten the proof already. I was miserable. When I went to see him, I was floored when I looked at the photos and saw Bruce with two different women. Not only was the bastard cheating on me, he was turning it into an Olympic event."

She moved around and to the couch. Her friends followed.

"I remember taking the envelope containing the pictures, and going home. Anastasia was still here, so I hid the photos in the sideboard in the dining room. I'd planned to move them to the safe later, after she left and before Bruce got home. Not like *he'd* ever see them in the sideboard, but I didn't want Anastasia to see them. The thought of that getting out mortified me."

Caroline kicked off her shoes and pulled her feet up underneath her.

"This is where it gets dicey. The next memory I have is spotty. I remember I had a migraine, no big surprise there. Then I remember Bruce came home. We had a dinner thing and he'd gone in to shower and get dressed, and then...nothing. The next memory I have is waking up in the hospital. The doctor said I'd been in a coma for ten days, and that's all they would tell me."

Caroline fidgeted with her necklace. "The police came to see me before anyone else was allowed in. They told me a call had come in to 911 from a neighbor with a complaint of screaming, and they'd been the officers to respond. When they arrived, Bruce was already dead and I was unconscious. The paramedics called for a helicopter, and I was medi-flighted to the hospital. Anastasia was the one who found us; it was apparently her scream that had the neighbors calling the police."

As Caroline told the story to her friends, she relived it in her mind. "They were sorry for my loss, and went straight on to say there were a few questions they needed to ask, some things they wanted me to explain. They wanted to know what had happened. I couldn't tell them, because I didn't remember."

She looked into the eyes of each friend, in turn, to judge how they were taking it. Gina's face held nothing but concern, while Amy's eyes glistened with unshed tears.

"Apparently amnesia isn't all that uncommon in patients who have been in a coma. The doctor told me he expected my memory to return, though couldn't say when. He also said that I'd already slipped into the coma before I arrived at the hospital."

They waited for her to continue. When she didn't, they looked at each other and both opened their mouths at the same time. Gina nodded at Amy to go first.

"Oh Sweetie, we had no idea. Why didn't you tell us?"

"It's not something you want to admit. Besides, I had no idea until I saw him get out of that cab. That was the day before the coma." Her excuse sounded weak even to her own ears. It had been a year and a half since that whole thing happened. The truth was, she was embarrassed that he'd been having affairs right under her nose and she'd not seen anything.

Gina set her wine glass on the coffee table. "You've been living with this for a long time."

The hurt evident in her voice, Amy picked up where Gina left off. "You know you could have come to us. We're your friends, Caro. You can trust us."

"Caro?" Caroline questioned. She'd never been called anything but Caroline by anyone in this town, including her friends.

"Yeah. Caro. I've thought of you that way for a long time. Is that okay?"

Caroline thought it was the sweetest thing anyone had ever done for her. She'd never had a nickname before. She smiled. "Yes, it's okay. More than okay. I rather like it."

"Caro fits you." Gina chimed in. The three raised their glasses in a toast.

CHAPTER TWELVE

Tom turned off the shower and shook his head vigorously. Water droplets took flight, peppering the walls and shower curtain. As he pulled the curtain back and stepped out, he plucked a towel from the clean stack in the linen cabinet and dried off quickly.

It had taken longer to change the oil in his truck than anticipated, putting him behind schedule. Today was the day they were scheduled to begin the smell therapy with Katy.

He dressed in clean, worn jeans and a grey t-shirt before heading down the hall to see how the lasagna was coming along.

"Andy, your turn for the bath," he called.

"Help me, please," a voice replied from the kitchen.

He headed that direction. As he pushed through the swinging door, he saw Andy lying on the floor. Tom hurried over. In one fluid motion he scooped her up and set her gently back in her chair.

"Andy, what happened? Are you okay?" His hands ran down her arms, torso and around her legs, feeling for anything out of place.

"I'm okay, yes. I was reaching for the potholders to take the lasagna out of the oven, do that for me quick please," she said, continuing on while he did as she asked. "As I leaned forward, a sharp pain shot down the back of my right leg. It caught me by surprise; I jerked and fell out of my chair."

He set the pan on the cooling rack before turning off the oven. As her words registered, he spun back around to face her. "You got a sharp pain down your leg? Andy, that's great news. Is the pain gone? Are you alright now? Where down your leg?"

She realized with everything else that had happened, she'd not told him about the strange sensation she'd experienced in her legs after she'd found his note and thrown her temper tantrum to an empty room. *That's over and done, let it go,* she told herself.

"I had one shortly after I woke up yesterday, too, only it wasn't pain, it was more like..." she frowned, not quite sure how to describe it. "Kinda like pins and needles, a little bit, is the only way I can think to put it into words. Yesterday's feeling went all the way down to my toes. Today's was definitely pain and shot down through here," she leaned to the side, "and stopped about here." Her finger drew a line from her butt cheek to the back of her knee.

Tom picked her up out of her chair and swung her around; she wrapped her arms around his neck and held on tight. "Whoo hoo! Andy, the feeling is coming back, you'll be back on your feet in no time," he twirled her in circles, holding on tightly to her, his excitement too much to be contained.

She laughed. "I know, I can't wait. I need you to stop with the circles, though, unless you'd like me to throw up all over the place."

He stopped immediately. "Oh, sorry." Looking into her eyes, he felt something slide into place, like he'd come home again. Not home as in at his house, but home within her. There was one more conversation they had to have before the air would be clear on this. He set her back down in her chair. "There's something else. Let's talk in the living room."

Tom held the door for her and followed her in, settling himself on the couch. She put the brakes on the wheels of her chair and hoisted herself over to sit next to him.

"You had your say this morning. I've got something I'd like to say, as well."

When she opened her mouth to speak, his upheld hand stopped her. "No, just listen for a minute, please."

She blew out a breath before nodding. She sat back, then pushed her bangs away from her eyes and waited.

"I'm sorry, too. Dealing with everything hasn't been easy for me, either, but that doesn't give me the right to hit you. I feel terrible about that. It's not how I was raised, it's not who I am. I'm doing the best that I can, and I promise from here on forward I will not ever hit you again. I'm not that guy."

"We need better communication. We're in this thing together, and we need to stop holding things back from each other until we explode. Both of us. Let's try to talk more every day," she whispered, hoping he would understand how much it took her to admit she was wrong and that they needed help.

"Talk more? To each other?" His tone of voice was incredulous.

Her body tensed as she looked up at his face. The smile was so big, she laughed out loud herself. "Yes, to each other, you goof."

"If you think that will help..."

She smacked his leg. "Oh, you."

"Speaking of talking, I still want you to see a therapist. It would do you good to be able to talk it out to someone who doesn't have a stake in it at all."

Her sigh was exaggerated, resigned. "I guess. If I'm going to do that, I'd like to start fresh with a different therapist, not the one I used before. I was fine talking to him back then, but now, I don't know...maybe a female would be in a better position to understand where I am now in my life." *That's not it. But what is the problem? Why do I, all of a sudden, feel uncomfortable with the thought of talking to Dr. Phillips? There's something wrong here.* The harder she pushed to grasp the reason, the more elusive it became. Then it was gone.

"Good. We can ask at the hospital tonight for a recommendation, if you like." Tom was relieved that she'd taken to the idea of talking with a therapist. The load lifted from his shoulders a little bit. *Every little bit helps*, he thought.

CHAPTER THIRTEEN

Tom wheeled Andy into the hospital, the warmth of the lasagna radiating through the insulated carrier held on her lap. The smell permeated slightly, but not enough to attract the attention right away of the people around them if they moved quickly, so they did.

As the elevator doors opened, they exited to see Dr. Alister standing at the nurses' station. He turned and saw them moving toward him.

"Hello Tom, Andy. Perfect timing." His smile was warm, genuine. "Dinners have been distributed, so we're good to go. Are you ready?"

"Yes. I hope this works, it was difficult to get it here without eating it on the way," Andy smiled.

"She's right. If we would have had forks..." Tom laughed.

"Let's go, then. It does smell good." Dr. Alister led the way to Katy's room. "I'm interested in the results, myself."

"So how should we do this? Tom?" She held the insulated container up for him to take, then locked her wheels.

"I'll open this and set it on the bed next to her head, where the smell will have its best chance to make an impact. That's what the article suggested, anyway." He turned to Katy. "Now, Katydid, don't knock this off the bed, okay? Andy made it special for you. It would be a shame to see it splattered all over the floor, and a definite low point in my life as I scooped up the top layer and ate it right there."

He unzipped the cover, removed the foil from the top of the pan, and fanned the steam toward Katy's face. Almost immediately the aroma infused the room.

Dr. Alister strode the few steps to the door and closed it gently. "That smells delicious; any minute now we'll have nurses circling the doorway like vultures if I don't close this."

"I'll take that as a compliment," Andy smiled as she said it.

"You should." His own smile lit up his face, adding a twinkle to his expressive eyes.

"While we're waiting to see if anything happens, doctor, maybe you can answer a question for us. If you were to recommend a therapist, who would it be?" Tom asked, his eyes never swaying from Katy.

"What type of therapist?"

"Psychologist, psychiatrist, along those lines."

"Let me think on that for a minute. I don't normally make a habit of recommending one over another, as they all have their strengths as well as weaknesses. Is there a specific reason that one is being sought, or general purposes?"

Andy reached out and took Katy's hand. "I would like to speak with one in a general sense; stress is becoming a problem for me, and talking with a therapist may help relieve some of that."

The doctor stroked his chin. "In that case, might I suggest Dr. Shakespeare. His office is located on Park, in the seven-story glass building near the circle."

"I'm sure he's a fine doctor; I was hoping to see a female, as a preference."

"Hmmm. Dr. Leslie is in the same building over there, and she comes highly recommended. Her husband is a professor and we've run into each other a few times at fundraisers and other events."

"Thank you. I'll give her a call."

Tom continued to fan the smell toward Katy. "The article you gave me on smell therapy didn't give any time frames; how do you think it will work? Can we reasonably expect to see something today, if we're going to see progress? Or do you suppose it will take a few days, weeks, or longer?"

"This is new territory for me, though I've done a bit more research since we initially talked about this. There have been a couple of cases where the patient responded within days. One case in particular, the patient woke up the same night. Hard to tell, as we're in uncharted waters here. None of the case studies had been comatose for anywhere near as long as Katy has."

Tom nodded, and Andy continued to pat the back of Katy's hand.

"Has there been any change in Dr. Stoltz's condition? Any determinations made yet as to what caused his coma?"

Dr. Alister nodded. "Dr. Stoltz had a sister. She flew in once she heard what had happened. In going through his important papers, she found his living will saying he didn't want any life-saving measures taken if something happened to him. He was taken off the machines yesterday and within minutes passed peacefully with a smile on his face. To me, that said he did not have the will to live; he didn't want to come back. I believe he saw something on the other side and went willingly—entirely understandable, given the circumstances. As far as the cause, that's still a mystery."

"I believe whether a person wants to live or not plays a huge part in when, or if, they come back from something like this. What circumstances made his decision understandable, if you don't mind my asking?" Tom inquired.

"Ah, I suppose since he's passed it won't be a confidentiality breach. He had a wife and a daughter, both of whom passed before him. They both fell ill, and he couldn't save them. If they were waiting for him, that's a good indicator of his lack of will to return to this plane. In that situation, if that was it, I believe I, too, would have made the choice to stay where my loved ones were, as well."

"I had no idea. Yes, I believe I would have made the same

choice, were I given one, under those circumstances. I take it you're a believer in the afterlife?"

"Absolutely. My thought is that we don't die, only our host body does. Our souls move along to another plane where we start over or continue on, in whatever form it takes for us to learn the lessons we missed this time around. I also believe that when a patient is in a coma and they come back with stories of having seen people they love who have passed, they've really seen them, and it's been on another plane." Dr. Alister cleared his throat. "I don't normally discuss my beliefs like this. Not everyone is ready to hear what I think in that respect. I hope I haven't changed your opinion of me and that I haven't overstepped my bounds."

Andy turned her head and looked at the doctor. "I think everyone is entitled to their beliefs. I like to think there's more after this world. Having been in a coma, I tend to believe there's more than we can possibly know from here." *Not to mention seeing who and what I saw while I was in that comatose state. There's no way anyone will ever be able to convince me that there isn't another plane, an in-between, and a whole lot more than anyone who hasn't been there can imagine.*

"I, too, am comforted by the thought of moving on instead of dying." Tom added. "Though I'd like to think that Katy's not ready to move on, and by her not letting go and her body not dying, I would also like to think she's going to come back. When she's ready, or when she can, whatever the reason is that she hasn't done so yet. Maybe when she does, she'll be able to tell us what it was that kept her away or why it took so long to return."

The trio grew quiet. Several minutes passed by as they watched and waited.

A knock sounded on the door as it opened. "Miss Katy, it's time to…oh, hello, I wondered why the door was closed." Julie, the nurse on duty and scheduled to look in on Katy slowed, sniffed, and smiled. "Now I know. What's going on with the lasagna? I thought I was smelling things when the scent made it out to the station."

"Smell therapy," Dr. Alister answered. "A technique that has had limited success in coma patients, as reported in an article in one of the medical journals."

"Really. I hadn't heard of this." She took a couple of steps closer, craning her neck to see. "It looks amazing."

"Hey, Julie. Andy and I planned on leaving the pan for the nurses, if you ladies would like it." Tom smiled.

She did a little shuffle. "That," she nodded vigorously, "would be awesome. If I may, it's time for vitals. I just need a minute."

Andy put Katy's hand back on the bed and moved out of the way so the nurse could do her job. After taking and recording her pulse, she checked the drip and then shined a small flashlight into Katy's eyes. Julie inhaled deeply again and sighed. "Holler if you need anything, I'm not going far."

She took her leave and Andy rolled back up to the bed. "I'm glad that Katy has nurses assigned to her that take their jobs seriously."

"We're fortunate to have a staff that is very good at what they do." Dr. Alister picked up the chart and read through the notes. "Her pulse is almost the same now as it was before we started the experiment; it picked up by two beats per minute. That may or may not be something; it could be as simple as the nurse's count. Time will tell. I'll look in on her again before I leave for the night and pay special attention to her vitals." He checked his watch. "It's been twelve minutes since we began our experiment. If it's going to work, I believe we've done what we can to help it along."

"Thank you, doctor." Tom shook his hand. "If there's a change, or anything happens at all, feel free to call. I'll have my cell phone on and it'll be next to the bed when we go to sleep later. Any time of the day or night, don't hesitate."

"You've got it." Dr. Alister left the door open on his way out.

As Tom replaced the foil on the pan, Andy patted Katy's hand again. "Go ahead and take that to the nurses, I'll wait here."

"You sure?"

"Yes. I'll be fine."

"Okay, be right back then." Tom brushed a hand over Andy's hair as he passed her.

When she was sure he was gone, Andy spoke quietly. "Katy, we need you to come back. Tom's at the end of his patience, and my accident isn't helping things between us. It's caused problems with my attitude and patience, too. He needs you back, I need you back, and if there's any way, there is so much to come back to, so many reasons I can't even begin to name them all." She squeezed Katy's hand. "Please. Please, come back."

Tom rounded the corner into the room and could hear Andy's whisper, but wasn't able to make out the words. "Alright, you ready?"

Andy jumped. "Ah, yep. Sure." She tucked Katy's hand under the blanket. "You be good, and we'll be back tomorrow."

Tom said goodnight to his sister. "If you want some of that lasagna, you'll have to get up pretty quick. There were several nurses already attacking the pan when I left their break room." Like his mom used to do, he tucked the blanket against her body and tight down along her sides. "Snug as a bug in a rug. See you tomorrow, Katydid."

Turning her chair toward the door, Andy rolled slowly, waiting for Tom to finish saying goodnight.

He caught up to her in the hallway outside the room. They left the hospital, neither speaking before they'd both buckled their seatbelts and Tom had the truck in gear.

"Do you really think this smell therapy will do any good?" Andy asked, her voice soft and hopeful.

"I don't know. The cases cited in the article are all easy enough to verify by other means on the internet, and I did that just to make sure they weren't made up. I hope we have the same results with Katy as those people had with their family members."

"I do, too. Right now, though, I only see one major problem."

Tom glanced over. "What's that?"

"We only made one pan of lasagna. What are we going to eat for dinner now that ours is being demolished by the nursing staff?"

CHAPTER FOURTEEN

It had been a long day. Karen turned off her computer and pulled her purse out of the desk drawer. A quick scan of her calendar reminded her that tomorrow morning she had to get Caroline Hanson on the phone and try to set up a meeting to interview her. The line had been busy earlier and she'd put off trying again. At least she could say she was working on it if anyone asked. Not that anyone would tonight, seeing as she was the only one left in the building. The place had cleared out about half an hour ago or so.

Karen checked her watch as she strode toward the elevator. *If I go home first, I'll be late for our reservation. I'm not going to do that to him.*

Ben made their dinner reservation over six weeks ago and she didn't want to ruin it for him by not showing up on time. He said he'd heard about Pierre's Skyway, a swanky new restaurant near downtown Oklahoma City, from a guy at work. The waiting list was long, so he'd put their names on a table for the first opening, and that was tonight. The restaurant itself was in a glass walkway that spanned across the canal, ten stories up, connecting two of the newer buildings. She couldn't help but think that the idea was a bad one and it would only be a matter of time before a tornado or earthquake shook the foundations and brought that bridge crashing down into the canal and onto the lower patios, taking everything in the area out of commission. Hopefully there wouldn't be any people there when it happened. Either way, it was a news story bound to happen.

As she waited for the elevator she checked her reflection in the mirrored doors. She smoothed the wrinkles from her skirt then leaned close to her reflection and scrunched her lips back to check her teeth for lipstick. *How long has that been there?* She pulled a tissue from her purse and wiped a smudge off of her front tooth. *I've only talked to every co-worker here and no one said anything. Hopefully it just happened. That's what I'm going with, anyway. See if I tell anyone they've got broccoli in their teeth next time it happens.*

When the elevator opened at the garage level, Karen stuck her head out and looked around. It was still light out, the sun sinking lower in the sky but not below the horizon yet. She didn't see anyone around and didn't hear any sounds that were out of place; regardless, her heart rate ratcheted up a notch. Stepping out, she quickly made her way to her car, keys and pepper spray in hand. Parking garages were one of her least favorite places. Could be her vivid imagination, or it could be the stalker she'd picked up a few years back.

As she got within a few steps of her car she clicked to unlock the driver's door. Getting in, she closed and locked the door behind her. Sliding the key into the ignition, she froze. Fear flooded her body and her pulse raced, her heart slamming against her ribcage.

There was a rose laying on the dash of her car, right above the steering wheel. It was black, and it was dead. Sweat popped out across her forehead and her hands were instantly clammy. Her hair spun around as she whipped her gaze across the back seat, relieved to find it empty. As her stomach rolled, she concentrated on not throwing up. Even without a note she knew exactly who had put it there. She choked on a sob. *He's never going to go away... never...*

The roar of a motorcycle going on the street startled her. Fumbling with the key, she cranked over the engine and got the hell out of there. *I can't take this anymore, I have to tell Ben and then I have to talk to Ted. I'm NOT going to play the victim ever again.*

The waiter took their order, picked up their menus and left. Ben looked across the table at Karen, seeing her faraway gaze for the third time since he'd arrived at the restaurant and found her waiting in the parking lot in her car.

"How was your day?" Ben settled back in the booth.

Karen didn't respond, didn't even blink.

He tried again. "The weirdest thing happened to me. On my way in to work this morning there was a car pulled off the side of the road. The lady standing next to it flagged me down, so I pulled over to see if she was okay. When I got out of the car she ran over to me, threw her arms around me and told me we were having a boy. Isn't that great?"

"Mmm hmm."

"Then when I told her I was having dinner with my girlfriend tonight, she told me I should tell you I didn't want to see you anymore because we were going to live on a chicken farm in South Dakota near her other husband and six children. I told her if you wouldn't agree to move up there with us that that would be a deal breaker for me. So what do you think?"

She twisted her earring, staring off into space.

"Karen?"

"I'm sorry, what did you say?"

"Baby, other woman, South Dakota, chicken farm? Are you in?"

"Sounds like I should have been paying better attention. Want to start over?"

Ben smiled at her. "What's going on with you tonight? You're a million miles away."

"I know, and I'm sorry. There's something I haven't told you and it's really time you knew."

"You were abducted by aliens. I knew it."

Karen laughed a thin laugh. "If only."

"What's got you so distracted?"

"Can we talk about this after dinner? I'd hate to ruin a perfectly lovely dinner." Her smile faltered.

He slid his hand over hers on the table. "Sure," was the only response he could muster, with his thoughts sailing all over the place. *What could it be that she felt she needed to keep secret?*

They made small talk through dinner, but Ben could see she wasn't really there with him. After they'd finished eating, he suggested they go back to his place. She hesitated a fraction of a beat before nodding; not long enough to be counted as an "I don't want to" but just long enough for him to notice.

She followed him in her own car. Once they were inside, Ben poured them each a glass of wine and moved into the living room. From there he let her take the lead.

What she had to tell him could potentially end their relationship. What if he wasn't interested enough to stay with her once he found out what kind of baggage came with her? Not to mention the size of the monster inside one of those bags...

She looked around, gathering her thoughts before she spoke. "When I lived in Philadelphia, my name was Shalia Carpenter. There was a man I'd dated who got drunk one night, showed up at my place, and tried to take advantage of me. I said no. He wasn't interested in that answer. The situation escalated. He hit me, I screamed, and a neighbor called the police. He began stalking me, leaving notes on the door to my apartment, taped to my windows, and eventually he found his way inside and left a rose on my kitchen counter. All of this I reported to the police. There was nothing they could do unless he tried to hurt me. They suggested I move, change apartments, find a different complex or rent a house. So I did. Things were quiet for months. I thought maybe he'd finally moved on. I was wrong. One evening I was carrying a sack of groceries between the store and my car, and suddenly he was just there, right in front of me, tilting his head to the side and smiling like..." She shuddered involuntarily at the memory.

Ben clenched his teeth, his jaw muscles working overtime. He quietly seethed at the thought of anyone doing to Karen what had been done, but he stayed still and refrained from commenting. He didn't want to interrupt her, not now that she'd gotten started.

"He had a knife. I froze. He put the knife to my throat and told me if I ever made him look for me again, he would kill me. As he pulled back, he cut a strip of my hair, caught it with his free hand and rubbed it on his cheek, then laughed softly as he walked away. I was terrified. I drove straight to the police station and filed for a VPO."

Her eyes were distant, staring at something only she could see.

It took everything he had to leave the silence unbroken.

"Victim Protective Orders are only paper, though. It couldn't protect me by itself even if I was granted one, and I didn't feel any safer. The next day I cleaned out my savings account, packed a few things into my car, and took off. I had no plan, no idea where I would go, but I needed to get away. I knew he was serious about killing me; it would only be a matter of time. I drove for almost a week before I ended up in California. Somewhere in Missouri, I think, I stopped at a hair salon to get started on a change to my appearance. I would have kept going if I could have, I was that scared."

He couldn't stand to see her eyes fill up with tears. His heart ached. Unbidden and untimely, he knew without a doubt that this was the real deal. The thought slammed home, his heart bouncing off his ribcage in acknowledgment. He was head over heels in love with this woman and would do anything and everything in his power to wipe that pain off her face and make what had happened to her a distant, unrecognizable memory.

"When I got to California I filed for a name change. There was an ad in the newspaper for a receptionist position at a local television station, which I applied for and got. A year and a half went by quietly. During that time I found that I truly enjoyed the television industry. I thought maybe one day I could become a reporter." Her smile was thin. "One of the reporters took me under her wing and taught me the business. I worked up the courage to go on-screen. It was a small station, local, so what was the harm, right? As soon as I did, I knew I was doing what I wanted to do. I loved every aspect of it."

He clenched his hands, knuckles turning white. Punching something sounded really good right now.

"One day I clocked out and walked out to my car, where my old nightmare shattered my new life. There, under the windshield wiper, was a single white rose. It had three thorns on the stem, and each thorn had blood on it. That same afternoon I packed my car and drove, once again leaving everything and everyone I knew behind, and started over fresh. I left because I had to; I was being stalked from coast to coast by a man who was getting scarier and scarier, and the police weren't much help. I've been freaked out enough to change my entire life twice."

"Oh, Karen." Ben found it hard to talk around the lump in his throat. The urge to protect her was overwhelming. He needed her to know that he would keep her safe.

She blew out a shaky breath. She'd come this far, she had to tell him the rest. "When I got to Oklahoma City, my car broke down—in front of a mechanic's shop, no less. What more could I ask for in a sign? I walked into the shop, talked to the owner. He came out and looked at it, said he knew what was wrong and that he could have it fixed the next day. He pointed me toward a café down the block, and after I'd gotten a sandwich the waitress pointed me toward a safe motel for the night. The next day I went back for my car, which was running smoothly again. The mechanic, Dave, asked if I would be willing to organize his office in exchange for fixing my car; his secretary had quit the week before and he had no idea where anything was, or what she'd done with his unpaid invoices. Right then I knew I had a choice to make: keep running, or stop in a place where I'd found kindness. I worked for Dave for several months, and rented a small apartment nearby. I colored and cut my hair again, worked out daily to change the shape of my body, and bought colored contacts to change my eyes as well. My savings contained enough to get some minor plastic surgery done, just enough that I felt safe."

Her hand fluttered near her face, gently touching her chin, cheekbone, and finally rested on the side of her nose. "Chin and cheeks aren't what they used to be. Nose, I kept, as a reminder to stay vigilant. He gave this to me," she said, her finger tracing the bump that had healed slightly crooked.

Karen flicked her eyes across his; the concern on Ben's face had Karen looking down, around, and anywhere but at him. The last thing she wanted to see was his face when he realized she was damaged goods and he would be better off without her, so she toyed with the stem of her wine glass instead, twisting it back and forth, staring at it like it would reveal the secret to life itself.

Ben leaned close and wrapped his arms around her, drawing her in.

She hesitantly set her glass down and let him pull her close. This could be the last time he held her this way. She allowed herself this last moment to melt into him. *Don't cry, damn you. Hold it together.*

"You're here with me now, I'll keep you safe." His words were spoken soft and low.

She didn't seem to have heard him. With a deep sigh, she pulled back.

"There's something else."

"Whatever else there is, we'll deal with it."

Karen closed her eyes. "You don't understand. I'm telling you all of this because he's found me again." One lone tear tracked down her cheek. Ben wiped it away with his thumb.

"What do you mean, he's found you?"

She took his hand in hers. "Remember back when we first met, that night at the banquet?"

"I'll never forget it. You turned me down for a date."

A ghost of a smile touched her lips. "I remember. How silly of me."

He smiled. "What about that night?"

"When Keith walked me to my car I got in and fumbled my keys. It was dark where my car was parked, so it took me a minute to find them. Once I had them in my hand again, my car wouldn't start. I looked for Keith, but he was already out of sight. So I got out, lifted the hood, and saw the battery cable just lying there, loose, off the battery. I wiggled it back on, got back in the car and the engine started right up. The hood release is inside the car, and the car was locked. It had to have been someone either with a key or who was adept at breaking into cars, because battery cables don't just randomly pop off the battery. Nothing had ever happened like that before this incident, and nothing since."

Finally, Karen brought her gaze back up to Ben's, her eyes locking on his. Fear emanated from within, emotions laid bare in a way she hadn't allowed him to see before.

He felt his heart break for her.

She continued. "That is, until today. When I got in my car at the parking garage after work, there was a black rose, dead, on the dashboard. Once again, my car was locked. I can't do this again, I can't deal with it, I want this to stop and I'm not willing to move again. I've found a place where I am happy and I've found you and I'm so in love with you. I don't know what to do."

Ben brushed his thumb over her fingers. "Technically, I found you."

"I'm serious. I can't do this."

"I'm sorry, honey. Humor is what I use when I'm processing. You don't have to do this alone. We're going to find him and take care of this once and for all."

Her breath caught in her throat. "What?"

"I said, we'll take care of this, you don't have to do it alone." His voice was low, soft, and comforting.

She wasn't sure she'd heard him right. *He's not going to leave me?* All at once the tension drained out of her body. "You're going to help me?"

It was Ben's turn to falter. "Of course I'm going to help you. I love you, Karen."

She leaned in and kissed him, then buried her face in his chest.

Ben wrapped his arms around her and formulated a plan.

"First thing tomorrow we'll go to the police. There has to be a way to make them listen. Do you still have the rose?"

"It's on the passenger seat, although I don't know what good it's going to do."

"I don't know either but it's a start. You won't be alone tonight, you'll stay with me, and tomorrow we'll get this thing worked out. We're also going to stop by the car lot and trade in your car."

Karen leaned back and looked at him for a minute without responding.

He watched her carefully. "What?"

"I can't believe I didn't think about trading in my car. That's the only thing I brought from my old life. Damn it. That has to be how he found me again. It had to have been the damn car."

Ben felt the need to keep in physical contact with her. He ran his hands down her arms and squeezed her hand, working his thumb over her knuckles.

"You can come to me with anything, you know that, right?"

The last piece mentally clicked into place. Relief and belief filled her. She smiled a real smile for what felt like the first time in days. "I do now. Going to the police station brings up another topic of discussion, though."

"You're on the most wanted list?"

"Ha ha, funny guy. No. I need to warn you about Ted."

CHAPTER FIFTEEN

'Andy, what are you doing here?' Katy screamed with her mind. Though her face felt frozen in a perpetual smile reminiscent of The Joker from the Batman series, her thoughts and feelings were anything but positive.

Why can't I say anything with my mouth? Where's the sound? Have I forgotten how to speak?

Katy's brain was firing on all cylinders, overtime, twice as fast as ever before.

Could it be that a dream—or what passes as a dream here, since there's no real sleep—can conjure up my best friend and bring her to this place, this "in-between," as Andy called it?

I can hear Andy's voice when she talks to me in the hospital room, though I can't move or answer. Being physically unable to move is part of the price of admission to the coma zone, the in-between. I hadn't planned to hide away in this level forever, just until the people responsible for what happened to me had been taken care of. Now that the threat was gone, I have no reason to stay here any longer. Why can't I cross back? Andy, can you help me? I want to come back, I don't want to stay here any longer. I'm trying to find my way, but I'm lost. Help me...

Andy was reaching for her, hands out, arms open, mouth forming words that couldn't be heard. As she tumbled backwards, Katy knew she'd been pulled back to the land of the living. Katy *followed as far as she could, stepping to the edge of the precipice, watching Andy's soul reunite with her body, seeing the nurse there next to her and the doctor running in, and Tom...she could see Tom, her brother, the one person who had stood beside her through everything, making sure her earthly body was taken care of in such a way that if, when, she was able to return, which at this point she highly doubted would ever happen, that the vessel she would return to would be ready and waiting. The television was left on all the time, unless a new nurse was assigned to take care of her, then it was stupid soap operas during the afternoon, or, worse, shows about who was the daddy of the babies, who was sleeping with whom, what kind of jobs people did and kept secret from their loved ones...*

"Andy..." she wailed behind her mask of perma-smiles. Please, save me, I don't know how to come home. She lifted her hand, using all of her concentration to make it happen, Andy connected with her body and was brought back to life, in the real world, no longer a part of the in-between where Andy could see her, if nothing else.

It seemed like only a second or two passed before she smelled the lasagna. Wandering through the non-time, she'd not found a way to see her own body in a good long time, or so she imagined. Apparently it was true, as she'd not realized Andy was in a wheelchair. Why was she in a wheelchair? And oh, yeah, why had she been in the in-between to start with at all?

The smell of lasagna. How she missed that. She'd not smelled anything but stale air for so long, it was like a dream filling her senses so full that she was unable to feel or smell anything else. For a moment she'd been above her body, in the room with Tom and Andy, smelling homemade lasagna and feeling Andy's hand patting hers. Why couldn't she open her eyes? 'Because I'm not in my body,' she answered herself. How could she get back into her body? It was time, the deeds were done. No longer were the people responsible for her condition even remotely alive. She'd seen their souls fly past her level, her plane, and slam face-first into The Never. She could hear their cries, their screams...why couldn't she find her way back to her body? Was there something else she needed to do, something she'd forgotten or didn't know needed to be done?

She concentrated with every fiber of her being. Move, damn you... MOVE.

CHAPTER SIXTEEN

Tom walked past the empty nurses' station. It wasn't unusual for the station to be unmanned at this time of the morning. They were probably making their rounds, checking in on their patients, updating charts, reacquainting themselves with the details of each room's occupants in the event there had been any changes since the last time they'd been on shift.

Katy had been here long enough that she was grandfathered in to the "one patient, one room" theory. *Thank goodness,* Tom thought. *It would be harder with another person in a coma sharing her room, the beeps of their machines, the sobs of family members, and the lack of privacy from having to share a room at all. Katy's situation was different than most coma patients: she wasn't hooked up to as many machines as the rest of them, nor was she wasting away as so many others were. Muscle tone being lost, facial features changing, sinking in on themselves, arms and legs reducing to sticks covered by skin.*

He rounded the corner of the doorway and entered her room. "Hey, Katy, I didn't see you..." He stopped in mid-stride. Something was different. What was it?

"Nurse," Tom called out, louder than was probably necessary.

"Tom? Is everything okay?" Cameron ran down the hall, knowing a stressed voice when he heard one.

"No. Who moved Katy's arms?" Tom pointed, and Cameron

immediately saw what he was talking about. "Nobody, as far as I know." He rushed into the room and reached for the clipboard hung on the end of the bed. Flipping through pages, he scanned the writing for a couple of days' worth of time.

"Nobody, as far as I know. There's nothing here that mentions changing her position. There's no reason for anyone to move her except for the physical therapist, and she comes three times a week. She's not been here since Thursday... she's scheduled for this afternoon. I can call down if you want, see if she came early."

"Do that, please." Tom's voice sounded foreign to his own ears. "While you're at it, call Dr. Alister and ask him to meet us here. I'd like to talk with him about this."

"Will do." Cameron moved as quickly as a hummingbird, running back to the nurses' station and making the requested inquiries.

Tom stepped closer to the bed, examining his sister for any other changes that were out of the norm. He didn't see any, though that didn't mean there weren't things so subtle that he was missing them. His heart beat hard against his chest. Changes could be a good thing, but he wouldn't know until the doctor arrived and did whatever he needed to do. Frustration at the clock's infernal ticking set his teeth on edge.

Cameron flitted back into the room. "Dr. Alister's on his way, he said he's five minutes out. He's coming straight to Katy's room, and would like you to wait for him here."

"I'm not going anywhere. Thank you."

Cameron retreated to the corner of the room. He wanted to stay close, to be nearby in the unlikely event something else happened that would require his presence and action before Dr. Alister arrived.

Tom closed in on the bed, moving to within inches from Katy. Reaching out with a trembling hand, he felt her pulse. It was jumpy, as if she'd run a marathon. *What else could cause a heart rate to accelerate like that? Could it be the smell therapy taking hold?* He didn't dare allow himself to believe.

Tom stood there, holding Katy's wrist and feeling her pulse jump. It was better than listening to the seconds tick by. The next thing he knew, Dr. Alister was standing next to him, his hand resting on Tom's forearm, softly saying his name to capture his attention.

"Doctor. I didn't hear you come in. Did Cameron tell you what happened?"

"Good to see you, Tom. He did; why don't you tell me what you experienced?"

"Well, I walked in, like any other day, exactly the same as I've done for years now, only today her right arm was above her head, like that, and her left is bent at the elbow, right there," he pointed, though it wasn't necessary. Dr. Alister had already seen the difference. "She's not been moved by outside sources, or so I'm told. She hasn't been touched at all. Could it be that she..." his voice broke.

"It's entirely possible; you've read the article yourself. What do you think could have caused her arm to move, if it wasn't her?"

"I don't know, but feel her pulse. It could have been mine I was feeling when I checked hers, but…" Tom's sentence trailed off while the doctor checked Katy.

"You're right. Her pulse is all over the place. Tom, I know you're not going to want to leave, but I'm going to ask you to step back." Dr. Alister pushed the call button and asked Cameron to bring some sort of machines, Tom didn't know what they were but he trusted Dr. Alister.

CHAPTER SEVENTEEN

Karen fired up her computer and headed for the break room to make a fresh pot of coffee.

When she got back to her desk, her monitor was blinking and ready to go. Before she called Caroline Hanson, she checked their database and found a clip from several years back where Mrs. Hanson was standing by her husband's side while he accepted an award for something or other. Another clip from a year and a half ago was there. General footage outside her house from when her husband had died and she'd been admitted to the hospital... in a coma.

Karen's heartbeat quickened. *She'd been in a coma around the same time I was, and from the looks of this, there was just as much mystery surrounding what happened with her as there was with my situation. How odd is that?* She scribbled a notation.

There was nothing else on her through the television station's archives, so she pulled up what she could from newspaper articles. There were a couple of articles from the time period of her husband's death, though not any more information than what the television station had provided. All she found between her husband's death and now was a photo and short blurb about a ribbon cutting ceremony at the opening of a health center.

One last search brought a telephone number and address. She added those to her notebook, and sat back. Tapping her pencil against her desk blotter, she took a minute to ponder. *What are the odds that two random people can wind up in comas within a couple days of each other, in the same town, and both under circumstances that were no more than a string of strange occurrences? She told the police there were empty blocks of time surrounding her events, just like there were mine. Is this a total coincidence, or is there more, and we're connected on some level? That's ridiculous, Fielding. What could connect a socialite and a news reporter? Still...no harm in asking a few questions, feel out the situation. Bob sent me after a fluff piece; wonder what would happen if I came back with more than that? Hell, I know what would happen. A promotion and a raise, that's what.* She had the nose of a reporter, and it was twitching. *Certainly can't hurt.*

Before she made the call, she got up and grabbed a cup of coffee. The news room was filling up, the noise level increasing with it. It didn't bother her most days, though making calls was more difficult as the day wore on, so she made it a quick trip.

Back at her desk, she dialed.

"Hello?"

"Hello, Mrs. Hanson?"

"Yes. Who's this?"

"Hi, I'm Karen Fielding, a reporter with Channel 9. I wonder if you would have time to meet with me. I'd like to talk with you for a few minutes."

Silence from the other end. Just when Karen thought she would hang up, Caroline sighed. "To talk about what?"

"I'd like to find out how you're doing after the death of your husband." Karen lowered her voice. "That's the official line. I've also noticed something...strange, something about the timing of your coma and, well, mine, that I would like to follow up on, if you're willing to speak with me, that is."

Karen held her breath for several beats.

"Yes. I'll meet with you. If you can come by my home, I'll be here until ten o'clock, when I must leave for an appointment."

She glanced at the clock. It was almost nine o'clock now. "I'm on my way. Thank you."

~~*~*~*

It was early enough that Caroline was still drinking her first cup of coffee when the telephone rang. Naturally, she'd assumed it was Anastasia calling to ask if there was anything she needed from the store on her way in this morning. The call being from a reporter caught her totally by surprise.

As she dressed for her day, she wondered what, exactly, had prompted this call. The timing couldn't have been more of a coincidence, as she'd just told Amy and Gina yesterday about the situation. The fact that Ms. Fielding mentioned that she'd been in a coma... well, it was hard to believe. *Could it be an angle, some new way to get the foot in the door, or could she be telling the truth?* There was only one way to find out, and her interest was piqued enough that she wanted to hear more. *I'll play it by ear, and if anything sounds the least bit off, I'll throw her out so fast she won't know what hit her.*

The trip down memory lane was exactly the same today as it had been every other time she'd taken it. There were no memories at all during the time period where both she and Bruce had been injured. *That's not really the right word, 'injured,' but what IS the right word?* Forcing the memories did nothing but frustrate her. The newspaper articles didn't help, either. How could they? The only person left alive that was in the room that evening has amnesia. Amy and Gina wanted to help her get her memory back. It was time to do everything possible, or forget about it and get on with her life.

The more she thought about it, the better the idea sounded of having lunch with her friends. At least give them a call, get it set up. They wanted in? They were going to be in.

Looking at the clock again, she gauged whether her friends would be up and drinking their coffee or if they were more likely to still be in bed. There wasn't any telling; perhaps a text message would be better. Dashing a group message off to them, she set her phone down next to her purse so she wouldn't forget it on the way out the door later. No sense being late for an appointment with Georgio because she had to turn around and retrieve her phone.

She hadn't taken three steps before her phone pinged twice, back to back. Looking at her text messages she saw that both of her friends were awake and responding, and both were free for lunch. Tapping out time and place, she dropped her phone back onto the counter as she heard the dainty ding of the driveway alarm she'd had installed. The sound alerted her to the approach of a car in her driveway. Stepping quickly to the door, she checked her hair and make-up in the hallway mirror, patting an imaginary stray hair into place.

As she opened the door, a young woman was striding up the walk. She was pretty, well put-together, and appeared to be somewhere in her twenties. Caroline didn't get the normal vibe she would have expected from a reporter. Most of the ones she'd dealt with in the past had a sort of sheen—something about them that left a bad taste in your mouth, and a feeling of having been taken for a ride without quite knowing why. She didn't get that from the first impression.

Twenty four minutes later, Karen pulled into Caroline's driveway. She arrived alone; not bringing Keith, her camera man, was a calculated risk on her part. She thought she could talk to Caroline, and then if all went well, she could come back with Keith for a short piece to appease the news gods.

Getting out of her car, she hurried up the walk. Before she had a chance to step up on the porch, the door opened.

Caroline was prettier than the photos in the newspaper had led her to believe, though every bit as put together.

"Ms. Fielding?"

"Yes, hello Mrs. Hanson. Thank you for seeing me."

"Please, come in."

"Thank you." As she followed, Karen looked around in awe. She hadn't known what to expect, but the rooms that were visible through doorways as they walked down the hall were subdued; the down to earth decor caught her by surprise.

When they reached the sitting room, Caroline waved her hand toward the couch before moving toward the counter. "Make yourself comfortable. How do you take your coffee?"

"Black is fine. You have a lovely home, Mrs. Hanson."

"Thank you." Turning, she brought two steaming cups, handed one to Karen, and sat in the wingback chair across from her. With that, she pointedly looked at her watch and waited.

Not one to miss the obvious signal, Karen nodded once. "Right." Setting her cup on the coffee table between them, she cleared her throat as she pulled her digital recorder from her jacket pocket. She held it up, and received a nod. Turning it on, she gave both of their names, the date, and the time before setting it on the coffee table next to the cup. "I'd like to talk with you about how you're doing."

"Why?" Caroline sipped her coffee, leaned back and crossed her ankles. She seemed as at home in the company of a reporter as she appeared behind the overly large scissors at some ribbon-cutting ceremony or other in the newspaper photo.

"To be honest, Mrs. Hanson, there's not much in the way of big news, and the boss thinks a story from you would help tide us over." Her eyes widened. "And I'm not sure why I just said that. I'm sorry. Is it too late to start over?"

Caroline's laugh was full-bodied, and unexpected. "Yes, it's way too late to start over. I like your honesty. Call me Caroline."

Breathing a short sigh of relief, Karen lifted her cup and drank. "This coffee is good, and I very much appreciate your time. I'm not normally that frank with people, especially on the first meet. At least I try not to be, especially when I'm recording. What I mean is, never mind. I'm going to get through this first part. Would you mind if I brought my camera man by to do a story on you for the nightly news? The public is always interested in the lives of our own citizens, and your story would be a quick follow-up on how you're doing since the last time we saw you in the news, when..." Instead of saying, 'when your husband died', she backed up and rerouted, "…you were found in a coma."

Caroline sipped again. "I prefer the privacy of not being interviewed on camera, so I'm going to regretfully decline your request. I will tell you that I'm doing well and am recovered. I appreciate the public's interest, though I'm not much of a story."

"I understand. Thank you." Karen was about ready to ask another question, and Caroline pointed at the recorder. Reaching over, she turned it off and pocketed it.

"You've got your quote for the story. I'll thank you to leave anything else we may discuss off the record." When she got a nod from Karen, she continued. "You mentioned on the phone that you were in a coma, as well. Tell me about that."

Karen wasn't used to being the one on the receiving end of the questions. It was...different. "Well, that's the thing. I've got blocks of time surrounding the situation before the coma, information that still hasn't come back, and I'm trying to figure out what happened. All I remember is walking toward a meeting with a confidential informant, then nothing that makes sense until I woke up in the hospital. I remember an intense headache, and I've been told that I shot a man who was trying to rob me. There's no information on why I fell into a comatose state, or anything that the doctors can find to tell them what happened."

She looked at Caroline. "What happened to you?"

After a moment's silence, Caroline spoke. "Off the record."

Karen nodded. "Off the record."

"I've spent the last eighteen months bouncing from 'trying to remember' to 'searching for answers' and back again. Haven't learned anything new about what happened with me, either. No one knows what happened, and I certainly can't remember. I'm told it was Anastasia, my maid, who found us, which makes sense. She would have been the only other person with a key, and was due in to work that morning. I'm also told I was then medi-flighted to the hospital, while Bruce was already dead by the time the paramedics arrived. I was unconscious when we were found, and comatose before reaching the hospital. The only thing I remember after arriving home that day before whatever happened, happened, is that I had a headache, too."

They were both quiet for a minute, reflecting on the parallels between their situations. "It's because there was no one here with you and your husband. That's the reason you haven't been able to make any progress, correct? Or is that in the black hole too?"

"Anastasia tells me I was home when she left, and that Mr. Hanson wasn't here yet. She also tells me that no one came to the door, and when she left, as far as she knew, I was alone. She said I was acting a little strangely that afternoon, but she didn't ask what was wrong. Before Bruce died, she was no more than a maid. I didn't know much about her, except that she cleaned house well and kept to herself. I kept her on when I was released from the hospital; she's been a godsend. Had it not been for her..." Caroline's voice cracked. "If Anastasia hadn't found us when she did, I might very well be dead, too."

Karen gave Caroline a minute before continuing as she thought out loud. "The doctors...did they find anything at all, any abnormalities, or lesions, dark spots, anything, on your brain?"

"Not on mine. They said for all intents and purposes, I was

healthy and there was no reason they could see that could have caused a coma."

"They said the same thing to me. No physical reason, tests were clean. Nothing they could identify."

Caroline checked her watch, then stood. "As I said on the phone, I've got an appointment I'll need to get to, though I've found our conversation interesting. I would really appreciate your keeping it to yourself, and again, off the record."

Karen smoothed her skirt as she rose. "I've enjoyed our conversation, as well. Don't worry, I was only here to get the quote on the record that I got. Everything else will stay private. Thank you for your time, Caroline."

"You're welcome, Ms. Fielding."

"Call me Karen, please."

"Karen."

Caroline accompanied her to the front door and showed her out. As Karen walked toward her car, she turned back and waved, receiving one in return. *This is so odd, knowing her coma mirrored my own. With there being two of us, I have to wonder, are there more?*

Karen backed out of the drive and turned toward the station. Mid-morning traffic wasn't as thick as rush hour, either in the morning or the afternoon, and she made all but one of the traffic lights while they were green, though she didn't notice. Her thoughts circled around the conversation she'd just had with Caroline, and the possibility of there being more to the reason for their comas than met the eye.

Before she realized she'd made the drive, she was putting the car in park in her own space at the station's garage.

The front desk was unmanned when she walked in the door.

Instead of waiting around for the receptionist—whatever her name was—to show back up, she made a right and headed down the hallway to Bob's office.

Karen rapped on his door and heard the familiar, gruff voice bark out. "What?"

She stepped in, closing the door behind her.

"Well?" Bob wasn't one to mince words. He was leaned back in his chair, feet propped on the corner of his desk, and had a cigar in one hand and a lighter in the other.

"I talked to Caroline Hanson. She doesn't want to do an interview." She hadn't been invited to sit, so she stood, hands clasped in front of her. *All the better to make my escape.* These kinds of conversations never made Bob happy.

"So do a thirty-second piece outside her house. With or without her."

"When do you need it?"

He leaned further back, the chair creaking ominously, and stared at the ceiling.

"Tomorrow. We've got enough crap to fill tonight's air."

"Yes, sir."

"Well, what are you waiting for? This cigar's not gonna smoke itself. Go on." He shooed her out.

Without another word, she turned and left, closing the door behind her. A smile crossed her face as she tread lightly down the hall. He was an old codger, but as long as you did your job, he wasn't all that bad.

The reception desk was still empty, and she shook her head as she passed. This one would never make it if she didn't keep that chair warm. *Not my problem*, she thought. *As long as I'm not the one pissing off Bob.*

She bypassed her own desk in favor of catching up with Keith. The camera men hung out in the studio, unless they were on assignment, so that's where she looked first. When she arrived, she saw three camera men, none of them hers. Two of them were in one of the side studios, with one out on the sound stage checking equipment. As she started across the room, her heels clicked on the bare cement.

Matt looked up. "How's it going, Karen?" Matt was one of the younger members of the crew. Keith had taken him under his wing and taught him what he knew. He was short and stout, with a baby face that made everyone think he was fresh out of high school. Not many knew he was twenty-eight, married, and that they were about to have their first baby.

"Good, thanks. Are things alright with you? How's Maggie?" She stopped when she was close enough to talk without reverberations.

"Yeah, it's all good. Maggie's ready to pop, or says she is. The last month has been hard on her, with the baby kicking non-stop and keeping her up half the night. Other than that..." he yawned.

She smiled. Maggie was a sweet lady. "It won't be long now. She's got, what, a couple more weeks until her due date? Sometimes they come early."

His eyes lit up. "Really? It could be any day then. To tell you the truth, I'm ready to meet the little guy."

"Aww, it's a boy? I thought you guys were waiting."

"We are. I'm wishful thinking." His smile was infectious.

"I'll look forward to the call, then. Let me know when it happens, okay?"

"Yeah, you bet. What brings you down here?"

She looked around. "I'm looking for Keith. I'm surprised he's not here with you guys."

"Oh, he's got today off. Do you need a camera? I'm free."

"That's right, I forgot, he mentioned he was out. No, I'm good thanks. I wanted to check his schedule."

"Okay, if you change your mind, I'm happy to help."

"Thanks, I'll keep that in mind. Catch you later."

As she walked away, she heard him start a dialogue. "Honey? Guess what? Some women go into labor early..." Karen couldn't help but smile. Young love, new parents-to-be, she couldn't help but be happy for them.

When she cleared the back room, she headed toward her desk, pulling out her cell phone and dialing.

"Yo."

"Hey, Keith, we're doing an on-site tomorrow morning. Can you meet me at..." she gave him Caroline Hanson's address and they set up for eight o'clock a.m. When she hung up with Keith, she dialed again.

~~*~*~*

After Karen left and the door was closed, Caroline made sure the locks were engaged and then took a moment to collect her thoughts before she grabbed her purse and keys. *She'd seemed nice enough, genuine, even, if my radar can be trusted.* Though a lot of reporters could charm a snake and make them like it. Maybe she was trustworthy, maybe not. She would definitely need to talk with the girls; she had no idea what to make of this.

After jotting a quick note to Anastasia to please pick up the dry cleaning tomorrow on her way in, Caroline set it on the kitchen counter and headed for the garage. Appointments were tight at Extensions; she needed her nails touched up today, so she didn't dare show up late.

The drive was easy. She'd been lucky enough to catch a car leaving the parking lot by the salon, and pulled in quick. Georgio was in the shop, and she was able to schedule a personal appointment with him for a color and cut the following week. He stayed so booked up, it was rare to find an opening in his chair at all, let alone when you needed it. She'd managed to catch a cancellation as it happened. It worked out well, because the lady who walked in behind her needed the appointment Caroline just cancelled with the other stylist. Mindy was good, but Georgio was better.

Once her nails were filled and polished, she scheduled her next nail appointment and walked out of the salon ten minutes earlier than she'd anticipated. Cincilla, the newest nail technician, was the quickest she'd ever seen; not very talkative, but that was alright. Caroline had other things on her mind today. In a sudden flash of brilliance, she knew what she needed to do.

Climbing back into her car, she carefully opened her purse. She didn't want to smudge her new polish. She didn't see her phone. Turning her bag upside down, she dumped the contents on the passenger seat; still no phone.

I left it on the counter. She knew it as surely as she knew her name—remembered setting it down after receiving texts back from Gina and Amy, and hadn't picked it up with her purse and keys.

Turning the key in the ignition, she cranked the engine and turned the car toward home.

Before she knew it, Caroline was in her garage. *I really need to pay better attention. How long have I been here?* Her question was answered as quickly as she'd thought it, as the garage door finished its descent.

She entered the house to hear Anastasia singing somewhere in the back. It was nice to know she enjoyed her job and felt comfortable enough to let down her hair while she worked. Just then, the vacuum cleaner was turned on and the singing grew louder to compete. Caroline smiled.

The house phone began to ring.

"Caroline, hi, it's Karen Fielding."
"Hello, Karen. How are you?"
"I'm well, thank you. You?"

"I am well, too. What can I do for you?"

"I've spoken with my boss, and he's asked me to go ahead with a video spot, with or without your presence. I know you would prefer not to be on camera, and I'm not asking you to; I wanted to call and let you know that I'll be outside your home with my camera man tomorrow morning at eight o'clock. Wanted to give you the heads up so you can plan around it, or make sure the curtains are closed during that time period."

A short silence followed. "Thank you, I appreciate your thoughtfulness. I wonder, would you be free for lunch?"

It was Karen's turn to be caught off-guard. *Unexpected. I wonder why.* "I am."

"Wonderful. I'm meeting a couple of friends at Pompeii. Would you be interested in joining us around twelve-thirty or so?"

Curiouser and curiouser. A glance at the clock above the door told her it was after eleven now. "I'd love to."

"See you then."

As she clicked off, Karen couldn't help but wonder if this had to do with the comas or if there were something more to it. She would know soon enough.

For now, she had a little bit of time to finish up her research on the kid, and dig a little further on Caroline's coma and surrounding situation. She had the afternoon off; she could call Ben, and if he had time today they could swing by the car lot and at least look at some cars, see what kind she might like. If she were going to do that, she needed to change shoes. If she ran home to change before lunch, she could go straight there from the restaurant.

There were too many people in the general vicinity to make that call to Ben right now. They would be clearing out again shortly to get their stories ready for the noon or six o'clock broadcasts. She'd wait until that happened to make that call. For now, she dug back in to the research.

~~*~*~*

The thought came to Caroline in the middle of the conversation. Now that she'd invited Karen to lunch, she really should let the girls know that she needed them there at noon and not to be late, that they would have company joining them at twelve-thirty.

As predicted, her cell phone sat on the island counter, right where she'd left it. She sent another text, and again their responses were quick to come back. How they did it so quickly, she would never know; it was almost as if they had their phones programmed with the answers before she ever asked the question. *I guess that comes as part of the package, growing up with cell phones. Maybe if I'd had one when I was in high school, if money hadn't been so tight...* She let the thought go at that. No sense revisiting that particular portion of the past. Can't change it no matter how hard you try.

Speaking of the past, she dialed the phone and waited.

"Aston Black."

"Mr. Black, Caroline Hanson here. How are you?"

His voice warmed. "Mrs. Hanson. I'm well, thank you. How are you?"

"Terrific, thanks. I have a request, if you have a few minutes."

"Always. What is it I can help you with?"

Caroline explained what she needed, and agreed to stop by with the fee he quoted her. Aston had been the private investigator whose office she'd found herself in front of when she realized Bruce was cheating on her. He'd been the one who'd shot the photographs she'd planned to use as proof of infidelity when she filed for divorce. Though the way things unfolded, she hadn't needed them. She'd inadvertently become a widow instead. Not before Bruce saw the photos, though. *Wait. How do I know that? I never showed him the photos. When did he see them? Where did that information come from?*

She was more perplexed now than she'd ever been. She could ask Aston. No, he wouldn't know. There were only two people who would ever know the answer to that one: she'd been at home with only Bruce for company when whatever happened, happened.

She left again, Anastasia never having been the wiser that Caroline had even returned home. If she were going to make it to the restaurant on time herself, she needed to go.

~~*~*~*

After Karen changed her clothes, she stopped at the dining room table long enough to jot down her thoughts on Caroline's story.

You may recall the story we broke in the winter of 2012 about Caroline Hanson and her husband, former District Attorney Bruce Hanson. They were found by their house staff when the staff arrived to work. Mr. Hanson was deceased prior to the paramedics' arrival, and Mrs. Hanson was unresponsive, and medi-flighted to the hospital. She slipped into a coma, where she remained for several days before she awoke without her memory of the surrounding time frame.

I've spoken with Mrs. Hanson and though she has declined to appear on camera, she asked me to relay that she has recovered and is doing well.

A happy ending is always fun to report. I'm Karen Fielding, for Channel 9 news.

Tapping her pen against her teeth, she read it over a second time. Not bad for a first draft. *This should cover the fluff for Bob, and allow me to keep my promise to Caroline. I'm not providing any information that wouldn't be readily available through other sources, just doing it in front of her house.* As she read it over once more, she timed herself. She would need to add a few more sentences to bring it to the thirty-second slot filler that would be required. There would be time for that after lunch.

Maybe Ben could free up some time this afternoon, as well, to go with her to look at cars. He would know better what to look for under the hood.

Karen slipped on a pair of flats and picked up her purse as she pulled out her phone. She dialed, pressing the speakerphone button, and slipped through the doorway between the house and the garage, making sure to lock it behind her. As she got in her car, she listened to it ring.

"Hang on." She knew he hadn't looked at the readout when he'd answered; he'd answered her before like that, and she understood it meant he was juggling. Voices in the background, then he was back. "Hello?"

"Hey, you." She backed the car out of the garage and hit the button to bring the door down.

"Hi, is everything okay?" Ben's voice was on alert.

"Yes, fine. I've got a lunch appointment, and then I have the afternoon free. How's your workload?"

"Pretty light at the moment; just got the guys lined out—gave them instructions for their project—and got them going. Once I finish this report, I'll be good. What did you have in mind?"

The change in his tone of voice from cautious to intimate brought a blush to her cheeks. A gleam shone in her eyes.

"I thought I'd slip into something more comfortable, and wondered if you'd like to help me..." she let the open-ended sentence hang in the air.

"Your place or mine?" The hum in his throat, raw sex coating his words, was worth it.

"Shelba's Deals on Wheels. Around, say, two-thirty?"

His booming laugh caused her to burst out, as well. "That's kinky. You know I love that 'new car' smell. Let me finish up here, might take until two-thirty before I'm through. How about I meet you there at three?"

"See you then." Smiling, she ended the call and slid her phone into her pocket. With a self-satisfied laugh, she headed out to meet Caroline.

~~*~*~*

As Caroline walked in, she spotted Amy and Gina sitting down at a table near the back. Her long strides covered the distance quickly.

"Hello, glad you're already here. We have half an hour before Karen Fielding will be joining us."

Gina arched an eyebrow quizzically. "That wouldn't be news reporter Karen Fielding, would it?"

With a nod, she continued. "That's the one. She called me out of the blue this morning and asked for an interview. I let her come over and we talked. The station manager wanted fluff to fill in the dead spots between big stories, since there haven't been as many robberies, carjackings, murders, or whatever else they fill their air time with, as they would like. I gave her the standard line about liking my privacy and I'm doing well, thank you for asking."

"She was happy with that?" Amy stood up and switched her chair for one from the next table. "Uneven legs," she answered to their unspoken questioning looks.

"For the story, she was. After she turned off the recorder, we talked for a few more minutes. Turns out she was in a coma right around the same time I was, and hers was under suspicious circumstances, too; complete with holes in her memory she can't fill. Then she wanted to hear more about what I'd gone through, if I wouldn't mind telling her. She knows it was off the record, so I told her a little bit about what I knew. She doesn't know about Bruce's illicit affairs," Caroline waved her hand as if the topic were a bothersome gnat, "because that doesn't have any bearing on what she asked. She doesn't know about the pictures, either."

"Why is she joining us for lunch?"

"I wanted you two to meet her, as well. I need your take on her, whether you think she can be trusted, and what kind of a vibe you get. I may be too close to the situation, but I'd like to talk more about what happened to her, without giving anything else away about me. Maybe we can figure out what happened back then and find a way to fill in the holes in both of our memories."

"Alright." Amy's tone of voice was thoughtful. "We'll let you do the talking when it comes to the reason she's here, and if either of us feels weird about it, we can change the subject. That can be the 'tell'."

"Good idea."

"That'll work." Caroline looked up and raised a hand in greeting. "Here she comes now."

"She's early," Gina tapped her watch.

They watched her cross the room, as did every man in the place. That could have been because she was a television personality, or maybe it was that she was a pretty lady.

"Hello, Karen, I'm glad you could make it." Caroline stood, motioning for her to take the empty chair. "This is Gina, and Amy."

Flashing her smile, Karen shook their hands. "Hello, nice to meet you."

"Likewise." Gina flashed a brilliant smile.

"Nice purse, is that a Kirkistan Original?" Amy asked.

Karen grinned. "Good eye, yes, it is."

"Gorgeous."

"Thank you." She took her seat and they took a minute to look over the menus.

Karen broke the silence. "I don't know why I bother. I always order the same thing here."

Caroline smiled. "I do, too. When I find something I like, I tend to stick with it."

The waiter materialized to take their orders.

After he'd gone, Caroline got down to business. "I'm sure you're wondering why I've asked you to join us. I am curious to hear more about the time frame surrounding your coma—if you don't mind my asking, of course. Amy and Gina are trying to help me figure out what happened during the time of my own to trigger it, and I thought if we compared notes we might find something we had in common during that time, something that may have been the catalyst. Though I'd still like to ask that anything we say be kept off the record."

"I'd like to find out what happened to me, too, and would like to try your idea. I've tried everything else I can think of; nothing has worked so far. The black hole is frustrating. No problem keeping it off the record. I'm not writing about mine, either."

As the two went over more of what they did remember, Amy and Gina stayed quiet, listening.

Their meals came and went. The plates were cleared. Finally, the details were exhausted.

"Well that was a bust." Caroline tapped her fingernail on her water glass. "I'd hoped we had something, anything, in common from the day or even week before."

"I shared your glimmer of hope. Still, there has to be something."

"What about blood work?" Amy ventured.

"Blood work?"

"When you were in the hospital, did they do a workup on your blood to find out what caused your comas? Maybe there was something in there that could have been the cause."

Karen answered first. "They did on me, but not until after I woke up. They thought mine was due to whatever happened in the alley, which is where they found me, so they didn't think to run anything exploratory. They had no reason to suspect foul play. Did they do any blood work on you?"

"Yes; but I'd been unconscious for a while, at least, by the time I was found, and sufficient time had passed for anything that might have been in my blood to have passed on through my system."

Gina spoke up. "Karen, you said 'foul play.' Do you two think that's what happened? That somehow there was foul play? That would mean it was done on purpose. How can that be, if there weren't any common places or events in your schedules?"

All four women were quiet, contemplating potential reasons or situations that would lead to any type of foul play as the cause.

"That would be a stretch. For these to have been somehow caused on purpose, there would have to be someone seriously pissed off at both of us. I can't imagine who would be that mad at me," Caroline pondered. *Except maybe a mistress. Now that's something I can have investigated—the backgrounds of Bruce's other women.*

"Though being a reporter, you may have made some enemies. Do you think you've made someone mad enough to try to kill you?"

Only one person; but he's torturing me on a regular basis without the cloak and dagger approach. No, he gets his kicks by watching my reaction to his own techniques. She shook her head. "No one that's smart enough to get away with anything. I wasn't even on the cop beat back when this happened, so I'm sure it's not got anything to do with my job, either."

"I know it's been a long time, but do either of you remember what you ate last, or where, before your respective incidents?" Amy interjected.

Caroline frowned, thinking back. "I had lunch with you two and Monica the day before. I don't remember if I ate again after that and then and that night, though I probably did, since it was the next night. I remember Bruce and I were supposed to go to the Carlsons' for a dinner party; needless to say, we didn't make it to that."

"I'd been to a quaint little Italian place with Ben immediately before mine. I don't think it was the food that caused whatever it was, since we'd eaten at different places and at different intervals before the incidents."

The ladies grew quiet, each lost in their own thoughts.

"I'm not seeing any consistencies between our situations.

Different schedules, locations, people...nothing even remotely similar. I've been thinking about the potential of more than just the two of us who had things like these happen and ended up in comas. That's not looking likely to me, either, since there's not even one parallel that we can find between us."

Caroline looked at Karen. "Even playing devil's advocate and saying there's something we're missing, something that was the same in both of our lives on each of our days, I don't have the first idea about how we would find others who went to the same place or ate the same food, or even bought gas at the same station. It feels like we're looking for a conspiracy when there's really only a coincidence."

"I have been thinking the same thing since we touched on that potential this morning. I hate to say it, but we seem to have hit a dead end. Maybe it *was* a coincidence. Could be possible, I guess." Karen sighed. "I was hoping against hope that we would come up with something tangible when we put our heads together."

Gina caught the waiter's eye and motioned for their checks.

"One more question. Where would I go to get a look at the clips from the television stations that covered what happened at my house? Maybe there's something there that I don't remember, something that might tip the scales. I'm not holding my breath, but I feel that I should exhaust every avenue before I give up and wait for time to bring my memory back."

"Let me see what I can come up with, and I'll clear it with the boss to let you come down and take a look." Karen looked at her watch. "I've got an appointment this afternoon, but I'll look into that when I'm back in the station tomorrow."

"I appreciate that." Caroline stood as Karen did. "Thank you for coming. I wish we could have come up with something, anything, to shed some light on this mystery."

"I do, too. I guess we'll know when our minds are ready to tell us. If they ever are." Karen picked up her purse. "Even without learning anything, I still enjoyed this. It was nice to meet you two," she smiled at Amy and Gina, "and I'd love to do this again."

"I would, too." Caroline smiled as well. "Let's talk next week, set something up."

"Great, I'll call you." Karen pulled cash out of her wallet, set it on the table near her glass and gave a finger wave to all three as she turned and strode out.

"I liked her." Gina spoke up first. "She seemed genuine to me, and not at all like what I'd imagined a reporter would be. I expected pushy, but didn't get that at all."

"I liked her, too. She sounded like she really wanted to figure out what happened, not only to her but to you, too. She's also got great fashion sense." Amy grinned.

"She does come across as genuine. I'm glad you two liked her as well. She's nice, and even being a reporter I get the feeling she cares about privacy and being respected for her word. If you want to be there, I'll let you know when we set up lunch again."

"Love to."

"Sounds great."

Karen and Ben met with Shelba, the owner of the dealership. She was an icon in Aspen Grove; her father owned a dealership back in the day where she'd learned everything she knew and thrown half of it out the window. Shelba's motto was to treat the customer right: let them walk upright, not bend them over. Make more money in the long run instead of screwing them to the wall on one car purchase. Anyone who'd ever bought a car from a different lot then came to see Shelba for their next was a customer for life.

"We've got all day, however long it takes to get you into a car that you want," she continued, her smile lighting up her face. She and Karen were the same height, and looked as if they could be sisters with their identical haircuts and business suits.

"Won't take all day at all. I like that Jeep Cherokee over there. What do you think?" Karen looked at Ben.

"I don't know, what about that truck there?" He pointed toward a jacked up four-wheel drive model that she would have needed a ladder to get into.

She rolled her eyes. "I'm going to test drive this one. You can stay and drool on the truck, if you would rather."

He didn't need any further discussion on the subject. "Alright then. You girls have fun. I'll be right there when you get back." Planting a kiss on Karen's check, he bounded over toward the testosterone-oozing pick up

Turning toward Shelba, she shook her head. "Men. So tell me more about the Jeep."

"I love it, personally. I drive one myself. This one's got..." They walked together back into the dealership office to get the keys.

CHAPTER EIGHTEEN

Tom hated that he had to go to work, especially today when there'd been progress. If Mrs. Chambers hadn't been on the cruise she'd won, he would have called in sick. Right now he was the only one with keys to the library, and he wouldn't do that to the children.

As he parked his truck in the lot, he reached for his extra set of keys from the glove box, the ring he kept the library keys on. He jogged across the lot and opened the doors, flipping on the lights and turning on the computers on his way toward the office. He knew it was going to be a long day of waiting and wondering.

Once he'd unlocked the office door, he rounded the desk, picked up the phone, and dialed. Running a hand over his too-long hair, he listened to the phone ring while he thought how best to tell Andy about Katy's movement. With his distracted mind it was all he could do to drive to the library, he hadn't wanted to add another distraction to the mix. Distractions make people into statistics.

"Hello?" Andy answered, quizzically.

"Hi, Babe, it's me. I'm calling you from the office phone in the library." Tom answered her unspoken question. "My brain is going a hundred miles a minute right now."

"What's wrong?" Fear threaded through her voice.

"Nothing's wrong. I think, anyway. When I arrived at the hospital to visit Katy, her arms were moved."

"Moved? How? By who?"

"I don't know, that's the thing. I asked the nurse to check the chart, and to ask the physical therapist if she'd been in earlier than her scheduled time. She hadn't. Cameron, the nurse on duty, said nobody had been in her room, but her right arm was above her head and her left arm was bent at the elbow. So I checked her pulse, and it was jumping all over, like…" As he spoke, his words came faster and faster.

"Oh my God, she moved them herself? She's awake?" Andy's excitement overflowed as they talked on top of each other.

"No, as far as I could tell she was still in a coma, but the movement… that's got to mean she's close, right? We have to think that."

"How will we know? Did you call Dr. Alister, let him know what's going on?"

"I did, he came while I was still there. He—"

"Wait, her pulse was different, too? This is fantastic—"

"—checked her, yes, it is, Dr. Alister checked her pulse and felt the same thing I did. He was running some more tests, and scheduling others, when I had to go. I hate it that Mrs. Chambers isn't here this week, I mean, I'm glad she won the cruise but it would be so much easier if I could be at the hospital, in case, you know…"

"I'll call my mom, see if she can take me up there."

"That's good, yes, if she isn't busy. I'll call you later and see what's going on. I can't believe, after all these years, she could be waking up any time." The lump in his throat made it hard to talk. Tom took a deep breath. *Wouldn't it be wonderful if Katy woke up? If she came back, finally, to live her life?*

"Okay, I'll keep my phone close. This is so exciting. I'm going to call my mom right now, before she gets tangled up in shopping or lunch with the ladies or bridge club activities."

"I have to get to work, I hear voices. I'll talk to you later. Love you."

"Okay, love you too."

Tom took several deep breaths before he left the office. Work now, think later. *Come on, Katy.*

Andy hung up with Tom, so excited she could hardly think. Pressing the speed-dial number for her mom, she wiggled in her chair while it rang. As soon as she picked up the call, Andy started talking.

"Mom, you'll never guess what happened, Katy moved her arms and her pulse was different, faster, than usual. I just talked to Tom, he went to the hospital this morning before work and found her position changed, then felt her pulse and found that too. Can you take me up to the hospital? Please?"

"Well good morning to you, too." Denise laughed, loving the excitement in Andy's voice. It had been so long since she'd heard that, it made her heart swell.

"Sorry, hi, good morning, how are you?"

"Miss Manners, I'm fine. Now, about this trip to the hospital, what time can you be ready to go? I'm always happy to spend time with my daughter."

"Give me ten minutes," she looked down at herself and realized for the first time since the phone rang that she was still in her night clothes. "Wait, make it forty-five. I need a bath and out of these pajamas."

"I'll see you in forty-five minutes. Love you."

"Thanks, mom. Love you too, see you then."

Andy rolled her chair down the hall and started the bath water running. While the tub filled, she picked some clothes out of the closet and tossed them on the bed, then ran a brush through her hair. Tipping her head to the side, looking at herself in the mirror from several angles, she decided a hair tie would do just fine, no need to mess with washing her hair this morning. She expertly flipped it up into a messy top knot then turned back toward the tub, slid herself in and made quick work of the bath.

She pulled the plug to let the water out and hoisted herself onto the side of the tub to towel off. Once she was back in the chair, she rolled back into the bedroom and grabbed clothes out of the dresser. As she pulled on her t-shirt, the doorbell rang twice before she heard the key in the lock.

"It's just me," her mom called. It had been easier to give her mom a key than to have to go to the door each time she came over. Tom was alright with it, as well, since she didn't abuse the privilege. Denise never showed up unannounced, nor did she let herself in without announcing she was there by ringing the doorbell twice. That was her code.

"Hi, I'm back here," Andy called out. "Almost ready, be right out." She worked her way into a pair of yoga pants, then quickly donned her socks and sneakers. When she exited the hallway into the living room, Denise was waiting on the couch.

"All ready?" She smiled.

"Yes. Let me get my keys, and we can go."

When Andy's accident occurred, once Andy woke up from the coma and it was realized that she couldn't walk, Denise had leased a van that was handicap-accessible. It made it easier for her to take her daughter places while Tom was at work. There's nothing Denise wouldn't have done to help the kids. Tom was like a son to her, and she was happy that he and Andy had fallen in love. She couldn't have asked for a better man for her only daughter.

They chatted about inconsequential things on the ride to the hospital. When they arrived, Denise helped Andy out of the van and locked it. Taking the handles on the chair, she rolled her daughter toward the entrance.

"Mom, if you've got things to do, you don't have to stay." Andy looked at her mom.

"I'm right where I want to be, young lady. Let's go check on

Miss Katy." She didn't say she'd rearranged her day so that she could spend it with Andy. There was no need.

"Okay, if you're sure." Andy knew without Denise saying so that things had been moved. She loved her mother, and was glad they were so close. It was a different kind of awesome, being friends with your mom.

"I'm sure. Is she still in the same room?"

"As far as I know. Tom didn't say they'd moved her, though he did say they were going to do more tests."

Denise rolled Andy past the nurses' station and into the room. Katy lay there looking much the same as she had every other time, only her toes were out from under the covers.

"Mom, can you call the nurse and ask why her foot is uncovered?" Andy asked, nerves racing.

"I'll be right back." Denise hurried toward the first nurse she saw. "Hi, I'm visiting Katy, and we've just arrived. Is there a reason her foot is out from under the cover, please?"

"Let's take a look."

They walked quickly back to Katy's room where the nurse took a look at the chart. "Yes, she just had a visit from the physical therapist; I'm sure that's why."

Andy's disappointment was evident on her face and in her voice. "Oh, okay. I guess I'm glad that's all it was."

As the nurse left, Denise put her hand on Andy's shoulder. "I know you wish it had been more movement on Katy's part. Remember, she's been asleep for a long time. If she wakes up, when she wakes up, it could take one minute or it could be as long as, well, as long as it takes."

Her sigh was deep and heartfelt. "I know there aren't any rules about this sort of thing, I just sort of hoped..." She brushed a tear away. "Tom needs something good to happen, something positive to go his way. Every time something happens in his life, it turns to shit."

"Not everything, honey. You are a good thing in his life," she stated as fact before moving around to face her. Tilting Andy's chin up, she waited for her to look up before continuing. "You, young lady, are a good thing in Tom's life. This, the paralysis, the wheelchair, the whole situation, is temporary. You'll walk again, and the two of you will go on to live a full and happy life. We have to take one step at a time, and take it as it comes. Some things cannot be controlled from where we are."

Andy knew her mom was right. She was so smart it was hard to believe she was ever wrong. She nodded. "I know. It'll get better for both of us. It's just going to take some time."

Denise stepped back and moved Andy's chair closer to the bed. "Have your visit, I brought my book and will be right over there."

Andy nodded and turned her attention to Katy. "Come back to us, come on. Now would be good. I'm going to call your brother when mom and I leave here today, and I would really rather tell him that he should come right away because you're awake instead of telling him that nothing's changed since he left, except the therapist giving mom and me a heart attack, but you're being stubborn about the whole waking-up thing. Your call. But," Andy looked at her mom over her shoulder, "*if* you wake up now, I'll bet mom would make lasagna for dinner, and you could totally come over. Or, we'd even bring you some."

Denise laughed. "Way to bribe your friend with what she loves."

"Remind me later to tell you about the smell therapy," she countered. "That could be what's bringing this on."

"Smell therapy? Alright," she said, quizzically.

Dr. Alister walked through the doorway. "Good morning, ladies."

"Hi. Doctor, this is my mom, Denise Parker. Mom, Dr. Alister." Andy made the introductions. ", Dr. Alister took over for Dr. Stoltz."

"Nice to meet you."

"You as well." They shook hands across the bed, then the doctor turned his attention to Katy as he checked her pulse.

"Tom was here this morning and called me from work. He told me her arms were positioned differently than they'd ever been before, and the physical therapist wasn't due to arrive until after his visit. Then, when mom and I got here her foot was out from under the covers. The nurse checked her, and said it was probably from the physical therapist who'd just left."

"Could her movements be from her trying to wake up?" Denise asked, holding out hope.

Dr. Alister gently opened her eyelids one at a time and shined the light in. "It could be. People who spend time in comas like the one Katy is in are very few and far between. We don't have much data on what I refer to as a voluntary condition."

Both ladies opened their mouths to speak but, before they could, he continued. "What I mean by 'voluntary condition' is that there is no medical reason for her to still be in the coma. All signs point to her being able to wake up, and we have no idea why she hasn't. I believe she will wake up, in her own time. Certainly, she's taking her time about it. Right, Miss Katy?" He notated her chart as he spoke.

"Is there anything we could be doing, that you know of, to help her along?"

"Nothing that isn't already being done. The smell therapy may be helping. I would suggest we continue that with another round," he looked at Andy, "when you and Tom have time to do it."

Denise spoke up. "This smell therapy...Andy mentioned that right before you arrived. Would this be the same sort of thing as playing her favorite music or rubbing her hand the way her mom did when she was young?"

"Yes, to an extent. There has been a recent study where certain smells have shown to bring positive results, such as movements made by the comatose patient. One young man woke up from his coma when his mother brought in a warm apple cobbler and set it on the table next to his bed where he would be able to smell it."

"I think that's a wonderful idea."

"I thought about baking her a cake." Andy looked at Denise. "Can I have your recipe? I've been meaning to ask you for it, and now is a perfect time."

"Of course. We'll run by the house and I'll get it for you on the way home."

Dr. Alister hung the chart back on the end of the bed. "We'll keep a closer eye on her, and set up a time for the cake."

"Thank you, doctor."

"Anytime." He turned toward the bed. "Miss Katy, always a pleasure."

After the doctor left, Andy turned her full attention back to Katy while Denise curled up in the oversized armchair in the corner, pulled the paperback out of her purse and delved back into the story.

With her voice lowered, Andy talked about nothing in particular and everything in general. While she talked, in another part of her brain she contemplated the idea of going back into a coma, herself, and coming back out voluntarily after she'd had a chance to see Katy and talk to her again. *Is it possible? Can a voluntary coma be achieved and reversed at will, or would drugs be necessary to go there? I want to help Katy find her way home. Could this be the answer?*

Half an hour passed, then an hour. The sun outside the window rose higher in the sky and heat waves shimmered on the asphalt surface.

CHAPTER NINETEEN

I have to get to her. Katy, where are you? I know you're here, somewhere, I can hear you calling me, help me find you. The snow was falling heavy, thick as fog, hindering visibility. If only I could see, I could find her. The cold seeped into every fiber of my being, making me shiver uncontrollably. I never realized cold could bring bone-deep pain, so much pain, I can't walk Katy, you have to come to me, help me help you, I can barely breathe. Walking through the pain, one more step, just one more...the ground dropped away, an unseen hole, falling, falling, falling, I had time to wonder if falling from so high and crashing into the ground in dreams would kill me in real life. In the blink of an eye, the snow and fog cleared—I saw clearly for the first time in what seemed like hours, and watched helplessly as the inside of the ice cave rushed up to meet me with its open maw and stalagmite teeth...

The pain ripped through, followed Andy out of the dream and into reality. *Holy Jesus, I've never felt pain like this before.* Her brain wasn't firing; every fiber of her being focused on the hot, searing scream of pain so intense it stole the air from her lungs and her ability to move.

She didn't know how Tom knew, but all of a sudden his face filled her vision. Andy lay still, her body taut, straining, consumed with raging pain. The agony coursed through her back and shot down her legs.

"Andy, what's wrong?" Tom's voice, groggy for only a moment before it filled with fear. "Honey, talk to me."

Sweat popped up across her face, chest, and back. The tears streamed down her face, mixed and mingled with the salty sweat. Tendrils of hair, drenched as if from a sudden rainstorm, was plastered to her forehead. Bodily fluids quickly soaked the sheets. Eyes squeezed tightly shut, she concentrated: *relax, ride the wave, control the pain.*

As suddenly as it came on, it receded. It didn't go away, not completely; enough though so her lungs weren't cemented closed and she could breathe, and she managed to make a sound. Her breath came out in ragged gasps.

"Pain. Shooting. Down my legs. In my back. Couldn't breathe. Couldn't move." It was all Andy could do to try and explain to Tom what the hell happened, all the while hoping it didn't come back.

His hands roamed over her body, carefully, slowly, afraid of causing additional pain. Andy scooted herself up the bed, pulled the pillow behind her back and pushed a little further up with her feet.

Tom's eyes went wide. "Oh my God, Andy..."

In the same instant, it crashed down on her, and her expression mirrored his. "Tom? Did I really just use my legs? Am I awake?"

"Yes, you did, and yes, we're both wide awake. This is fantastic." The whoop he let out bounced off the walls and ceiling of the bedroom.

I want to be as happy as you are. I'm trying to be, but the pain isn't gone yet. It's hanging on. I'm still not in charge of my own body at this point, I want this to be real, but I'm having a hard time believing.

"The pain...it's still in my legs and back. Not as bad as it was when it first happened a little bit ago, but it's not going away, Tom. I'm scared."

Petrified is more like it. Oh, god, not petrified. I've been petrified for weeks. Terrified, I mean terrified. Karma, don't hear what I said, please don't hear that.

"Let's get you to the hospital. I'll call Dr. Packard, let him know we're on our way." Tom fumbled his cell phone off the end table. It clattered to the floor, under the bed. He scrambled after it, and came up dialing.

All Andy could do was sit still and will the pain away. She didn't want to stop concentrating on suppressing it, didn't want it to take over again. Tears continued to stream down her face. Something else she wasn't able to control.

Tom finished his call and threw on a pair of jeans and a t-shirt. "His service said he's already there, he's on call tonight. How are you doing? Let me get your chair..."

"I don't know if I can move. I'm seriously scared, Tom. What if I move and then I can't move anymore?"

He pulled the wheelchair closer, then sat down next to her on the bed. Tom took her hands in his. "I don't think you're going to go backwards with this. I think your body is ready to be healthy again, that's why its acting the way it is. Let's get you to the hospital, and see what the doctor thinks. I'm sure he's as interested in your recovery as we are. Maybe he'll see something this time that didn't show up on the last tests, and he'll be able to tell us what will happen from here. We have to try, Honey. As scary as things are, I'm right here with you and I'm not going anywhere. Whatever he says, we'll handle together. But I think you're on the road to recovery."

Andy squeezed his hands. "You're probably right. Positive thinking." Taking a deep breath, she held it for a ten-second count and blew it out. Now or never. "Okay. Will you hand me my yellow dress, the one hanging on the end of the clothes rack, just inside the closet door? I can't wear these pajamas to the hospital. I could use a baby wipe, too, please, to clean some of this sweat off me."

~~*~*~*

When they arrived at the emergency room entrance of the hospital, they were ushered directly back into an exam room. They weren't there two minutes when Dr. Packard came through the door.

"I hear you've had an eventful night," the doctor greeted Andy. "Tell me about it."

"It scared the hell out of me. I was having a nightmare, and the pain pulled me straight up out of it. I couldn't move for I don't know how long, couldn't breathe, the pain was so intense. It was all up and down my spine, and through both of my legs. Tom woke up and was talking to me, I remember that but I don't know what he was saying, I couldn't concentrate. Finally, the pain eased off just enough where I could breathe and talk. Then it eased a little bit more, and I pulled myself up to a sitting position on the bed. Then, without thinking, I pushed myself up a little more, using my feet. I did it without realizing what I was doing."

"How are you feeling now?"

"The pain is lingering. It stretches from here," she leaned forward and pointed to a place just above her hips on her spine, "and follows through all the way down to my toes. I've got some intense tingling, too, like my legs have been asleep and are waking up, the pins and needles feeling."

"Can you wiggle your toes for me?"

She wiggled all ten, then rolled her ankles in careful circles. "This feels so weird after not being able to move or feel them at all."

"This is good, Andrea. I'll tell you what I'd like to do. I'd like to run some tests, see what is different now than the last tests, gather some data and see if we can figure out what happened and what's going on now. Are you up for that?"

She nodded. "I think so. Which tests? I've had more than a few since this first happened."

Tom slipped back into the room as the doctor rattled off the tests he would like to perform. He'd stepped out to call Denise, Andy's mom. As soon as the edge wore off of the situation, Andy would want her to be here. Idly, he wondered if the timing between Katy's movements beginning and Andy's feeling returning was coincidental, or if somehow they were connected. There's only been a couple of days between the two. What if...*That's crazy,* he told himself. With a shake of his head, he brushed off the thought. *Totally nutso.*

CHAPTER TWENTY

"I'm not sure why I still need physical therapy. I've been here every day for the last week, since the feeling came back. My balance is back, the pain is almost gone, and I'm walking further each day." Andy's temper flared any time Tigger used that sing-songy voice. *Sure, it probably made the kids who had to work with her feel better, but for the love of Pete, did she not know the difference between working with children and working with adults?*

She clapped her hands together and smiled. "Because Dr. Packard says it will help, and he was totally right about getting the feeling back, wasn't he? We should just do what he says, and we'll be all better in no time," she smiled and nodded while she talked, bouncing that pony tail up and down.

Andy wanted to give it a good yank. Instead, she channeled that anger into movement. Grabbing the bars, she steadied herself while she pushed herself out of the chair and stood. Sometimes the pain worsened when she stood, sometimes it didn't. Today, not so much. Good. She hovered her hands above the bars as she walked between them, in case her legs gave out or the pain returned. She didn't want to crumple to the ground.

Reaching the end, she turned and walked back. Sure, it took all of her concentration and energy, but seven steps each way without stopping was definitely an improvement. She didn't want to admit it to anyone else, but the bars on either side made her feel safer while she got her legs back under her, so to speak.

"Yay, you did it," Tigger bounced as Andy reached the starting point. "Now let's try the leg press. Have a seat, I'll wheel you over there."

A growl emitted from low in her throat. Tigger didn't seem to notice. "Come on now, let's go." Smile, head bob. Andy imagined what it would feel like to knock her block off.

~~*~*~*

"We had a good day, didn't we?" Tigger sang to Andy as she wheeled her into the waiting room. Her smile brightened when Tom looked up. "It was a *great* day!"

"Get me out of here before someone gets hurt."

"Buh bye now, see you tomorrow," sing song, pony tail bounce, and triple skip, all before Tigger disappeared behind the doors again.

Tom wheeled Andy toward the doors. "I swear, one of these days..."

His laugh drowned out her muttered complaints. "Let's go see Katy. I think it's time you tell her you're walking again."

They drove down the street and parked the truck in the lot. "Do you want to walk, or take the chair?"

"I think the chair. I'm still a little noodly from the PT." Truth was, she didn't want to be without the chair yet. It was her safety net, in case things went south with her legs. She wasn't as convinced as everyone else that there wouldn't be a relapse; how could she be, when they didn't know what caused it in the first place? What if it happened again?

Tom opened her door and held his hand out for her. She stepped carefully out of the truck on her own, and sat down in the wheelchair. "You'll be out of this in no time," he said, as he closed the truck door and wheeled her toward the entrance.

She just nodded.

As they entered Katy's room, Tom greeted her with his standard opening. "Hey, Katy, I didn't see you there."

"Hey, Katy," Andy made her voice light and happy. "Got some news for you."

Tom set the brake on the wheel and held his hand out for Andy. "Want to show her?"

Grasping his hand, she stood and walked to the edge of the bed. "I'm getting feeling back in my legs, isn't that great?" She pushed as much happiness and positivity into her voice as she could manage.

"I know you two have a lot to talk about, so I'm going to step out for a minute, see if Dr. Alister is in the building. I'll be back," Tom said more to Andy than Katy as he pulled a regular chair closer to the bed for Andy. He gave her a kiss and a pat on the butt before heading out the door.

"Hey, so, I'm sure you probably already knew, but I've had more nightmares about you." Andy started. "I need you to come back. Tom needs you, too. If you would only come back, we could all move on with our lives. With my health making an upswing, Tom is starting to look hopeful again. That's something I hadn't realized was gone from his eyes until it came back." She sat down and leaned forward, lowering her voice. Her tone became wistful. "Now, if you'll come back, if you can, please do, it would mean the world to both of us. You've got so much life to live, I don't know why you're spending it in the in-between. What's stopping you from coming back?"

She reached out and stroked the back of Katy's hand. "Everyone is gone that hurt you. There's no reason you can't wake up. I know you're in there, I *know* you can tumble. I did it. I don't know how, but there's got to be a way for you to do it, too."

Tom didn't see anyone in either of the hallways and the nurse's station was currently deserted. *I'll check back on the way out. That's just as easy.*

As he returned to Katy's room and took one step in, something in Andy's tone of voice stopped him in the doorway. He backed up and stayed right outside the doorway, where he couldn't be seen by Andy. He strained to hear what she was saying.

"Tom is going to want to set the wedding date again and, damn it, I want you to be there while I'm having the happiest day of my life. I have to wonder if what happened that day on the way to the church wasn't karma or something else holding us back from getting married. That may sound crazy, but..."

...the sun warmed my face. A slight breeze ruffled the veil draped over my arm, tickling as it shifted. The weeds growing up through the cracks in the sidewalk danced happily before me. I lifted my skirt a little higher to keep the hem from brushing against them, and stepped down off the curb and between the two cars. This is as good a place as any to cross, I thought as I neared the middle of the street. Tires screeched as the car barreled around the corner. I froze, unable to move, as fear dug its fingers into my psyche. I couldn't help but watch as the car bore down on me. It was screaming toward me so fast. I froze in place, couldn't move even if there was time. I can't get out of the way. The driver would see me, how could he not?

Andy gasped. "Oh my God, I just remembered the car that hit me," she exclaimed.

At that, Tom rushed in. "You remembered more?"

"I did. I had a flashback. I was talking to Katy about the day of the wedding, and all of a sudden I remembered the car coming around the corner. It was an older model, but I don't know what kind, I'm no good with cars. They all look pretty much the same. It had rust on the bumper, I remember that. I wish I could remember more."

"We'll call the detective, see if he can use this."

"Do you think he can?"

"I don't know. We'll have to see."

"I'm going to call him. Why don't you visit with Katy for a few minutes, I'll be back." Andy stood and walked back to the wheelchair, dug in the side pocket and came up with the detective's card and her cell phone before situating herself and rolling out the door, dialed as she coasted out into the hallway.

~~*~*~*

Tom watched Andy leave before turning back to his sister. "Well that's some good news, isn't it? Not only is she getting the feeling in her legs back, but she's getting her memory back, too."

He settled into the chair Andy had vacated. "So. Are you ready to read the newspaper, or have you already done that today? You haven't? Alright then." He snapped the paper open and began their ritual.

"Let's see. Okay, how about this. *Friends of the Library are hosting a huge garage sale at the community center in Crosstown Park, located on the South side of Aspen Grove, the first weekend of each month this summer. Donations can be delivered to the back entrance of the Center each Friday from 2:00 pm - 4:00 pm. Proceeds from the sales will be used to buy new books for the library and the schools.* "That's a great idea, isn't it? I think I've got some boxes of things in the garage that I could donate. No, don't worry, I won't give away any of your stuff."

He turned the page, and a circular fell out. "There's an ad here for...wait, it's not Sunday. Nope, we don't read the Wednesday ads. Don't you ever tire of this argument?"

Tossing the sales pages into the trash can, he continued on. "Huh. Check this out. *Another earthquake shook the area shortly after midnight last night. The USGS rates this latest shaker at a 3.1. No damage has been reported.* I slept right through it. Wouldn't have known we had one if I hadn't read this article. Did you feel it? No? Not surprising. You've always slept like a log. Remember how your alarm clock used to go off for an hour without waking you up? Mom would have to come in and drag you out of bed for school."

Tom smiled at the memory. Katy was the deepest sleeper he'd ever seen. He used to listen to their mom, every morning, trying to wake Katy up. Their bedrooms were next to each other, and the walls weren't that thick. He could hear her alarm, *beep, beep, beep,* on and on and on, and then would hear their mom go in. That was fun to watch from the doorway. Mom shook her shoulder, rubbed her back, then finally pulled the covers off her and tickled her feet. That usually got her moving. We both knew 'Operation Wake Up Katy' was a success when her hand shot out and silenced the alarm clock. Once she was awake, she was a whirlwind, but until she came out of her dreams, she didn't hear anything.

Breaking out of his reverie, Tom turned the page, snapped the paper and continued reading. "Well, look at this. There's going to be a political rally. The anti-gay people are meeting on the steps of the Capitol building next Friday in protest of the ruling that came down about same sex marriages being recognized in Oklahoma." Tom looked over the top of the newspaper at Katy and shook his head. "Everyone deserves to be happy, and we all deserve to be treated equally. How hard is that to understand? Oh, I know, I'm not getting started. I don't have the energy today to get on the soapbox."

He scanned down and across the articles. "Here's another good one. The zoo has re-opened the stingray exhibit for the season. Did you know they have stingrays out there? I didn't. It's been too long since I've been to the zoo. A couple years ago they built a new elephant enclosure, and I haven't even been out there to see that yet. I remember hearing about a baby elephant being born. Now there's a baby gorilla out there, and a brand new baby rhino, too. Hey, do you remember when mom took us that summer it was so hot, and we raced from mister to mister, laughing and ending up soaking wet? Good times. If I have kids, I'm totally taking them to the zoo."

I wonder if Andy wants kids. We've never talked seriously about having them or not having them, and if she wants them, how many.

Hmmm.

Tom continued. "Next, we have the Police Blotter..."

Andy ended the call. She'd done all she could do, reporting what she'd remembered. Surely she would remember more. He said he'd look into it, but without any distinguishing features like the license plate number, it would be hard to narrow down who had done it by the vague description she'd given him, especially with the case being cold.

Not the answer she'd been looking for, but what did she really expect?

She reversed direction and wheeled herself back down the hall toward Katy's room. When she arrived, she paused directly outside the door when she heard Tom reading the police blotter aloud: An attempted burglary thwarted by the homeowner waking up; a murder/suicide; and a body found on the bank of the lake. Her thoughts returned to the flash drive. For the umpteenth time she wondered what had happened to it.

As she listened to her fiancé read through the newspaper stories, her mind wandered to her own problem at hand. Now that she was getting the use of her legs back, she could look toward finding out what she could. First things first, she needed to visit the scene of the crime. *It's been weeks since I was hit. What are the odds of finding the people who were around that day and might have seen what happened? Why haven't I read the articles that were written about me? I can talk to the medics that responded, and if I can find out who called the police, maybe I can talk to him or her, as well, to see what they remember. If the newspaper archives don't have their names, the police report should. There should also be notes about anyone else they spoke with that day. First things first. When we leave here, I'll ask Tom to take me to work with him. I can spend the day at the library, reading the newspapers. It hasn't been long enough for them to have been micro-fisched yet...that takes six months or longer, and definitely works in my favor here.*

Tom folded the newspaper as Andy rolled in. "Alright, Katydid, be good and I'll see you tomorrow." He tucked her covers around her, smoothing them down.

"See you later, Katy. Hopefully next time we talk, I'll have more progress to report. You work on progress, too. Bye."

They left the room and waved at the nurses on their way past the station. As they neared the truck, Andy spoke up. "If you don't mind, I'd rather go to work with you today than back home. I'd like to spend some time reading."

"That's fine with me. I'm glad you're interested in getting out of the house. Nice to see you returning to your old go-go-go self." He smiled at her as she stood by the truck door while he folded the wheelchair and set it in the back of the pickup bed.

"I never realized how much we use our legs until I didn't have the option. I'm glad the feeling is coming back. I'd like to get back to doing things on my own again."

"I'm glad to hear it. Can you climb up in there yourself, or would you like some help?"

"Just let me rest my hand on you, but I want to do it." She managed to lift herself up with the help of his shoulder. "There, see?"

Her hundred-watt smile was a welcome sight to him. It had definitely been too long since she'd smiled like that.

"Were you interested in reading something in particular, or did you want to wander the stacks?"

"Don't worry about me, I'll find some way to entertain myself. I thought maybe I'd check out the newspapers, see what's been happening while I've been out of the loop."

They talked about nothing in particular for the twenty minutes it took to get back to Aspen Grove. Tom helped her out of the truck and rolled her into the library. "I'll be in the rare books room today, if you need me." He gave her a kiss and walked off, leaving her to her own devices. *The view as he walks away is even better today than it was the day we first met,* she thought. A familiar warmth spread through her, one she hadn't felt since the accident. *Well, well, well... glad to know the feeling there came back, too.* A flush crept up her neck and across her cheeks. With a smile, she turned and headed toward the newspaper archives.

The next time she looked at the clock, it was after noon. *Two hours? Time flies.* She folded the scrap piece of paper and tucked it in her pocket before returning the latest newspaper to the rack. Stepping back over to her wheelchair, she'd just lowered herself in as Tom stepped through the doorway.

"Hi there."

"Hi yourself. Are you getting hungry? I'm going to take a lunch break. Want to grab a burger?"

At the sound of food, her stomach let its situation be known. "Apparently I do, if that growl translates correctly." She smiled.

"Great," he said, flashing his dimple. "Let's go."

After they'd ordered their burgers and fries, Tom spoke up. "I've been doing more research on smell therapy. There was a couple in Ireland not long ago whose daughter had been in a coma for two-plus years. They finally convinced the doctors to let them take her home for Christmas, thinking that since it was her favorite holiday, and they were considering taking her off life support due to no brain activity, she could spend the holidays at home with them before they made the final decision. It took a couple of nurses splitting up shifts, and several specialists moving the equipment to their house, but they did it. They set her up in the living room near the Christmas tree, played her favorite carols on the stereo, and cooked her favorite foods. They did everything to make it the Christmas she would have chosen had she been conscious. When the parents came downstairs on Christmas morning, they found the nurse asleep on the couch and their daughter awake in the bed. She was sitting up, staring at the tree in wonder, and the first thing she asked was how long she'd been asleep. It had been the end of summer when she'd been involved in a rock climbing accident."

"So you want to try more lasagna, is that what you're saying?" Andy watched him closely.

"I'm thinking more along the lines of dessert this time. The lasagna got a reaction, I wonder what German Chocolate cake would do. What do you think?"

"That's exactly what I told my mom at the hospital yesterday. We stopped at her house and she copied her recipe for me. I think it's worth a shot. I want Katy to wake up as much as you do. If we can help that process along, I'm all for it. Let's talk to Dr. Alister about when would be the best time. I'd really like to eat a piece of the cake, before the rest is turned over to the nursing staff. They sure didn't waste any time on the lasagna; they scarfed it down in no time flat."

"They were definitely hungry, weren't they? You know, I'd like to run this by him as soon as possible. Do you mind if we stop by the hospital on our way home this evening?"

"I was thinking about calling my mom and asking her to pick me up, see about doing some shopping. If she's not busy, I'll have her come get me from the library and drop me at the house when we're through. You can go by the hospital. I'll get dinner started and we can eat when you get home."

"Sounds like a plan." Tom was relieved that the old Andy was resurfacing. It had been a very trying period between the un-wedding and now. He breathed a little bit easier knowing she was coming back to him. It was about time things went his way. Now, if only Katy would wake up.

Speaking of the wedding, when Tom overheard Andy telling

Katy she wasn't ready to set the date again until Katy was awake, he vowed to himself to do everything possible, try any remedy whatsoever, to wake her up. If there was anything he could do from here, from this side of her coma, he wanted to do it—no matter how silly or unorthodox it seemed. He'd tried everything the doctors had suggested up until now; it was time to do everything he could find, even if the doctors hadn't suggested it.

Their meals arrived. After the waitress set their plates down and left, Tom asked the question before he could talk himself out of waiting. "So, I know this is coming out of left field, but I was thinking this morning while reading the paper. Do you want kids?"

Andy choked on a French fry. After she coughed it out, she answered. "What?"

"Sorry." Tom looked sheepish. "I didn't mean to catch you off guard like that, but I was reading to Katy and there was an article about the zoo, which took me back to when we used to go to the zoo when we were kids, and from there I wondered if we would be having any."

Another French fry made it to her mouth before he finished his sentence. She chewed thoughtfully. "I've always wanted a family. Two kids, or three. Maybe four. Being an only child, I spent a lot of time with my invisible friends. I want my kids to have siblings to talk to and play with."

He breathed a sigh of relief. "Great. I would love to have a baseball team, myself, but we can start with two or three or four, work our way up from—"

The pickle slice whizzed past his head, barely missing him, and hit the wall with a splat. "Hey," he laughed.

"A baseball team, indeed." She rolled her eyes, then smiled. "Let's discuss numbers after we're married. But yes, I do want children."

With renewed purpose and hope, he turned his thoughts back to the wedding, and then even further back to Katy. He decided that if

Denise picked Andy up this afternoon, he would spend some time in his office doing more research of his own for any other possible options he hadn't yet found. Katy had to wake up. Soon.

CHAPTER TWENTY ONE

Overhead lights reflected off the rhinestone earrings and mesmerized Andy as she turned the cardboard card they hung from this way and that.

"What do you think about this one?" Denise stepped from behind the curtain and struck a pose.

"Oh, I don't know. It's kinda flowery, don't you think?"

She studied herself in the full-length mirror, rotating back and forth to see every angle. "Yeah, I guess you're right. What if I add a belt?"

"No, I don't think you're anywhere near old enough for that dress yet, mom."

"Hmm. Good call." Looking at her daughter in the reflection of the mirror, Denise smiled. "So you said you'd remembered another piece."

"I did." Andy filled her in on the details while she disappeared behind the curtain to change into her own clothes. By the time she'd finished explaining, Denise was hanging the dress back on the rack.

"You couldn't see who was driving, I take it?" Taking the handles of the chair, she wheeled Andy out of the store and back into the mall.

"No. I called the detective who'd investigated the hit and run, and told him what I'd remembered."

"What did he say?"

"He didn't seem to be overly concerned, said there isn't much information to go on with the description being so vague."

"Maybe you'll see more soon. Do you think there's more missing from your memory?" They paused in front of The Stork's Bundle store and looked in the window at the display before continuing on.

"I don't know." *There has to be more.* She didn't voice her thought aloud—didn't dare. Someone else she didn't want to explain the flash drive and its contents to would be her mom.

"Well, if there is, it'll come. Give it time."

As usual, the food court was a bustling beehive of activity. They skirted around the edge and continued on, people parting and moving around them in waves. "Do you ever wonder how so many people can be at the mall in the middle of a weekday afternoon?" Andy pondered out loud as she watched the masses.

"Every time I'm here," Denise muttered. "Are you ready to go, or is there somewhere else you want to stop first?"

Her watch read four thirty p.m. "I'm good. Will you take me home? I told Tom I would start dinner."

"Of course."

The two continued toward the exit doors, and out into the parking lot. As they neared the crosswalk, a car horn blared, the driver—intent on taking the right of way—was driving too fast…

…and erratically. Time slowed to a crawl, then leapfrogged forward, skipping seconds, and the view didn't make any sense. My veil can't be on that tire, its right here on my arm. Why am I seeing the underside of that car, and the curb? Oh no, that's my flash drive over there. Mister, get that for me, please. I need it. Wait, come back, where are you going?

Andy let out a shriek as Denise yanked her chair back away from the edge of the curb.

"Oh my goodness, are you okay?" asked an older lady who exited the mall after them. She was wearing the exact dress Denise had put back earlier, with her reading glasses hanging from a string around her neck. Her purse was clamped tight between her elbow and ribcage. "Young people these days, they have no respect for anyone."

"We're fine, just startled. You're alright, right, Andy?"

"What? Yes, just startled." She parroted.

"Well, that's good, honey. You two take care now."

They watched the woman cross to her car. "You know, I think you were right. That dress is a little bit too flowery for me. Are you sure you're alright? That was scary."

"I'm okay. If I could have kicked that car, I would have. Stupid punk. He's going to get someone killed."

CHAPTER TWENTY TWO

"Tell me more about Ted." Ben knew that he'd been instrumental in Karen's sanity four years ago when she'd first moved to Aspen Grove, but wanted to be on firm ground for this meeting. Her cryptic answers to his prodding this morning while they were getting ready for work were disconcerting. There was more to Ted than she was letting on, he was sure of it, though he couldn't imagine what it might be.

"We're almost there, you'll see." Karen laughed as she parked her brand new Jeep in the police station visitor's lot.

He shook his head imperceptibly. She wasn't usually this stubborn. "Alright, woman," he said, giving in. As if he had any choice in the matter.

Releasing her seat belt, she leaned over and gave him a quick kiss. "Let's go."

They walked hand in hand toward the building. Climbing the steps, Ben gave her hand a squeeze before letting go to open the door for her.

"After you." He swept the air with his hand in an overly large arc, bending at the waist at the same time.

"Thank you, kind sir." Her curtsey was pronounced, and she giggled.

They approached the front desk where an officer sat, feet propped up on the corner of the counter, newspaper open and held high in front of his face.

"Officer Dunphy, get out here," she bellowed, her voice bouncing off the walls like a ping pong ball.

"What are you *doing*, hollering like that?" His shocked whisper bounced off the walls, following hers around the almost-empty vestibule.

The newspaper crumpled between hands the size of bear paws. The boots hit the floor with a loud thud, and the man in the uniform stood. Granted he was standing on a platform behind the desk, but he would have been just as intimidating had he been sitting in a pit three feet below ground level.

"Jesus, Karen," was all Ben could say.

"Get over here young lady, right now." The commanding voice left no room for argument.

Several other uniforms appeared in the hall; they'd obviously heard the commotion.

Ben quickly stepped in front of her, holding her back. "Surely she didn't mean to yell so loud, officer. This room," he gestured at the empty walls and high ceilings, "is perfectly built for echoes."

Pinning him with a look, the officer growled. "Are you the 'young lady'? No. I'm not talking to you. Move."

Ben gulped audibly, at a loss for words in this never-before-experienced situation. He didn't see any other choice; he moved.

Karen approached the desk, stomping her heels with each step. The officer came around to the front and swept her up in a hug, lifting her feet off the floor.

"You are such a troublemaker," he said, loudly enough for his words to reach Ben.

It all came together. He breathed a sigh of relief and approached. "Officer Ted Dunphy, I presume?"

The twinkle in Ted's eye as he set Karen back down and reached his massive hand out to shake Ben's was enough for Ben to know that he'd been had, and that the two of them would get along just fine.

"Nice to meet you, Ben. I had no idea what she was going to do, though I figured there'd be something. I saw the two of you as you came up the stairs out front. I was ready."

"I wasn't ready, she caught me by total surprise." He turned to Karen. "He's right, you *are* a troublemaker."

Her laughter surrounded them.

"Now that you've had your fun..." Ben smiled. "Shall we tell him?"

Karen sobered. "Ted, we need to talk. Seriously."

By her tone he knew she was through joking. "Sure. Nunez, catch the desk?"

Nunez nodded. "Sure thing."

As Dunphy led the way and Nunez was sure he wouldn't be seen by Ted, he shyly waved at Karen. She gave him her camera smile and waved back as she passed.

"Who was that?" Ben questioned quietly.

"He embarrassed himself last time I was here and got called on it by Ted. That was his apology, and my 'no worries'," she whispered back.

They followed Ted into the same small, glassed in room she and Ted had used on her previous visit. He closed the door behind them.

"What's up?" The crease between his eyebrows deepened with concern.

"That stalker I thought was being quiet? Not so much anymore. He somehow got into my car and left a black rose on the dash. The car was locked; I always lock it. I'm fanatical about locks, but they don't keep him out."

Ben held her hand while she composed herself. She drew strength from the contact, felt his support through the connection. With a gentle squeeze of his hand in thanks, she continued where she'd left off. "Ben went with me down to Shelba's where I traded in the car. That's the only thing I've kept with me each time I've moved, so that may be the way he's been able to track me."

"Good call, trading the car. It may not stop him for long, if he knows where you live and work. If you've got an easily accessed designated parking space at either place, you'll want to see about parking elsewhere for now at one or both places." Ted looked at Ben. "Does he know about you yet?"

"If he does, he hasn't made that known to me."

"Nothing unusual or unexplained in the last few weeks? Something left or taken, or even moved?"

Ben thought seriously. "Nothing comes to mind."

"Good. This type of guy, once they fixate on the fact that there's a man in the picture, trouble usually escalates. We can't do anything legally until he attempts harm, but stepping up the patrols is something I can, and will, ask for. The captain is quick to approve requests of this nature. I'll need your address before you go, Ben, so your place can be added to the request."

Ben nodded. "Sure, thanks. Anything to keep Karen safe."

"It's very frustrating that he can do these things to me, freak me out, make me paranoid like this, and there's nothing that can be done."

"I know. Between you and me, if I catch anyone near your car or your house, or even yours now that you're a part of her life, there will not be a need for a VPO and you'll never be scared of him again." Ted's words made her feel a little bit better.

"I've still got the rose, if you think there would be any use for it." Her eyes were cautiously hopeful.

"There's probably nothing we can do with it, but bag it and put it in the evidence room. I'd like you to fill out a report, anyway, so we can have a record of what he's doing for when we catch him. I'll get the forms."

"There's blood on the thorns—do you think that might help?" Ben leaned forward in earnest, resting his arms on the table, tension visible in the way he held himself.

"The blood isn't yours, correct?"

Karen shook her head.

"If we catch him, and the blood is his, that will help, sure. It will put him at the scene, breaking and entering at least. If that's all we can get on him, it's enough to put him behind bars; if there's more, it will add time for the crime."

"The flower is in the car, I'll go get it. Be right back." Ben patted her leg and went to retrieve the rose.

Karen nodded. "Okay. Let's fill out a report. At least it's something. I wasn't sure the rose would do any good, but Ben thought we should bring it anyway. I'm glad we did."

"You'd be surprised what a drop of blood can give us these days. With the advancements in technology, even I'm amazed sometimes what the labs can do."

Ben came back in with the rose, a napkin wrapped around where his fingers held it. "I didn't want to taint the DNA, if it's there, by touching the flower. I used a napkin to pick it up."

"That's great. As long as neither of you touched the thorns where the blood is, there's no problem, though if there's a question we can get your fingerprints or DNA at that time."

They both nodded. "No problem. I just want this bastard caught." The muscles in Ben's jaw clenched.

"Me, too. I can't do this anymore. I'm too tired from all the running, and I'm ready to make a life here." Her eyes tracked from Ted to Ben.

Half an hour later they were finished filling out the paperwork, and Ted stacked the forms together. "I'll walk these through myself, get them in the system. I take it since you're going through the steps, reporting this," he tapped the pages on the table, "that you're planning to stick around and see it through, am I right?"

Karen's eyes moved from one man to the other. "Yes. I'm not going to run anymore. It's obvious that he's not going to stop, no matter where I go, and I've found a town, met friends, and have established a place where I'm liked as well as respected; I also have a good man in my life who loves me, and who I love. It's time to put my foot down and live my life on my own terms. So, yes. I'm here to stay."

Before she knew it, she was wrapped in a huge hug. "Good to hear. Maria is still waiting for your call. Make her phone ring, will you? I'm not sure how much more of the badgering I can take."

She held up her hand in a mock salute. "I'm on it, as soon as I get home."

Ben reached for the doorknob.

"And Karen?" Ted spoke softly.

She turned. "Yes?"

"I'm glad you're staying. I've missed you; so have Maria and the kids. They overheard me telling Maria that I'd seen you, and asked when Aunt Karen was coming to visit."

Her smile lit up her face. "Awwww…tell them I said 'soon.'"

Ted turned his attention and steely-eyed glare to Ben. "Don't hurt her."

Without hesitation, Ben returned the unblinking stare. "Not in this lifetime. She means everything to me, and I'll be damned if anyone else will hurt her, either."

One second ticked by, then two before Ted nodded and the two shook hands. "That's what I wanted to hear. We'll see you at dinner, too, then. Maria will be thrilled."

"Wild horses couldn't keep me away."

~~*~*~*

Karen closed the sliding glass door behind her and moved toward the porch swing, where Ben already relaxing. "Alright. I just got off the phone with Maria. We're set for dinner at their place a week from Friday. You are in charge of bringing the beer and chips, I'll be making potato salad, and she and Ted will take care of everything else. As long as there isn't a burn ban, we'll have burgers on the grill."

"Sounds like a plan."

As the sunset lit the sky with its brilliant pinks and oranges, Karen snuggled in next to him, giving the swing a gentle shove. Gliding lazily, they enjoyed the scene.

"I've seen sunsets all over the U.S., but none seem to compare to the ones we have right here in Oklahoma."

Ben draped his arm around her shoulders, pulling her closer. "Gorgeous." Dipping his head, he nibbled on her ear. "Tasty, too."

A warmth flooded her body. "Mmmm. You know, you keep that up and I might not leave tonight."

"That's the plan." His hand slid lower, gently brushing the side of her breast with his fingertips.

Her hand caressed his thigh. "As much as I'd like to stay, I've got to be on location early tomorrow morning for a quick spot. I don't have my copy for that, and there's a story I've been working on that's at my place that I need for the staff meeting tomorrow afternoon. I don't want to have to tell Bob I don't have either of the stories. Those are not words he likes to hear."

He worked his way down to her neck. "How detailed is your early morning spot? Can you do it from memory?"

Heat bloomed, racing a direct line from his touch to regions south. "Shouldn't be too difficult."

Moving down, he continued. "Good. Then, how about tomorrow morning, on my way to work, I swing by your place and pick up your story, and we can have lunch, and you'll have your story for your meeting?"

It wasn't easy to fight through the cloud that was filling her brain. "You'd do that for me?" was all she could manage.

"Mmm hmm..." His journey continued slowly, torturously, down to her collarbone.

"Ohh. That's nice. Are those fireworks?" The huskiness of her voice let him know he'd won. She would stay.

"You see fireworks?"

"Mmmm hmmmmm. Don't you?"

"Now that you mention it..."

"I think they're coming from the bedroom."

"Should we check?"

"Could be dangerous if they're left unattended."

The sun continued to set on a beautiful day. The night was just getting started.

~~*~*~*

Karen's heels ticked off her steps, one at a time, like drumsticks cracking against each other. The night was cold; exhaled breath plumed, holding its shape as it drifted away like a heavy cloud.

Goosebumps stood out on my arms. Rubbing my hands vigorously up and down my arms didn't help; it was as if I hadn't done it at all. The darkness surrounded, bringing with it a presence; something I can't quite put my finger on, something lurking in the shadows, causing the hair on the back of my neck to stand at attention. My thin, sleeveless top wasn't anywhere near appropriate for the time of day, nor for the freezing fog that crept steadily toward me. The short blue suit skirt did little to protect my lower body from the ice cold temperature, either; a fact brought front and center by the ice cold bite of wind as it slid past my calves. Uncontrollable shivers erupted all over my body—even my teeth, clenched together as they were, clacked against each other like shaken dice.

The scene took on the familiar glow of a street light. Somehow, there were moths fluttering around the frosted glass globe, the light dancing off the ice crystals forming on their wings. As one fell to the ground, the added weight of the ice too much to bear, another would take its place. It was like a train wreck—I wanted to look away, but the macabre nature of their dance with death held my gaze, tethered by a fine silk thread I could feel and see.

A shift in the fabric whispered frigid air in a whirlwind around my body and released that thread from the globe. My gaze followed the thread, fascinated, as it floated through the breeze. The loose end landed on the ripple of time as it rolled through like an ocean wave. In an instant it became clear where I was and who I would find, as my gaze continued to follow the thread.

`A nightmare, that's all this is,` *said a tiny voice in the corner of her mind.*

`Are you sure?` *Another voice taunted in a whisper as cold as the air around her.*

`Yes, you're not real. You're only here in my head. I'm sleeping. Any minute now I'll wake and you'll be gone.`

`In Dreamland, you don't call the shots. I do...`

`You are my subconscious. I am in control.`

`No. You aren't.` *As if making that point clear, the kid stepped out from behind the dumpster, bullet holes showing up as gaping wounds across his body, many more than the reports said there had been, undulating like snakes in a macabre dance, as if they were alive instead of the result of the bullets used to stop him.*

`"If I weren't real, could I do this?"` *His head changed. In a shift of space and time, the face was no longer that of Darnell Taylor; as if looking at the reflection in a funhouse mirror, the bullet holes shimmied up, up, up, stretching and molding, changing flesh and bone into that of her one-time date and long-time stalker—the cause of bone-deep fear. A final snap, eerily similar to the sound of a rubber glove makes when pulled onto a hand, brought his features into perfect focus. Tilting his head back, he laughed slowly, with purpose; an evil sound that slithered around her face, caressing her cheeks, kissing her lips.*

Her scream echoed from one side of the alley to the other, surrounding and suppressing her.

The terror was as real in her asleep body as it was in her awake mind, only she couldn't make herself wake up.

~~*~*~*

Ben held her, not knowing what was causing her to whimper, only knowing he needed to be there when she woke. But weren't you supposed to let a dreaming person wake on their own? Or was that only for sleepwalkers?

Following his gut, he wrapped his arms tighter around her, rubbing her arms and back, cooing softly to her and calling her name. If he wasn't supposed to wake her, he hoped his voice would bring her out of wherever she was; if she got much colder, she would turn blue. Her lips already looked as if they held a tinge.

Her mouth opened as if she were going to scream. Instead, her body shuddered and took in a long, deep breath, as if she hadn't in too long. The convulsion scared the crap out of him. Raising his voice, he called her name over and over.

"Karen. Karen, Karen, KarenKarenKaren! Wake up, I'm here. Wake up, Karen. Come on, you can do it. I've got you, you're safe. Wake up, honey."

Her eyelids shot open but her gaze did not focus immediately; the utter fear he saw shining out of her eyes tore his heart in half. As her head whipped back and forth, she gasped for air. He kept holding her, talking to her.

"Here you are, it's alright now. You're awake, I've got you."

Focus slowly replaced fear. She concentrated on seeing Ben and only Ben, wiping everything else out of the picture. The shudder turned to shiver, and he pulled the blanket from the bottom of the bed all the way up and tucked it under her chin and around her shoulders, continuing to rub heat back into her body.

"Oh, God..." Karen leaned on him, her own weight too much to bear.

"Shhh, shhh, relax." It took several minutes before her breathing was anything close to normal. She pulled away slightly, enough so she could sit up, and leaned back against the headboard, bringing him with her. The moonlight streaming in the window was enough for them to see each other; no artificial light was necessary for her to see the concern etched into every detail of his face, nor for him to see the pain in hers.

Prompting wasn't necessary. She told him what she'd seen, who it was, and what had transformed from the initial scene. He listened.

The more details she shared, the more hatred grew in his core for the kid and the stalker. He'd never felt anything rake across his nerve endings the way this did. If he were given even the slightest chance, if he found this stalker before the police did, he vowed silently to himself that he would end this torment for her. This night, this moment, he made this promise to himself. And he would be damned if he was going to break it.

Karen's iron grip remained on his arms around her long after they'd lain back down. He held her until she slept, listening as her breathing returned to normal. His breathing slowed, as well, though his was from the calm that descended, coating him with its resolve.

CHAPTER TWENTY THREE

"Mrs. Hanson, there is a Mr. Glover on the telephone for you." Anastasia called.

"Thank you, I'll be right in." Caroline stood and brushed the dirt from the knees of her gardening pants. Weeding the garden was something she enjoyed doing herself. Peeling her gloves off her hands, she laid them and the trowel on the bench next to the back door before going inside.

Closing the French doors behind her, she took off her floppy sun hat, set it on the end table and picked up the call. "Hello?"

"Mrs. Caroline Hanson," asked a breathy, male voice.

"This is she."

"My name is Phillip Glover. I am an insurance agent with McGee's Insurance Agency. We carried the accidental death and dismemberment policy on your husband through his business. First, I want to give you my condolences on your loss."

McGee's Insurance Agency? Accidental death and dismemberment policy? When did he take that out? "Thank you for your concern, Mr. Glover."

"Yes. Well. The Certificate of Death has recently been provided to us, as well as the medical examiner's file and the police report. Our internal investigation has been completed, and we have a check for you, paying benefits under the terms of this policy. I wonder, Mrs. Hanson, when would be a good time to bring this by to you?"

"Wouldn't it be easier on your company to mail it to me?" His heavy breathing was irritating through the telephone; she could only imagine how it must sound in person.

"Oh, no, that is not permissible with an amount such as this one. Your signature will be required in person upon presentation."

An amount such as this one? "What amount would constitute a personal visit, Mr. Glover?"

"Ten million dollars."

"That is a large sum. I'll tell you what, Mr. Glover. Let me have your telephone number and I will set a time with my banker for us to meet with him, where you can present the check and I will sign your document acknowledging receipt of the same. When I've talked with my banker I will call you back."

She copied down his number, as well as his name and the name of his company.

"We'll speak soon. Goodbye, Mr. Glover."

Caroline set the handset back in the cradle before going to Bruce's office. When she'd had his personal effects delivered from his office, she instructed the movers to deposit everything in his home office. It had been a traumatic time, and as such she hadn't bothered to go through any of the boxes yet. She hadn't seen a reason before now.

After the unexpected call from Mr. Glover, Caroline couldn't help but wonder what *else* she didn't know about her husband.

With a twist of the doorknob she pushed the door open and moved her hand along the wall until her fingers touched the switch. The room was bathed in light from lamps placed strategically around the room.

A whiff of his scent hung in the air. The remnant from a time when she was blissfully unaware of her husband's true nature, she breathed deeply, mentally reached for what they'd had, longed to smell his cologne one more time. It was there for just a moment before it once again disappeared into her memory.

Her instructions to Anastasia at the time had been to leave this room out of her daily cleaning ritual. There was no reason to bother with a room that sat completely unused.

To her left was a beautiful oversized mahogany desk. The trim and designs engraved were ornately carved, held up by legs ending in claw feet—something she'd imagined belonging on bathtubs before she'd seen them on this desk. They fit perfectly within the design, lending a regal air to the overall feel of the piece. The chair he'd chosen to pair with the desk was every bit as ostentatious, with its brass buttons marching in lines down the arms, and the worn leather hinting at stories of its own. In front of that were two guest chairs, plain by comparison, though no one ever visited him here in a business capacity. To her right was a deep-cushioned couch, also made from the softest leather, and a matching leather recliner, both angled toward a gas fireplace. The wall next to her was floor to ceiling bookshelves, every shelf filled with legal volumes. The heavy curtains directly across from her were closed. She moved with purpose and pulled them open. Dust motes scattered at the disturbance, floating everywhere, as if gravity didn't exist. The added natural light gave her a better look at what she was up against.

The conversation pit between the recliner and the fireplace was filled with stacks of bankers' boxes which contain everything that had been in his downtown office. Whoever packed it up had taken time to note on the outside of each what was inside, or at least what part of his office the contents had been taken from. There were boxes labeled "knick knacks," "personal docs," and even one listed "photos," among the many that contained files.

Bruce hadn't been one to fill his space with memorabilia; her curiosity insisted she open this last box first.

There were several framed photos. The first was a picture taken at their wedding. The happiness on her face—on both of their faces—put a lump in her throat. They'd been happy. When had that changed? What had gone wrong to bring her to where she was now?

Caroline carefully laid it on a nearby end table and reached into the box to pull out the second frame. This was a candid shot from their fifth anniversary. The trip down memory lane took her to Bermuda, where they'd spent the week sightseeing and relaxing on the beach during the days, and dancing to the music of one fantastic band after another as they wandered from club to club until the early morning hours, before returning to their bungalow and making love before falling asleep in each other's arms just before dawn.

The week had flown by. When they'd arrived home Saturday evening, their friends were waiting with a surprise party. This picture was taken as they came in the door. She'd clutched his arm tightly, scared out of her wits until she realized it was a party and not intruders. The fear obvious to her must have been seen as surprise by everyone else. Bruce's face in this picture was all smiles, while hers was certainly not. *Why had he chosen this photo to display?* The answer hit her like a ton of bricks. *Of course, because he looks fantastic and I'm a backdrop. Even back then, he was all about himself.*

The last frame in the box held a photo of Bruce and another woman. She felt the heat rise in her face. How dare he frame a picture of himself with…

…her, who is she? Caroline yelled at Bruce, all the pain and shame spewing forth, unable to control it. He stood there stunned, mouth moving, no words coming out. For the first time since she'd met him, he was unprepared and had no answer.

She shoved the photo at him, not caring if he took it from her. The look on his face told her everything she needed to know. One after another, she flung them at him, each picture another blow to their crumbling marriage. The pictures drifted to the floor, landed face up, face down, on top of each other, on the coffee table, under the edge of the couch, they were everywhere. So many photographs, so much proof.

"Are you alright, Mrs. Hanson?" Anastasia stood in the

doorway. Her question brought Caroline out of her reverie.

That answered how I knew he'd seen the photos. Another piece, missing no more.

"Yes. No. I don't know. Come here, look at this please." She wanted to see the look on Anastasia's face, gauge if she knew this woman, if whoever she was had been here in this house as well as on her husband's arm. The face looked vaguely familiar, though Caroline didn't remember from where. *Surely he didn't have the balls to bring them here...*

Anastasia moved around the boxes and knelt down next to Caroline on the floor. "That's a lovely photo. Was Mr. Hanson good friends with Ms. Sanders?"

Of course. Cheryl Sanders, the model-turned-actress. "I don't know. He attended events without me sometimes. I hadn't seen this picture before. I'm not even sure where or when it was taken."

"There's the edge of a banner on the corner here," Anastasia's finger hovered over the photo. "It might be for the cancer benefit. That's what this symbol looks like to me."

Caroline looked closer. "I think you're right. That does look like their logo." Her thoughts returned to the flashback. Sudden realization at what must have happened dawned on her. "I've remembered something, Anastasia. That night, the night before you found us in the living room, I confronted Bruce about some pictures. Those pictures were strewn all around. The police never said a word about them."

Anastasia gave a slight nod. "Yes, ma'am."

"I have to ask, did you clean them up?"

"Yes, ma'am."

"Why?"

"You have always been kind to me. When I saw the pictures, I figured out what Mr. Hanson had done, and I hurt for you. It wasn't the business of anyone else. No one needed to see those pictures, so I picked them up very quickly and called the police. The lady said they were on their way, that someone else had called them already and said they heard a scream and asked if I was alright. I said it was my scream, and told them that you and Mr. Hanson were hurt. She said she was sending an ambulance too."

Her brow furrowed, Caroline tried to piece together more of what had happened that night. Nothing else came. "The photos, then. You have them?"

"No, Mrs. Hanson, you do. I put them in the bottom of the sideboard, under the silver serving tray."

Caroline reached out and clasped Anastasia's hands in her own. "Thank you." It seemed inadequate, only saying thank you for an act of kindness so huge, but what else can you say to express gratitude this deep?

"You are welcome." She looked at her boss, took in the sadness in her eyes and the tiredness she'd not quite managed to hide. Anastasia felt as if she and Mrs. Hanson were growing closer, perhaps they could be friends one day. "Would you like me to help you with these boxes? More hands make quicker work."

Caroline nodded. "That would be wonderful. Yes, please."

They emptied one box after another. It took several hours to get down to the last two boxes. These were the boxes that she was most interested in, where there would be anything else she needed to know.

As if sensing Caroline's hesitation, Anastasia sat back and waited. The air felt different, somehow, as if they were on the precipice of something important.

"I want you to know how much I appreciate you and everything you do for me." She looked at Anastasia. "I don't think I've told you how much it means to me that you stayed on, even after...after finding Bruce and me the way you did, then keeping everything going while I was in the hospital, and through recovery. Everything you did, even without knowing if we were—if I was—going to be alright, if you would still have a job, you still kept coming and took care of things here. After I came home, you took on more than your job required by taking care of me until I was on my feet again. And now, the pictures, I really don't have the words to express the magnitude of gratefulness I'm feeling right now."

She nodded. "You did tell me, Mrs. Hanson. Then you bought me a car, too. I am very thankful to work for you."

"Call me Caroline."

"Caroline. That will not be easy for me, but I will try, Mrs. Ha…Caroline." Anastasia smiled.

The dynamic of their relationship had drastically altered today. Caroline had an ally she'd not realized before now. With new eyes she looked at Anastasia. This week had been an exercise in trust; not only hers, but others as well. Now, seeing her long-time maid as someone she could rely on, another puzzle piece clicked into place. It felt good.

She drummed her fingernails on the box lid. "The call this morning was from an insurance agent. Apparently Bruce had an accidental death policy I didn't know about, and there will be a check coming from that policy. I came in here to see if there were any other policies, or even any other bank accounts, safety deposit boxes, stocks, bonds, anything else along those lines that might be languishing in these boxes. That's what prompted this sudden cleaning out of his things. These two boxes are the last, and contain his private paperwork from his desk. We need to pay special attention to any sort of policies or files that have information in them like that."

"He had secret money from you? I don't understand that. In my family, we all know about everything that has to do with money. We talk about it, and I have never thought about keeping money secret. Why would he do that?"

"Bruce did a lot of things secretly. A lot of it doesn't matter anymore. He was…" she thought how to put it, "a difficult man. I loved him, but some of the things he did, what he hid from me, I don't respect him or those things. I don't know why he did half of what he did. Trying to explain him to anyone else without understanding it myself would just be guessing. He's gone, and so are his secrets, unless we find them."

It was a step in the right direction. Healing took time, and it was definitely time to start. Though she wouldn't forget, she would forgive; not for him, but for herself. Caroline learned long ago that to achieve freedom from her past, she had to let go of the pain and hurt, come to terms with the fact that she'd been done wrong, and move past it. It wouldn't be easy, but she would tuck it away with the rest of the bad memories.

The two women went through the paperwork, sheet by sheet, until the last had been examined. There weren't any more insurance policies, though there was a letter from Cyrese Bank, located on the island of Grand Cayman.

Caroline held the letter and read it again. *This letter is dated six years ago. How much money has he been funneling to an offshore account? A better question is why he felt the need to hide assets. Was it from me or the government? Odds are on tax evasion, most likely. I may never know why, but I can damn sure find out how much. I never would have thought to look for money hidden overseas.*

After Anastasia left that evening, Caroline poured a glass of wine and took it into Bruce's office. She made herself comfortable on the couch and gave herself over to the onslaught of memories that had threatened to slow down the process of cleaning out the boxes today. For the first time, she allowed herself to cry for the loss of what might have been. If only she could remember the rest of what happened the night he died. The memories from that night may never be recovered, or they could flood back tomorrow, the doctors just don't know. Perhaps it was better left a mystery. Did she really need to know? Probably not. It wouldn't change the fact that Bruce was dead, nor would it change that he had cheated on her numerous times.

Of one thing she was certain: she wouldn't marry again. With the type of men she attracted, it wasn't worth her time or heartache.

Tomorrow would be soon enough to start the process of finding out how much money he—now she—had offshore. The letter from the bank contained the account number, so that was good. That would make it much easier. It was next to impossible to retrieve any sort of information from the banks down there without that.

Caroline finished her wine and unfolded herself from the couch. As she stood in the middle of the room, she turned slowly, taking a last look at what had been her husband's office. *Tomorrow I'll start looking for a decorator. It's past time to do something with this room. It would be a nice space for a personal library. I've always wanted a reading room.* The decision to let go and move on instantly lifted a weight off her shoulders, one she hadn't realized she carried.

As she made her way to the door, she felt a cool breeze. It only lasted a second or two, but seemed to her that it was the past saying goodbye. She turned off the light, left the door open, and walked away.

CHAPTER TWENTY FOUR

"That's a wrap." Keith lowered the camera, looking over at the 'Hanson Mansion,' as he'd dubbed it. "Can you imagine living in a house that big? I mean, come on, who needs three stories with twelve thousand square feet." Shaking his head, he turned away and stowed the camera inside the news van.

"Oh, I'm sure it's not twelve thousand," Karen countered, grinning at him. "Ten thousand, maybe. Come on, let's get this back to the station, I need some coffee."

They worked together to load their equipment back inside the van, then climbed in. Keith wove his way out of the ritzy neighborhood.

He cleared his throat, breaking the silence. "So, how's it going with Ben?"

The smile played around the edges of her lips as she turned and looked at him. "We're good. Why, is there something I should know?"

Shifting his eyes toward her for a second, he affected an innocent look. A slight blush crept up his cheeks. "No, nothing. That's good. I mean, no, not about you guys, but I thought maybe we could double date some night. I met this girl, and I'm usually good with asking them out but this one, I don't know. I can't seem to put my finger on what it is. I trip on my tongue every time I get close to her. I thought maybe if you guys were there, you could help smooth the way?"

"Really. A double date. I haven't been on one of those since high school." Enjoying his discomfort, Karen looked out the side window and watched the manicured lawns and oversized houses roll by. If Keith had been anything but good to her, she might have let him hang with this one, but he'd been an angel to work with, and somewhere along the line they'd become friends.

"Yes. I mean, if you don't mind. Or want to. Please?" He was getting more uncomfortable by the second.

Begging isn't his style. This girl must be special. It would be nice to see him find his happy.

She let him off the hook. "Sure. Ben and I would love to have dinner with you and your friend. There's this great little Mexican food place we know of, or there's an Italian restaurant with checkered tablecloths if she likes that better. They're both good for quiet conversation. Ask Ben if you want, he knows the names of the best and the newest places. Set it up with her, we'll be there."

The smile on his face could have lit up the town. "Thanks. Cool. Really, thanks."

Aspen Grove was a small enough town that rush hour wasn't a rush. Even with the cars on the road carrying their passengers toward day jobs in the City, there weren't enough of them to create a crush of cars anywhere.

Keith pulled the van around and behind the parking garage at the station, and to the chain link enclosure. He parked it inside with the rest of the company vehicles. The news vehicles, along with the tornado chasers, were kept under lock and key due to the large amount of money invested in the equipment kept inside each one.

Her cell phone rang. Pulling it out of her purse, she checked the readout before answering. If it had been an informant, she wouldn't have taken the call in front of Keith. It wasn't; it was Ben.

"I'm going to take this, see you later," She told Keith as she clicked to answer.

He waved and jogged toward the building.

"Hi, honey, we were just talking ab—," she managed before he interrupted her.

"Karen, where are you?"

"We just pulled back in at the station. What's wrong?"

"I'm at your townhouse. I need you to come home."

"Ben?" The worry washed over her in waves. She started toward her car.

"Now, please."

"I'm on my way." She hung up and ran around the side of the building to the garage, fishing her keys out of her purse on the way.

It took her less than ten minutes between the station and home. As she rounded the corner, Ben's car came into view in her driveway. She whipped her car in next to it and jumped out. As she ran up the walkway to the door, her heart pounded hard against her ribcage.

The door opened before she could reach for the knob. Ben stood in the shadowed entry, waiting.

"Come in, quick." He closed the door behind her. As he did, she gasped. Her townhouse was a wreck: furniture overturned, pictures that used to hang on the wall lay smashed on the floor, her favorite lamp shattered in the corner.

"What happened?" She turned toward him and her breath whooshed out of her, leaving her as deflated and empty as a two-day old helium balloon.

"Oh, my God, what happened to your face? Are you alright?" Closing the gap between them, she reached out and gently touched the lump on his temple. She looked him over, for the first time seeing the blood that had traced a line from a cut near his hairline to his blood-soaked shirt. His knuckles were scraped and bloody, as well.

He took her hands, stopped her before she could touch him. "I'm fine. Listen. I need you to look at something. I need you to tell me who he is."

"Who *who* is?" The confusion crossed her face for a split second before everything fell into place.

Ben took her elbow and steered her down the hallway. They reached the bedroom door before she saw the 'who.'

Stars clouded her vision as she stumbled back, hitting the wall full force. "No, no no no. Tell me he's dead, please tell me that."

He stepped between her and the man lying on her bedroom floor, blocking her view. "Look at me, Karen."

Blinking several times, she looked up at him.

"Who is he?"

"Stalker. That's the guy I dated, the one who…"

He nodded. "I thought so, but needed you to tell me for sure. Wait right here, don't move. I need to check on him."

"What? He's not dead?"

Ben stepped into the bedroom and squatted down, pressing on the side of his neck. First one side, then the other, and back to the first. "Yes. He's dead. He wasn't when I called you, but he is now. We need to call the police."

Full and total relief flooded her system. Pushing herself off the wall, she strode into the bedroom and kicked him in the ribs with all her might. "You bastard, you made my life hell for years. I'm glad you're dead." Her words flowed from her like venom, purging her of the poison he'd instilled in her.

It was then that the vase of roses caught her attention. They were spilled across the floor on the far side of the bed. Hauling back, she kicked him one more time, this time to the head. "I hate roses," she growled at the cooling body.

Stepping back out of the bedroom, Karen smoothed her skirt. "*Now* we can call the police."

"Tell me what happened." The officer stood next to the open door of the ambulance where Ben was being tended to by a young paramedic.

"I came by Karen's house to get the notes she needed. When I walked in, I must have surprised him; I heard something 'clunk' from somewhere back near the bedroom. It wasn't readily apparent if it was in this townhouse or the one on the other side of the wall. As I started for the hall to check it out, this guy came at me. We fought. He picked up a lamp and cracked me with it. I ducked, but not in time. He caught me with it here," he pointed to his head, "and I fell. He came at me again, and the fight was on. I came at him, he took off down the hall, and we ended up in the bedroom. The rest is a fog. I knocked him out, called Karen, and you guys."

~~*~*~*

Karen stood by the curb and watched the paramedic take care of Ben while she explained what she knew to a stout, fresh-faced officer with a buzz cut. "Ben called me and asked me to come home. I could tell by the tone of his voice that something was wrong. I didn't find out what the problem was until I got here."

The young officer made notes in his book as she talked. She couldn't tell by his face what he was thinking; *he'd make a great poker player*, she thought.

"Then what happened, Ms. Fielding?"

"When I arrived, he let me in. The first thing I noticed was that my living room had been trashed. I didn't know at the time whether it was a burglar or what. Ben, that's Mr. Brady over there," she motioned with her hand, "had blood on his shirt, which you can still see. He's got this bump on his head and I'm not sure what else, it's a blur now, but he told me he was okay and then walked me down the hall. I still hadn't connected the dots, didn't know what was going on. Then I saw *him*."

He nodded as he wrote. "Saw who?"

"Him." Karen pointed to the body bag on the gurney as it wheeled past. "I presume that's the dead man from my bedroom."

"Do you know the identity of that man?" His pen continued to scribble across the page.

"Of course I do. He's been stalking me for years and across the entire United States." Karen gave him details: places, years, and names—not only that of her stalker, but those of the officers who had taken statements previously.

"Officer, I'd like a moment with Ms. Fielding. Alone." Ted Dunphy's shadow moved across the two of them.

"Ted, I'm so glad you're here," Karen said.

The younger officer looked between the two for a moment. "Alright." He stepped away to confer with another officer.

Leaning down, Ted wrapped his arms around her and gave her a paternal hug. "What's this I hear about a dead man in your bedroom, and a boyfriend with blood all over him?" His eyes searched her for damage.

"Oh, Ted, It was awful. I'm trying to keep it together and professional, but this whole thing, I can't believe it's real. Ben came by to pick up my notes for my meeting this afternoon....oh no, I didn't tell anyone I was leaving, I have to call in..." She looked around frantically for her phone.

He produced his from his pocket, handing it to her. "Here."

As soon as she'd made her quick call, she handed it back to him. "Thank you. I was on my way into the office building when Ben called. He asked me to come home quick. He sounded...off.

Something was wrong, but I didn't know what. As soon as I got here, he opened the door and let me in. I saw the disaster area that was my living room, and then I saw Ben. He had this blood all over him," she started to lose it. Taking a deep breath, she reined it in and continued. "It wasn't all his. Ben said he was alright, and asked me who the guy was that was lying on my bedroom floor."

"Was it him?"

She knew who he meant without further explanation. "Yes."

As he wrapped his arm around her shoulder, she sunk into his embrace and took a moment to collect herself and her thoughts.

"He was dead by the time I got here. I haven't had a chance to talk about this to Ben, to find out what exactly happened. Would you go ask him? I know he's talking to the officer in charge, but I would feel better if I knew he was okay."

Ted nodded. "I'll be right back. You'll be alright while I'm gone?"

A quick nod from her was all it took to convince him. He strode over to where Ben was being treated by the paramedic.

The young officer returned; as if he hadn't been interrupted, he continued. "Is there anything else you can tell me about what happened here today?"

An almost imperceptible shake of her head gave him his answer.

"Alright, then. We'll be in touch if we need more information." He produced a business card, handing it to her. "Here's my card. If you think of anything, please call me, day or night." The line sounded rehearsed without sounding practiced.

"Okay. Thank you."

Karen hadn't spent any time alone since realizing her stalker was dead. Really, truly gone, not to return, no sequel, no prequel, no further chapters in her personal story that would include him. The weight lifted and left her feeling lightheaded. Even with the situation as it currently was, she found it easier to smile. Tilting her face up toward the sun, she closed her eyes and did just that.

She didn't know how long she'd sat there enjoying the pure relief and joy before she heard his voice. "Karen?"

She opened her arms to him without ever opening her eyes. "Ben. Hold me?"

Without another word, he stepped in and wrapped his arms tightly around her. They sat together quietly until Ted finished talking to the other officers as well as the detective who would be in charge of the investigation.

"Everyone good here?"

They both nodded. "What's the next step?"

He looked between the two of them before rubbing the back of his neck. "The next step is for Detective Peterson to decide, though I would imagine once he's read the reports and both of your statements from today, along with the information I've just passed along to him, it will probably be an open and shut case. I don't expect any charges to be filed against you," he looked at Ben, "and it shouldn't take the team long to finish with your townhouse, though I hate to think about the mess they'll leave behind with their dusting powder and paper booties tracking it everywhere. They did say they found where he'd jimmied the lock on the sliding glass door by the kitchen and let himself in, which will go a long way toward clearing any wrongdoing by either of you. You may want to hire someone to clean the place, and let the landlord know he'll have to replace that lock as well before you are safe to stay here again. Do you have somewhere you can go?"

Ted took care not to look at Ben when he asked Karen this question. Without hesitation, she nodded, placing her hand on Ben's. "I'll stay at his house. Thank you for coming, Ted. I appreciate your smoothing things out with the officers on scene, and taking the extra steps with everything else you've done that I don't even know about yet."

"Oh no, don't thank me. It's your young man here that you

should be thanking. He's the one who put an end to the tyranny, not me." He smiled at Ben. "Though *you'll* have to tell Maria about this...I'm certainly not going to mention it. She'll want details I can't even begin to give her, probably more than I'll ever want to know."

Karen laughed, long and deep. It felt good to have the weight gone. She'd had no idea what the pressure was that she'd been under for so long until now, until it disappeared. As the release took over, her laughter doubled and had her holding her stomach as tears rolled down her cheeks.

Ted and Ben looked on, uncomfortably, having never seen this side of Karen before.

When her laughter died out, she plopped down on the curb, spent. "Whew. Sure, I'll call Maria when we leave here. God that felt good. I haven't felt this relieved in years."

"Okay, then. Totally understandable. Are you alright to drive?" Ted couldn't help but smile at her.

"Sure, I'm great." She nodded and gave a double thumbs up. "Can I go in and get some things? I need more clothes, girl stuff—"

"—I'll clear it with Detective Peterson." Ted interrupted her list-making and made a hasty getaway. The quickest way to run off a man was talk about mysterious girl stuff.

"I'll go with you. You'll need anything of value, too, since the doors won't be keeping people out for a day or two."

As they gathered what she needed, Karen couldn't stop smiling. Karma had finally come for her stalker, and she couldn't be happier with the end result; though she couldn't help but worry and wonder how killing a man would affect Ben, in the short or the long run. Perhaps Ted would be willing to talk with him about it. She'd mention it when they got together for dinner. Though she should call her before then, or they would all feel the wrath of Maria for not telling her sooner. The thought only served to widen her smile.

CHAPTER TWENTY FIVE

Time skipped a few beats. It must have, since I went from standing frozen in place to horizontal on the road with no time between the two events. The screech of brakes and skidding of tires were background noise; a side note to my thoughts. What happened? The sidewalk is cracked. I don't want the heel of my shoe to get caught and scrape. That was my focus, then...I don't know what happened. The tires. Something about tires. Now, everything is sideways in my vision: a car stopped at an angle, my veil draped over the back tire, my purse under the car parked along the curb. Scuffed men's brown dress shoes staggering toward me. I watch them approach. The man squats down, he has brown eyes. What are you saying? You're mumbling. What are you...something about being sorry. Vodka isn't supposed to have a smell. It does, though. I smell it now. That's a weird thing to smell while lying on the road. I can't think straight, I don't know what he meant. I don't know what any of this means. Time skipped again. The car disappeared down the street, its tail lights winking out as it turned the corner. Where did the lady come from? Help me, please. Why can't I stand?

The flashback ended abruptly. The pounding in her head arrived in tandem. *What lady? Who was she? Why am I only now remembering someone else at the scene?* Frustration clawed its way to the surface and exploded out.

Andy looked around for her cell phone. *Crap, it's in the side pocket of the wheelchair.* With concentrated effort, one foot in front of the other, she walked out of the bedroom and down the hallway toward the living room where she'd left her chair earlier. Hand to wall, then on to the back of the recliner as she passed, careful not to fall. Sweat popped out on her brow and along her hairline before she'd reached her goal.

Dr. Packard told her not to push herself too hard, but she was at home and hadn't thought she would need to be anywhere in a hurry, so she'd left the chair by the front door, in the living room, at the furthest possible point from where she was when the flashback took over.

Her hand touched the arm of the chair and she let herself collapse into the seat. It might still be a little while before she would be able to walk distances without help, especially at this rate.

She dropped her hand into the pocket and wrapped her fingers around the phone. Another minute wouldn't make a difference. Before she dialed, she took several deep breaths in, then exhaled slowly to regulate her breathing and her heart rate. Calm and collected was what she needed.

In a town the size of Aspen Grove, if 9-1-1 was dialed, the call was as likely to be picked up by the Sheriff's Department as it was the local policeman on duty. The non-emergency phone number was handy to have memorized. To save time and frustration, she wanted to speak with the local authorities. If there wasn't anyone on duty at the station and there was no one to answer the phones, the calls were forwarded to an on-duty officer's cell phone. Handy work-around in a small town.

"Aspen Grove Police Department." The voice was that of Officer Benton, the town's newest hire. Alice Benton was his grandmother and also the owner of the local daycare. Andy had gone to school with him and they'd graduated at the same time.

"Benny, its Andy. How's it going?"

"Andy, hey. Going slow and easy, how's things with you?" His voice was caring. Not the tone you'd get from a big town officer, but one from someone who was genuinely interested.

"Getting better all the time, thanks. The physical therapy is helping."

"Cool, you're walking again?"

"Yeah, little by little. It's taking longer than I wanted, but the doctor thinks I'm going to be one hundred percent in a few more weeks. I'm dealing."

"Awesome. So, what's up?"

"I've got a question about something that happened when I got hit by that car. Are you at the station or on patrol?"

"I'm at my desk, at the station What do you need?"

"I need the name of the lady who found me that day. Now that I'm recovering, I would really like to go by and thank her. I hope her name is in the report. Would you mind looking at that for me?"

"No problem. Give me a sec while I pull it up." The sound of fingers on a keyboard filled the silence. "Okay. Two calls came in; the female caller was Mrs. Edna McGinty. The car hit you right in front of her house. The report says she was in her living room, heard the tires squeal on the pavement, and when she looked out, she saw you lying in the middle of the road. She was still with you when the officer and paramedics arrived. Her address is 124 Maple Lane. The other was a male caller." Fingers played over the keyboard in the background. "That call was anonymous; either that, or the name wasn't understandable. Sorry I can't help you with that one."

The radio squawked in the background. He answered the call. "Gotta run. Old man Jones' cows are out again."

"Thanks, Benny. Say hi to your mom for me, huh?"

"Will do."

She hung up and jotted the address down, then sat back to think. *I can't ask Tom to take me. I know him; he wouldn't understand why I would be asking about a flash drive. I don't think there's an answer that would satisfy his curiosity as to what was so important that I had a flash drive in my purse on our wedding day. Mom will take me if I ask her. She might even leave me alone with Mrs. McGinty for a minute, if I ask. That could work. I'll ask Mom to take me. Okay. What will I say to Mrs. McGinty? I'll thank her, of course. If she hadn't heard, and another car would have come around that corner, I might not even be here. No, stop thinking like that. Focus. Could she possibly have seen my flash drive underneath that car, and picked it up for some reason? Or did the car that was parked there run it over and the rain wash away the pieces? There's only one way to find out. Please let her have found it. I'll go crazy if I can't get it back.*

CHAPTER TWENTY SIX

"Thanks again, mom. You've been running me all over town and I appreciate it." Andy rolled her window down and held her hand out. The cool morning breeze flowing over and around her fingers felt was refreshing.

"You know you're always welcome. I'm glad you called me. So tell me who we're going to see. I don't recall a Mrs. McGinty."

"She's the lady who heard the car hit me when my accident happened. I want to thank her for getting help, and for coming out to the road to see if I was even alive. I had a flashback and saw a lady standing over me, then called down to the police department and asked who reported it. Benny Benton was on duty and looked it up for me. He gave me her address, too."

"Living in a small town comes in handy sometimes. In a bigger city, you wouldn't have gotten that information so quickly or easily." Denise pushed her glasses higher up on her nose while she kept her eyes on the road, watching the street signs for Maple Lane.

"I know." Andy moved her hand up and down as the air flowed past. *I hope she can tell me more of what happened that day. Someone has to know, and since the driver took off...*

Maple Lane led them through a small, quiet neighborhood, and ran parallel to the street where the church was located. The houses were on postage-stamp sized lots, with the houses close enough together for the neighbors to open their respective neighbors' windows and shake hands without ever leaving their homes. This wasn't the type of neighborhood Andy preferred; she liked more room between families.

"There it is, 124." Denise pulled up next to the curb, under the shade of a large tree. The house was painted canary yellow and had white shutters on either side of the large window. An oversized copper-colored wire butterfly hung to one side of the single garage door. There was also a wheelchair ramp that led to the front door.

"Are you ready?" Denise asked.

Andy nodded. "Yes. I'm excited, a little, and apprehensive too."

"That's to be expected. She may know more about what happened."

As Denise wheeled Andy's chair up the driveway and the ramp, a woman appeared in the front window. At first sight, she reminded Andy of Mrs. Claus with her white hair in a bun on her head and the wide smile on her plump face. The door opened before they'd reached the stoop.

"Why, hello." The lady from the window stood in the doorway, one hand on the screen door, the other clasped around a dish towel.

Denise smiled. "Hello. Are you Edna McGinty?"

"I am."

"I'm Denise Parker and this is my daughter, Andy. Would you have a moment to visit?"

"Sure, of course. Come in, come in." She held the door as they passed into her living room. The yellow extended from outside to inside, creating a wonderful open feeling to the room. The floral pattern on the couch and love seat gave the expectation that a butterfly could land on them at any moment. Andy couldn't help but smile when she saw the bright orange and black Monarch in the pattern on Mrs. McGinty's house dress.

"Have a seat. Would you like some fresh lemonade? I made it this morning." Mrs. McGinty waddled through the doorway without waiting for their answer. Denise and Andy smiled at each other.

Another benefit of living in a small town—people trusted one another.

Photos on the walls depicted a life lived, moving from black and white photos of a young couple through birthing of babies and children growing older. There were graduations, birthday parties, random vacation shots, all marching in order, through time, with the final photo being a slightly younger Edna and a man who could only be her husband. Their hands were clasped together as they smiled sadly at the camera. It seemed one or both knew the end was near.

"That's my Howard. We were married for forty seven years when he passed." Edna set the silver tray holding a pitcher and three glasses on the coffee table.

"I'm so sorry for your loss. These pictures are wonderful, and a tribute to what must have been a happy life for him." Denise turned back, encompassing all of the photos in the gentle sweep of her hand.

"Yes, it was a good life. We raised two children, Robert and Margaret. Robert is a doctor now. He's married to a nice lady and they have two children of their own. They live in Montana; we don't get to see each other very often. Just for Christmas, usually."

"And Margaret?" Andy rolled her chair closer and accepted the glass Edna poured for her.

"She passed on six years ago. She and her husband were coming back from visiting a sick friend and their car was hit head on by a truck driver. He'd fallen asleep at the wheel."

"That's terrible," Denise said softly as she touched the back of Edna's hand.

"Their twins were in the back seat, sleeping, and only bumped and bruised. Terrance and Jerald have lived with me since. They're good boys," she said, handing Denise her glass. "But as much as I love to talk about my life, that isn't why you're here, is it? How can I help you?"

"We're here so that I can thank you. I was the one who was hit by the car in front of your house earlier this summer, and you came to my rescue. If you hadn't, they say I might not have made it."

Edna's rings glittered as her hand fluttered near her neck. "Oh, dear, I'm so glad you're alright. That was quite a scare. I heard the car screech, and then something thumped. I'd been in the kitchen with the doors open, to let the breeze blow through, and by the time I got to the front window, I heard the car door slam and it took off, and that's when I saw you out there in the street. Oh, my, I was worried sick when I saw you weren't moving. I called the police and told them to bring an ambulance, and then I went out to check on you. I saw your eyes open, but you didn't look okay, not at all. There was blood, and your beautiful wedding gown was dirty and torn." Edna patted Andy's knee. "With the condition you were in, how on Earth did you know it was me who found you?"

"I called the police station and asked. The officer told me your name was listed in the report. I hope you don't mind that my mom and I have looked you up and stopped by."

"Goodness, no. I'm delighted to see that you're alive. I was going to go shopping with Beatrice that day, and at the last minute she had a spell and decided to take a short nap first, so we were getting a later start than we usually would. I believe everything happens for a reason, and I was supposed to be home to help you."

Karma.

"I'm certainly glad you were."

"Did the accident happen before or after your wedding, dear?"

"Before. I had parked my car down the road a bit, because there wasn't anywhere closer to the church. I didn't hear that car coming until it was too late. One second the road was clear to cross, and the next it wasn't."

"That was an awful thing to happen on your wedding day, and before the ceremony. Goodness me. I'm glad to see that you are making a recovery. Your chair...I hope your condition is only temporary."

"Yes, just until I'm strong enough. For a while we weren't sure, but the feeling is coming back and I'll be good as new."

"Oh, that's wonderful, dear. Life is so much easier with two working legs. My Howard lost one of his legs in the war, just below the knee. Sometimes he didn't much feel like strapping on his prosthetic, so he had his chair he used when that happened. It was more and more often, near the end. Can't say I blamed him. I wouldn't have wanted to use a wooden leg all the time, either."

Squeaky hinges sounded from somewhere in the back of the house, followed by wood thudding on wood.

"Grandma?" called a male voice as footsteps approached.

"In here," Edna called.

"I'm getting ready to mow the yard," he said as he came through the kitchen doorway. "Oh, hi."

"Terrance, this is Andy Parker and her mother, Denise."

"Hey, how's it going?" Terrance said, a dimpled smile creasing his face. He stood tall and lanky, with red hair and freckles.

"Hello."

"Hi. You're Terry...Marshall? We had a class or two together in high school, didn't we?" Andy tilted her head. "Or was that Jerry?"

"That was me. Art class. Mr. Abner. I was a couple years behind you."

"Ah, right."

He turned his attention back to Edna. "Grandma, you're out of gas for the lawn mower. I'm going to go get some, and be right back. Do you need anything from the store?"

"I don't think so."

"Okay. Back in a few." He turned to go.

"Good to see you again." Andy said.

"Yeah, you too."

The footsteps retreated and the screen door closed gently this time.

"Your grandson takes good care of you." Denise stated.

"He does. They both do. Just last week Jerald brought over a computer and set it up. I've never had one before. He built it himself, just for me, and showed me how to do something called 'surfing the 'net.' Last month Terrance brought a brand new washing machine in and hooked it up while I was at bingo."

I have to ask her about the flash drive. Andy drained her glass. "Mom, we should go."

The ladies stood. "I'm glad you were home that day," Denise reached out and took Edna's hand in both of hers. "I don't know what would have happened if you hadn't been here to call the ambulance right away."

"I'm glad I was, too. Karma works in mysterious ways. Who are we to question?" Edna squeezed her hand in response, then pulled her in for a hug.

"Would you mind getting the van? I'll be right out."

Denise nodded at her daughter, smiled at Edna and let herself out. As soon as she was out of hearing range, Andy voiced the question that had been on her mind since she'd first thought about it. "I can't thank you enough, Mrs. McGinty. I wonder, did you happen to find anything in the road that day after the ambulance took me away?"

"Did you lose something, dear?"

"My purse emptied, and I lost a bottle of nail polish and a flash drive."

"Funny you should ask. I did find a couple of things. There was a broken bottle of nail polish, which I cleaned it up and threw in the trash. There was something else, as well. What did you say it was? A flash drive? That's the computer thing, right?"

"Yes. Small, and plugs in to the side of a computer."

"That may be what it was. Let me look." Edna stepped over to a side board and sifted through a silver bowl, then moved to the other side and looked in an abalone shell on the shelf. She came back and held out her hand. "Here we go. Is this it?"

Relief flooded Andy's system. It took all of her control to keep her face neutral. "Yes, that's it. Thank you so much." Her fingers twitched as she picked the flash drive up from Mrs. McGinty's hand.

"Lovely, then. One more lost item finds its way home." She smiled. "I tend to pick up things that look like someone might miss them, and I hold on to them in case someone comes around looking."

"Thank you again, you have no idea how much you've helped me. If I can ever do anything for you, all you have to do is ask." Andy pulled a scrap piece of paper and a pen from the side pocket of the wheelchair and scribbled her phone number on it.

"You're a dear. Have you married your young man yet?"

"Not yet. I want to be able to walk down the aisle. We'll reschedule the ceremony for some time in the near future."

"Well, best wishes to you, dear. Stop by again if you would like to talk some more. I have more time than company these days and I enjoyed our visit."

"I would like that." Andy set the parking brake on her wheels and stood. She took one step forward and enveloped Mrs. McGinty in a warm hug.

As she rolled down the ramp and out toward the van, Denise smiled and waved. Andy turned to see Mrs. McGinty waving for all she was worth, and she couldn't help but smile and wave back.

CHAPTER TWENTY SEVEN

"Hello, Aston, it's Caroline Hanson. I received your voice mail this afternoon. I'll stop by your office tomorrow. Thank you for calling." Caroline clicked 'end' and set her cell phone off to the side. Not only was he quick, he was professional. *I'm thankful it was his office I stopped in front of that day. I'm also thankful, and lucky, that he was standing in the doorway. If it weren't for him being there, and that car almost running me over, I might never have met him. He's proven invaluable when it comes to private investigations.*

As she went about putting together a salad for dinner, her thoughts drifted to the meeting with the insurance agent and her banker, set to take place tomorrow morning. *Hmmm, I wonder if Aston would be able to find anything else that may be out there. He's found everything else I've asked of him. At this point I have no idea how many secrets Bruce kept, or where else to look, beyond what was in his personal effects. If anyone can help me with this, it's Aston.*

She would talk with him about this in person tomorrow; it was after office hours today, and she would be speaking with him soon anyway. This sort of request was best discussed in person, in her opinion, in place of leaving a message advertising that she may be worth more money than her appearance already led people to believe.

Caroline carried her salad and a glass of wine to the dining room. There had been a time when dining alone bothered her, though recently she'd grown accustomed to it and found that she enjoyed her own company. Eating dinner by herself allowed her to read while she ate, too. This was something else she found enjoyable.

Placing her napkin in her lap, she opened her current paperback, *The Rose File* by E.J. Rycer, to the bookmarked page and instantly found herself back in Boston. Detectives Jess Reilly and Greg Fisk were hot on the trail of a killer, and she found it engaging and entertaining, trying to figure out who that killer was before the detectives did.

ıl~*~*~*~*

When she'd concluded her business with the banker and the insurance agent, Caroline left downtown Oklahoma City and drove back to Aspen Grove. If it hadn't been for a mandatory meeting, she wouldn't have gone to the city at all today, though this was one of the best reasons she could think of to spend time making the drive there and back.

Aston was leaning against the doorway when Caroline pulled up and parked in front of his office. His pale linen suit complimented his dark skin and white smile.

"Beautiful day."

"That it is. You never know for sure in Oklahoma from one day to the next."

He turned and led the way into his office, closing the door behind her before taking a seat behind his desk. She'd been to his office twice before—once when she'd hired him, and the second time to pick up the proof. Perhaps it was a sign of healing that she wasn't uncomfortable with the memories that were invoked by her presence here; perhaps she'd gotten past the worst of the pain.

The center drawer of his desk clunked closed, bringing her back to the present.

"I've found the information you requested." He placed a large envelope on the desktop and slid it toward her.

"You certainly don't waste any time, do you?"

"Not usually, no." His deep laugh put her at ease.

She picked up the envelope containing background information on Karen Fielding as well as both mistresses from the original photos and tucked it in her purse. "Great. I've got another search I'd like you to run, as well." She outlined the information in which she was interested.

He jotted a few notes on a legal pad while she talked. "Why don't I give you a call when I've found what there is to find. This one may take a few days."

"That's fine. Thank you, Aston. I'll look forward to your call."

"You're quite welcome, Caroline. We'll talk soon."

Soft light from the lamp on the end table held the shadows at bay while Caroline flipped through three stacks of pages as she took in the information Aston provided for her. Background information on each of the three women told entirely different stories: The first in her early twenties, a runaway from a childhood riddled with abuse; the second, mid-thirties with two black widow divorces behind her and aliases that spanned several states; the third, her newest acquaintance, Karen Fielding.

Ms. Fielding, previously known as Shalia Carpenter, had been through her own tribulations. With great difficulty she remade herself more than once, only to be re-discovered again and forced to uproot her life, move on to start over in a place where no one knew her and she would have to prove herself again. Caroline felt a certain kinship with Karen from the first time they met. Perhaps it was like recognizing like.

Other than knowing one Hanson or another, the only thing these three ladies had in common was name changes. After she'd finished reading, she slipped two stacks back into the envelope and carried it down the hall where she secured it in the bedroom safe. The third stack went with Caroline to her office, where the shredder turned one page at a time into confetti. There was no need for information such as this to be saved. Karen was who she was through the actions of another; the thoroughness in Aston's research gave Caroline every confidence that she had nothing to fear from Karen. The last sheet of paper slipped through the razor-sharp blades.

~~*~*~*

Three days later, the phone call from Aston took less than a minute. He'd been unable to find any further bank accounts or offshore dealings in Bruce's name, nor any leads at all on finances within the U.S. There was, however, a home in Vail, Colorado, which, when traced back, was held in the name of a shell corporation and now belonged to Caroline.

Regardless of the fact that she enjoyed visiting locales with mountain views, she knew this house would be listed for sale sooner rather than later. Not for the money; she had plenty of that. No, she didn't want any property that may have been used as a love nest by him and his mistresses.

Her life was finally her own, without an abusive or cheating husband. She'd had one of each and was happy enough remaining single.

As soon as Anastasia arrived for work the following Saturday, Caroline stopped her before she could even pick up a dust cloth. Caroline showed her the photos of the house in Vail and two airline tickets in hers and her mothers' names that had been purchased online, and handed her an envelope with a mix of cash and Travelers Checks for their trip. Anastasia was adamant that the gift was too much. All it took was threatening to fire her if she didn't go before

Anastasia gave her a hug and scooted out the door quickly.

The time away would be good for both Anastasia and her mother, and Caroline would take the time to usher the ghosts out of her home and her life.

So, half an hour later when the doorbell rang she got up to answer it herself.

"Tell me you have coffee, Caro," Amy said, barely concealing a yawn as she hugged Caroline then made her way toward the kitchen.

Gina rolled her eyes. "Drama queen," she stage-whispered.

With a smile, Caroline hugged Gina. "Wait until she hears what the designer has suggested for the office."

Her eyes popped open wide. "What? Tell me..."

"What have I missed?" Karen stepped up onto the porch.

"Hi, come on in. Not much yet, we're going to start with coffee while I tell everyone what the designer thinks."

Gina's smile was warm and open. "Good to see you again."

"Thanks, I'm always up for coffee and decorating." Karen smiled back.

Karen and Gina headed down the hallway, chatting as they went.

Caroline closed the door. She stood where she was for a moment, listening to the voices chatting and allowing herself, for the first time, to feel loved. It was a wonderful feeling.

"Caro, you're out of creamer," Amy's voice floated down the hall.

Smiling, she shook her head. "Check the mini-fridge," she called back, and headed down the hall to join her friends.

CHAPTER TWENTY EIGHT

Andy closed the front door behind her and flipped the lock. *I have to check to see if the virus is still here, if the drive still works.* She rolled quickly down the hall and through the doorway, into the home office. One push of a button and her computer came to life. As it cycled through its opening sequence, she examined the flash drive for evidence of damage. Nothing jumped out at her; could it be that it still worked and the virus was safe, once again, in her hands where it belonged?

She inserted the drive into the slot, then clicked through to open the documents. From the looks of things, it was still here, and without a problem opening or running. *Yes, thank goodness. Now that I have it back, what am I going to do with it? That was a close call, and could have gone bad in a hurry. Someone else could have found it, someone with knowledge and a will to use it. And then? I would have been responsible for God only knows what. I can't carry it around with me, that's obvious. The question is, should I save it at all, or destroy it so the chance for it to fall into the wrong hands never happens again? I'm done with it. Really, what else would I ever need it for? Besides, I could always rewrite it. Right? Though this one copy took me three years to code. What if I just save it in a hidden folder on the computer, with a password required to access it? That would probably be the best option, just in case. Then I can get rid of the stupid flash drive and not have to worry about it anymore. Yes, that's the best idea.*

With several clicks of the mouse and a few keystrokes, Andy segregated a folder for her eyes only and locked the virus away. With the safeguards in place that she used, no one would stumble across it without her telling them it was there, let alone access the actual folder without her password. Even if all of that happened, which was highly unlikely, whoever it was would have to be pretty damn smart to know what the program even was, let alone what variables to enter in the prompts to make it work.

Relief once again flowed through her. Done and done. No need for the flash drive any longer. With a couple more commands, the flash drive was overwritten and no longer a danger to being compromised.

The front door opened and closed. "Hello, anyone home?"

It was Tom. Time for Andy to show him just how much progress she'd made. With a push, she backed her chair away from the desk and turned toward the doorway before she set the brake and stood.

"Hi, honey, I'll be right there," she called, and with one foot in front of the other, walked out of the room and down the middle of the hall, not touching the walls or banister. Smiling, she walked steadily toward the man who had put up with all she'd given and still come home, to her. He was amazing. Andy made a pact with herself right then and there: be the best person she could be, work every day toward being amazing to Tom, and not waste this second chance she'd been given to spend her life with the love of her life.

"Hey, look at you." Tom stood where he was, and watched her approach, strong and steady. "You're doing great."

"I'm working on it." Without warning, she twirled in a circle in front of him. For a second, he thought she was going to fall. Her laughter bubbled out. "See?"

Relieved once again, he grinned at her. "You're ready for the Miss Universe pageant?"

"My talent will be...walking from one end of the stage to the other." She laughed again. "Is that pizza?"

He held out the plain white box. "It is, indeed. I thought we should eat something before we take the cake to Katy."

"Good plan. I'm just going in now to frost it. Let me get it finished quick and then we'll eat. Want to help?"

"I thought you'd never ask."

CHAPTER TWENTY NINE

Tom wheeled Andy through the doorway and into Katy's room, the cake held carefully on her lap. The residual heat from the pan felt warm on her legs. The mouth-watering smell wafted up, teasing Andy and Tom with a promise of deliciousness.

The distance from the parking lot to the hospital room was still a little bit further than she could make on foot without help. It wouldn't be long, though, before she was one hundred percent again. I give it a few more days of therapy with the overly-happy physical therapist. If she had her way, she'd never go back. Hell, if she had her way the accident never would have happened; she'd be walking fine now. As it stands, tomorrow wouldn't be soon enough for her. I love her drive. Tom smiled.

Denise was already there, seated beside Katy's bed. "Hi, Andy. Tom. How's it going?"

"Hi, Mom. I'm glad you're here. I made your cake." Andy's face split into a cheesy, self-gratified grin.

"It smells heavenly." Her heart swelled with pride, and her face showed it. "Job well done, I can't wait to taste it."

"Denise, it's nice to see you. Thank you for coming." Tom enjoyed the easy relationship they'd developed, and was genuinely happy when she'd expressed interest in being present for this round of smell therapy.

Andy handed the cake to Tom. "Here, hold this for a minute,

please." He took it from her. She locked the wheels and pushed herself up from the chair, leaving it where he'd parked it. The chair on the other side of Katy's bed was ten steps away, and Andy made it without a falter or help. She stood next to the bed, one hand resting lightly on the back of the chair, the other on the edge of the bed.

"Hi, Katy. I baked you a cake. It's not just any cake, either. I used mom's German Chocolate cake recipe. The only thing is, you have to sit up to eat it. Oh, and I brought forks, so, if you want some, you'd better open your eyes quick, or I'm totally going to sit right here and eat it in front of you."

"Peer pressure. Good tactic," Tom laughed.

"She used to use it on me when she wanted her way. I figure this is payback." Andy giggled.

"Okay. Tell me, how do we do this?" Denise asked.

I can hear you, can you hear me? Katy's voice echoed off the unseen walls of her mental prison, bouncing around as if there were a dozen of her calling out. Something was different this time. She could hear their voices, imagined she could feel Andy's hand on her own. With all her willpower, Katy forced herself to run away from the hospital room, from Andy, and from Mrs. Parker. As soon as she reached the point where the tether wasn't tight, she turned and ran as quick as she could back toward the room. One second the tether snapped tight, almost strong enough to make her stop; she dug deep and pushed. The next thing she knew, the tether released its pull as something else tugged her toward her physical body. She tumbled over the edge, unable to control anything at all. It was almost as if the tether had switched directions now and she was falling/being directed to her new/old destination. Katy tensed, squeezed her eyes closed and gave herself up to whatever would happen.

She landed with a softness she hadn't expected. What, really, could one expect, with never having been in a coma before, let alone come out?

Katy felt heavy. *I can still hear them talking. I know I'm in my body now. Why can't I open my eyes? I have to let them know I'm here.*

Every ounce of concentration was focused on reaching for Andy. *She's so close...if only I can touch her, get her attention, she's come out of a coma, surely she can help me...*

Tom set the pan down on the moveable table and lifted the foil. "What we did with the lasagna was open the lid and set the pan on the bed, close to her head, then fan the smell gently toward her." He turned the table, positioned it closer to her face as he talked. "I'm thinking we can get better coverage if we cut the cake into pieces, put those on plates, and arrange them on this table so the smell covers more distance."

"There's a knife in the side pocket of my chair," Andy pointed. "On the left."

Denise removed the knife and slid it out of its plastic cover, and brought out the package of paper plates that were stowed there as well. She handed the knife to Tom and opened the wrapping on the plates. She set them out in a straight line across the side of the tray that was closest to Katy.

"Thanks. Here we go. You ready, Katy?" Slicing through the warm chocolate, he dished out five slices, laying them out one by one. He left the rest of the cake in the pan behind the cut pieces, the foil set to the side, and licked the frosting off his fingers. His approval was evident. "Mmmm."

As Andy sat down in the chair, movement caught her attention. "Um, Mom? Tom? Did one of you just bump the bed?"

Denise's brow furrowed. "I don't think so, why?" She turned her attention to Katy. "Oh, my..." was all she could muster.

"What?" Tom's voice was on high alert. He moved to where he could see what held their attention.

Katy's hand was dangling down the side of the bed, out from under the covers, and still swaying gently. Her eyes were still closed, though that didn't mean anything at this point.

"It's working. The smell therapy, the cake, it's bringing her around." His heart soared. Tom reached over and pressed the call button several times in quick succession. When the nurse answered, Tom responded, "Katy moved again. Can you come in here?"

This time three nurses showed up. "Are you sure she moved on her own?" the male nurse asked.

"Yes, Andy saw movement, and neither one of us," he motioned to himself and Denise, "were close enough to the bed to have knocked her hand out from under the covers," Tom explained. "There has to be a test or something that can tell us what is going on with her, whether she's awake and unable to move, or whatever. Or better yet, something to give her to help her wake up. Can you call the doctor please? This isn't her first movement, and I'd like him to be here if it happens again, or at least the one *responsible* for making a decision on what needs to be done to verify what's happening."

The nurses huddled amongst themselves, then left the room as one unit.

Denise's hand rubbed up and down on Katy's leg, while Andy reached out and grasped Katy's hand. "Katy, I'm here. If you can hear me, please squeeze my hand, let me know."

"Maybe it's the cake." Tom positioned the tray closer, slid the cake plates as close to the edge as possible, and gently fanned the smell toward Katy's face. "Come on, Katydid, you can do it. Fight through it, I know you're close, we saw your hand moving, come on baby girl, let's go…" He continued murmuring encouraging words to her as he fanned.

Both of the ladies watched, to no avail. Andy tried again. "I know you're in there, can you hear me? Don't make me come back into the in-between to find you and ask you personally. I'm not above doing that." *Am I? Is there a way to make that happen? Can I go back in, without a medical reason to do so? I wonder...*

"That's not funny," Denise chided. "Don't even joke about that."

Andy ignored her mother's comment. *If there were a way, maybe I could go in and bring her back this time, knowing what to expect. Would it be the same as last time? Could I come back out willingly, or would it take a roll down a hill to make the transition?* Her thoughts raced. *I can put people IN a coma, I'll bet I'm capable of bringing them out.* Computer coding began to take shape in her brain, some saved, others discarded, more rearranged. *Yes, I think I can.* A smile crossed her face, fleeting, as she continued to rub.

My eyelids are so heavy. I wish I could open them. Maybe if I rest for a minute. Getting loose from the tether and then forcing my hand off the bed took everything I had. Another minute, that's all. I'm so tired. My entire body feels like there's a weight on it, holding me still. That was the most effort it's ever taken for me to move. Thank goodness they noticed. I hope the doctor can help me from here. What is that smell? Is that chocolate cake? Mmmm...I love Mrs. Parker's German Chocolate cake...

~~*~*~*

"Come on, Katy, you can do it. Wake up," Tom turned the words into a mantra. Everything he had was focused on his sister. There was a real chance she could wake up; he did everything he could think of, including mentally willing her to do so. Tom wasn't a religious or a spiritual man—sending thoughts and wishes her way were about as close as he'd ever gotten to praying. Though praying was toward an all-powerful being, and the thoughts he sent were to his sister...*there's no explaining what I'm doing. Just wake up Katy. I need you. Andy needs you. Your life needs you. There's so much you need to do. Wake up, open your eyes, come on, I know you can do it.*

The male nurse returned. "I've paged Dr. Alister. He's on his way. We need you to step back now so we can give her a checkup. Please."

"Tom moved the table out of their way. Denise backed off, too, giving them full access. Andy stayed close by the bed, talking low, keeping constant contact. She wasn't in the nurses' way, so they let her stay where she was.

The two other nurses wheeled machines in while her visitors backed out of the way. They went about their tasks: a well-oiled machine that talked and acted in a strange language known only to medical professionals. The excitement level was elevated, even among the staff.

Dr. Alister arrived fifteen minutes later. "Another exciting day, have we?" He stepped directly to the bed and the nurse advised him of their test results.

"Sounds like Miss Katy is making progress. Her blood pressure is good, vitals are that of a healthy young lady, and her pulse is strong and fast." He checked the chart. "Faster than it has been, well, ever. Since she's been with us, anyway. What were you doing when the change occurred?"

Tom moved the tray back to where it had been when the nurses took over. "We'd just set the cake on the tray and cut several pieces. I thought making the smell cover more area would help in getting it to her, and that's when Andy saw her hand move off the bed and hang down the side."

"I started rubbing her hand then, and haven't stopped."

~~*~*~*

I'm so tired. Why is it so difficult to open my eyes? I can feel your hand on mine, Andy, and I'm trying to wake up. I'm back. It seems like too much trouble to even move one muscle, let alone all of them. I have to let you know I'm here. Tom, Andy, Mrs. Parker, can you hear me? Anyone? I can't feel my mouth moving, can you hear my words at all? Andy, listen hard, maybe you can hear me.

Katy gathered every ounce of energy she had left and pushed hard. Concentrated on doing one thing, let them know. With a burst of force, she pried her eyes open a tiny bit. As soon as she did, the tug from the in-between let go completely and faded away. She took a deep breath. It became easier: to breathe, to think, to move, to do everything. Pushing her eyes open further, she blinked several times, slowly, adjusting to the light. As shapes came into focus, her eyes met those of a stranger. He saw her and smiled.

"You're doing exactly what I would have told you to do. Touch and sound are as important at this stage as anything else," he said, then looked down at his patient and smiled. "Though it would appear the cake has done the trick...hello, Miss Katy."

The three turned and looked at her simultaneously.

Her eyes were open.

Tom let out a whoop loud enough to wake every patient in the wing. Tears of joy overflowed even as emotion clogged his throat. He and Andy converged as one, hugging Katy, talking to her over each other, laughing.

Denise stood back, her arms crossed tightly across her body. Her own emotions were strong; her daughter was walking again, gaining strength every day, and now Katy was awake. Things were looking up for everyone. She wiped a tear from her eye. It was wonderful to see the pure joy. She was glad she'd come down and been here for this.

Nurses converged on the room, filling it to capacity. Word spread like wildfire, animating all who heard. Hope renewed when a patient awoke.

"I know you're excited, I am too, but she needs to breathe. Give her some room, please. I'd like to check her vitals and have a word with her."

Staff who were not assigned to Katy made their way out of the room, talking animatedly. Tom and Andy stepped back, out of Dr. Alister's way so he could check her over.

"How are you, Katy? We are all very glad to see you. I'm Dr. Alister. I'd like to check your pulse and look in your eyes, would you mind?"

She blinked slowly, then shook her head once.

"I know you're tired. I would most assuredly be exhausted if I'd just awoken from a coma." He held her wrist and watched the second hand on the clock.

An unintelligible croak emerged.

Tom appeared on the opposite side of her from the doctor, with a hospital-issue cup in his hand. He held the straw for her. She sipped once, then again.

She looked at her brother. "Thanks. Hi."

His smile lit the room. "Hi, yourself, Katydid."

Andy stepped up next to him. "I'm so glad you're back. We have *so* much to talk about."

Katy nodded, smiling weakly. "I know. You were going to eat the cake in front of me? Harsh."

~~*~*~*

The doctor chased everyone out of the room half an hour after she'd awoken last night. Secretly, she was glad. It was exhausting, coming back. They'd be back today, they'd assured her of that several times before they'd actually left. Katy was as happy to see them through her own eyes as they were to see her awake.

Daylight began to break, and the light filtered in through the blinds that hung across the window.

Katy's mind had been awake most of the night as her body rested. It was getting easier to move her limbs and open her eyes, though getting out of bed and walking wasn't happening yet. Maybe tomorrow she would be more adjusted to the weight of being in a body again.

Through the night she'd thought about everything she could remember, everything she'd heard while she'd been in a state. A nurse brought her a pen and paper when she asked. She jotted cryptic notes about everything she could remember, in case it faded away. When she finished, she slid the paper and pen into the drawer of the table. *There will be time to flesh it out later*, she thought, as her eyes closed.

This morning, as reality dawned with the new day, her eyes held more than their share of sadness. *I knew mom and dad were killed, or they wouldn't have crossed through the in-between. Though it was wonderful to see them, and I know they've gone on to a better place, I have no idea what I'm going to do without them. Tom has had years to get used to the idea; I haven't. Not really. Seeing them pass by after they died is entirely different than knowing that now I have to go on without them. None of it seemed real while I was there. Where will I go, what will I do? The last real memory I have is of a snowball fight with Andy, outside the school, and then the alley. Oh, God, am I here because it snowed?* A shiver skittered down her spine. *Was it real, what they told me, about Darnell being killed? I didn't see him in the in-between. How can they be sure? I saw Jerome, dressed in a priest's robe or a minister's, or something, as he went by. He saw me, too, and I felt his regret. He let me go, didn't hold me like Darnell wanted him to in that alley; I know he didn't want to hurt me. I felt that from him as he passed through, too. What about the others? Were they really the shadows that slammed into*

The Never? That part seems like a dream now, and so hard to remember. Andy said there were more people, I know she did, but I can't remember who or what. Who were they? Surely she or Tom will tell me. I have so many questions to ask...

There was a soft knock at the door. She turned her head toward the sound as Dr. Alister breezed into the room. He seemed like a caring, gentle man to her.

"Good morning, Miss Katy. How are you today?" His smile was infectious.

Her voice wasn't strong yet. "Good morning, doctor. I'm still tired, but I guess that's to be expected, right?"

"We just don't know what should be expected, as you," his eyes twinkled, "are a very unique young lady. I would rather not prescribe anything to help you sleep at this point, as I have reservations regarding your stability." He checked her pupils and then her pulse.

"Oh, I wouldn't take it anyway, I don't like medications. Not even aspirin. I'll probably sleep better once I am in my own bed again and not being awakened every couple hours by nurses."

"That's probably true. I would like to keep you for a few more days. Mainly for observation, but I have a few more tests I would like to run, make sure everything is fine now."

"Okay."

"Very few people have traversed the pathway you have been on and, with that in mind, I would like to ask you some questions. If you're up to it this morning."

She raised the head of the bed and settled herself more comfortably. "Sure."

"Thank you." He sat in the chair next to the bed and withdrew a small notebook and pen from the pocket of his white coat. "First of all, do you remember anything from the time period you spent in the coma?"

"I do, a little. Some things. Most of it is a blur, but I do remember little things."

He made notations. "Is there anything specific from that time period, something that happened on the other side, where you were, or on this side, that stands out in your mind?"

Concentration wrinkled her forehead. "The television must have been on, because I remember an oil spill in the gulf, some sort of new health care program, and a tornado that ripped through Moore. Oh, and something about earthquakes. Are we having earthquakes?" Her comment came out as more of a question than an answer. "Seems there have been a lot of them…does that make any sense to you?"

"It does. All three of those incidences did, indeed, happen and yes, we've been experiencing earthquakes, as well, strange as it may seem." The pen scratched across the paper. "What else?"

"Rick Applecore married Kathy Green. Why do I know that?" Katy wondered more to herself than the doctor.

"Now that one I don't know," his face crinkled around his eyes as he smiled. "I'd like to ask you a question, now, about what happened before the coma. What is the last thing you can remember from that time period?"

She fidgeted, uncomfortable with the memory. "I was walking home after band practice. It snowed." Her wan smile told him she wished it hadn't. "I'd been waiting for it to snow. That's my favorite. So, I was walking by the flower shop, and there's an alley right there. Someone grabbed me. There were two kids I went to school with, Jerome and Darnell. Darnell hit me, and told Jerome to hold me. He didn't want to, he let me go. Then, I don't remember much, just that he hit me. Darnell did. Next thing I know, I'm in the in-between, and I can see my body in a hospital bed below me." She frowned, looking around the room. "It wasn't this room, though. Is that right? Have I always been in this room?"

More scratching of pen on paper. "I haven't been your doctor the full time, so I'm not sure. I took over when your other doctor…passed away."

There's more to it than that. If he doesn't want to tell me, and it's obvious by his answer that he doesn't, I'm sure Tom or Katy will fill in the blanks. If it even matters.

"Okay. I'll ask Tom. He'll be able to tell me."

"Mmm hmm. I'm sure he will. Can you tell me what the first thing you remember about waking up?"

"That's easy. Your eyes." Katy looked at Dr. Alister. "I saw you first."

"Thank you for talking with me about your experience, Katy. I would like to talk with you more about it later. For now, I'd like you to get some rest." He stood and pocketed the notebook and pen. "Doctor's orders."

A nod was all she could manage; her eyes were closing on their own. "I'm tired anyway." Her gentle snore punctuated her sentence.

Dr. Alister made a notation on the chart and stayed with her for a moment or two longer, watching her sleep. He had so many more questions, but for now they would wait.

CHAPTER THIRTY

"After all that, it's finally over. The stalker is gone, the kid that attacked me and I killed has been thoroughly researched and he wasn't a good man, and speaking of good men I have one who saved my life, and means the world to me. Things couldn't be going better for me."

"How do you feel about everything?"

A full-bodied laugh exploded from deep inside her. She didn't try to stop it. "To be honest with you, I feel fantastic. I haven't felt this good in... I don't know how long. Since way before I moved to Oklahoma, that's for sure."

"That's great, I'm glad to hear it."

"Only..."

The therapist sat quietly, waiting.

Karen sighed. "I wonder, will the nightmares go away? The last one combined the stalker with the kid. They were bad enough when there was only one of them bothering me at a time, but the situations have combined in my subconscious and the last nightmare was the worst I've ever experienced."

"Sometimes the subconscious takes a little bit longer to purge the bad from the brain. The situations in your conscious mind have been resolved, so my guess would be that the nightmares will stop soon. Nightmares are your subconscious' way of ridding your brain of excess negativity. I know it's hard to think of them as a good thing, though I believe they are."

The silence stretched on for nearly a full minute while Karen digested the information. "I hadn't thought of it like that. Well, then, with any luck that last one was the end of the parade."

"Perhaps."

"That's everything. As soon as the nightmares end, that is."

The therapist smiled, setting the note pad down on the desk. "That's terrific. I agree with you. From our session today, I believe we've gone as far as we can go together. It seems like you're ready to me. If you feel the need to talk, I'm always here for you."

"I'm glad you've been here for me over the past couple weeks. I know we only had a few sessions, but I feel like I've made progress and I'm comfortable with where I am mentally. That's what this is all about, right?" She stood, smoothing the wrinkles from her skirt.

Her therapist stood as well, mirroring her movements. "Yes, it is. It has been my pleasure to get to know you, Karen."

"Thank you." The women shook hands, and then hugged.

As Karen slipped out the side door, she took a deep breath. Freedom smelled good.

˷ ˏ*˷*˷*

Cicadas and crickets welcomed the night with their song as the stars winked on, one by one.

They sat on the back porch, as close as two people could be without sitting on top of each other. "I feel like I could talk to her a little bit more about the nightmares if they continue, though I'm not sure if they will now that I've done my research and you've killed my stalker."

Ben leaned in and kissed her. "Whatever you need to do, I'm one hundred percent behind you. If you want to continue to see her, then do it. Though you might be right, the nightmares may be gone now that there isn't anything to worry about anymore."

"We'll see what happens. I've always got the option to go back."

"Absolutely. But now, what do you say we go out for dinner tonight?"

"Sounds good to me. Where did you have in mind?"

"I'm thinking pizza."

"Stolley's Pizzaria?"

"Haven't been there in months. Works for me." He locked the doors and they walked around the house.

He brushed her hand with his and intertwined their fingers. This, their relationship, felt like the most natural thing in the world to him. An idea took shape. The more he thought about it, about them, the more positive he was that Karen was his forever, and he had a plan.

"Clear your schedule. We're going away for the weekend. After the last few weeks, we both need it. Hell, we deserve it. I've booked us a cabin at Aspen Lake. No, don't argue. There's nothing on fire at work that needs you there seven days a week, and you've got vacation time stacked up, right? I thought so. Put in for it. I've already cleared the time and the deposit is non-refundable. Good. Why don't you pack tonight after work, put your suitcase in your car, and come over for dinner? Okay, you can still pack tonight and put your suitcase in your car tomorrow. Alright, I'll see you then. I love you too."

Good. Convincing her went smoother than I thought it would. Ben put his cell phone back in his pocket and turned his attention to his own open suitcase on the bed. It had been a long time since he'd been nervous about spending the weekend away with anyone; but she wasn't just anyone. He chuckled. If he had anything to say about it, she would be the only woman he'd spend a weekend away with ever again, and he planned to be doing it for a long time.

~~*~*~*

They arrived at the cabin's rental office just before five o'clock p.m. Ben pulled the car in to the gravel lot, happy to see there were only two other vehicles present.

"I'll go get our keys. Be right back." He climbed out of the car and strolled toward the office. She watched him go, admiring the view before opening her own door and stepping out to stretch. From where she stood, she couldn't hear any traffic from the main roads or the highway. *Good. Nothing like uninterrupted country sounds to lull a girl to sleep at night.*

Around the side of the building she could see the beginning of a trail. It wound around and through the trees, disappearing behind a huge cedar. The area looked to be well kept; she was happy to see the pride that was obviously taken in the appearance of the grounds.

Ben came back out of the office. Two keys dangled from his hand as he approached her. "Our cabin is down this path. She said we're the only ones booked out of the five cabins on this twenty acres so it will be quite peaceful. There's a restaurant a couple of miles up the road; she asked if we needed reservations and offered to call them in for us. We're set for six o'clock."

"Sounds great. Shall we?"

They grabbed their suitcases out of the trunk and made their way toward the pathway. Ben reached over and interlaced his fingers with hers, matching his pace to her footfalls. She let him lead the way. They walked in comfortable silence, passing one offshoot that most likely led to another cabin. After following the path around a large stump and past a perfect picnic area, the path to their cabin showed up. It was probably thirty feet further on before the trees opened up to a fairy tale view.

The log cabin they were staying in was beautifully weathered and surrounded by a wraparound porch. To the left of the front door a porch swing hung from two iron chains, and to the right was a wooden patio table and two chairs that looked to be handmade.

Karen sighed. "Ohhhh. Isn't this beautiful?"

"The caretaker said this one is her favorite."

They stepped up onto porch and Karen set her bag down while Ben dug the key out of his pocket. She explored, following the porch around the side of the house as he opened the door. Picking up both bags, Ben went inside and set them out of the way.

He could see her through the window, trailing her fingers along the railing in appreciation. As she neared the back door, he stepped closer to the window to watch her while she wasn't aware. A hummingbird buzzed up to the feeder hanging near her head, and her laugh sounded like... home. *How could I have thought she wasn't 'the one'?* Reaching into his pocket, he touched the ring he'd been carrying for weeks. He'd tried to put it back in the safe several times, but hadn't been able to convince himself it belonged there. Apparently his subconscious knew something he hadn't acknowledged yet. His ring belonged on her finger. All he needed now was the perfect time to ask her to wear it.

While she was otherwise entertained, he unzipped the front pocket of his suitcase, pulling the small black velvet box out and nestled the ring inside that he'd been carrying around in his pocket. Now he was absolutely ready when the opportunity presented itself.

They took a walk after dinner before going back to the cabin. The path took them through a shady copse of trees and opened onto a slight rise, the edge of the gentle grassy slope giving way to a sandy beach along the edge of the lake. The sunset was throwing the most beautiful pinks and reds across the clouds, and the colors reflecting off the water as it lapped at the beach resembled liquid gold.

"I think you should change your name again." *Well, that's romantic. You'd better step up your game, Brady.*

With a hint of fear and a questioning look in her eyes, she turned to look at him. "Why? He's dead. He can't hurt me anymore. What reason would I have to—"

Ben pulled the velvet box out of his pocket and lowered one knee to the ground. As he opened the top, the last rays of sun from the sinking sun refracted through the diamond staring up at her.

"Karen Fielding, you are the most beautiful woman I've ever met. I want to be the one to hold your hand and your heart for the rest of my life. I want to share my life with you, make babies with you, grow old in matching rocking chairs with you. There has only ever been you. Please make me the happiest man on the face of the Earth, and say you'll marry me."

Her legs shook, threatening to give out. Tears overflowed and streamed down her face as she watched him, as if in slow motion, sink down to one knee and stare up at her as if nothing else existed. As he spoke, she saw for the first time that he wasn't looking at her with his eyes, they were just a portal. He was looking at her with his heart. She watched his lips form the words, and knew that she was where she needed and wanted to be. Right here, with him.

As she lowered herself to kneeling, Karen reached out and placed her hands on either side of his face, letting him see that she looked at him with her heart, too. This beautiful, strong face was the face she wanted to see every day for the rest of her life. It was as if the beating of their hearts melded, became one, at that very moment in time. She felt it and knew it was where she ended, and they began.

"Karen? Are you going to say something? Anything?" He was about to pass out from holding his breath, waiting.

"Yes."

"Yes, you're going to say something, or yes, you'll marry me?"

She laughed. "Yes, I'll marry you. I love you so much, Ben Brady."

CHAPTER THIRTY ONE

It had been a long week in the hospital after she'd come out of the coma. Katy was anxious to leave here, go home, and…and what? *Getting out of here is the most important thing right now. I can't wait to go home.*

"Katy, hi," Andy rolled into the hospital room for the last time. "Are you ready?"

With her feet swinging back and forth over the side of the bed, Katy sat waiting for them to take her home. She grinned at her friend, happy to be leaving this room, though she didn't feel the passage of time nearly as much as her brother, Tom, had. He had been the one to come visit her regularly. "Yes, I am. Where's Tom?"

She set the parking brake on the wheels and stood. "He's signing the paperwork and we've already parked the truck right out front. And, so you don't have to wait for a nurse to bring a wheelchair, I'm going to let you borrow mine."

"I've missed so much. We have a bazillion things to catch up on, like why you're in a wheelchair in the first place."

Andy gave her a hug and then sat down in the chair by the bed. "Yeah, about that. We do have a ton of things to talk about. Do you remember anything I told you while you were in the in-between? Or anything Tom told you? There's so much that's happened."

"Some things. Dr. Alister asked me the same thing, and I only remember a few details." *I want to talk to you about Jerome and*

Darnell, and the others, but I'm not sure if I want to talk about the flash drive or the virus, yet, Andy. Please don't ask me that question. I need time to think. "I remember some stuff from the news, bizarre things. I also remember—"

"What about—"

"—that rally car driver getting married."

"Hey, Katy, I didn't see you there. You know about the wedding of the century? I broke that news to you gently when it happened. It was in all the newspapers, even Aspen Grove's. Sorry to be the one to tell you." Tom's arrival interrupted Andy's question. Good thing, as she didn't want him to know about the flash drive at all and she had almost spilled the beans. All he heard was the sound of his sister and her best friend, his fiancé, talking over each other the way they used to in high school. No sound in the world could have made him happier.

"Tom, hi. I do know that, it's true then. Ah, well, the coma took me out of the running." Katy levered herself off the bed and met him halfway. "Are we ready to go? I can't wait to get out of here."

"Your chariot awaits." He unlocked the wheels and turned the chair for Katy. "Climb in. Andy, are you sure you want to walk out?"

"Absolutely. I've been practicing for this." She walked as if she were on a runway. "Remember when we used to practice our runway walks, Katy?"

Bubbling laughter followed the trio, echoing in the newly-empty room and down the hallway.

~~*~*~*

The light turned red. Andy slowed to a stop. "Are you sure that's where you want to go? Are you up to it? You've only been out of the hospital for a day." She chanced a sidelong glance at her best friend.

"Yes. I need to see." Katy sat in the passenger seat, facing forward, ignoring Andy's look. "The light's green."

"I know." She hadn't noticed, but was far from telling Katy how worried she was about the current developments. "We're expected home in about fifteen minutes," she tried again.

"It won't take long, I just need to *see*." Exasperation was evident in her voice.

"Okay."

They didn't talk again until Andy pulled to the curb in front of the flower shop. As the sun dipped below the horizon, the scene was left in a dreamlike state. Not quite light, not yet dark.

Katy opened the door and stepped out of the car. Andy followed. "Behind the dumpster?"

"Yes. That's what the police report said, and where the photos in the newspaper showed."

Forty feet behind the dumpster was a brick wall dead end. Katy strode into the alley, moving as if she were on a mission. "Here?" She stopped in front of a dark stain that, to this day, hadn't been washed away by rain nor snow.

"That's it."

"This is my blood, isn't it?"

"I think it is. I'm not—"

"My head—"

"—comfortable being here—"

"—cracked against that wall. This is where everything changed." Katy spun around, facing her friend. "Is this the first time you've been here, in this spot, since the attack?"

Tears stung her eyes. "No."

"Is that stain from my blood?"

Their eyes locked. Neither looked away. "Yes," Andy whispered, the first tear tracking down her cheek. "I was so scared. I've been here more times than I can count."

"Was it you?"

Eyes wide now. "Was *what* me?"

"Was it you who sought vengeance, made them pay, invoked

karma, after they were freed by the courts?"

Time seemed to stop. Not a sound was heard by either girl. Girls then, young women now.

A choice to be made, Andy stepped up and claimed her work. "Yes. I did, and I'm not sorry. They were all responsible for what happened to you. Two of them put you in a coma. Two others let you down with their lack of procedure. Those who took them out were guilty of their own crimes. *I did nothing wrong,*" Andy's venomous words poured out of her. "Not one of them deserved to live after what was done to you." Spittle flew from her lips and landed between the two on the asphalt where Katy had lain, so many years ago: beaten, bloody, unconscious, and eventually comatose—all because of the actions of others, and then the inactions of those to follow.

The women stared at each other, neither speaking for several heartbeats.

I knew you did, Katy thought. *I heard you tell me while I was in the in-between. I am so glad you told me again, now that you knew for sure I would hear you. I can't tell you how much it means to me, not without telling you I already knew. I remember so much, not only what happened in that hospital room, but what happened in the in-between, as well. I won't tell anyone what I know; they wouldn't understand. Thank you, my friend, for being honest and telling me. I've missed you so much.*

Katy broke the silence. "Thank you."

Andy nodded once.

With those two words, nothing else needed to be said. With the gap of time bridged, the friends clasped hands and then held on to each other in a long hug that healed all wounds.

CHAPTER THIRTY TWO

Candlelight flickered patterns across the wall. The sun was almost set, and Denise should be in the driveway any time to drop Andy off. Without her help, Tom wouldn't have been able to make this happen; well, without hers and Katy's help. An afternoon of pedicures and facials was worth the price it cost for the three ladies to spend some time together.

As if summoned, the van turned in. Though Andy didn't require the use of a handicapped-accessible vehicle any longer, Denise had yet to take it back to the rental agency.

The key in the lock surprised him. Why would she think she needed the key? His car was...in the garage and the only light was the flickering of the tiny flames atop the wax.

"I forgot my phone in your mom's van." Katy's voice floated down the hall from the front door. "Go ahead, I'll be right back. Hold on, Mrs. Parker," she turned and ran back to the van.

"Tom, are you..." Andy's question broke off mid-sentence. She'd seen the flower petals that led toward the dining room. His grin grew as he waited for her to push through the swinging door between the front room and where he waited.

"Hello?" Closer, still, her voice still filled with confusion and, was that a touch of wonder?

The door inched open. Tom waited patiently.

When her head poked through, he clicked the remote to turn on the CD player. Soft music drifted down from the speakers in the corners of the room.

"Hi there." Love filled her eyes as she took in the details: candlelight, soft music, appetizers, and the love of her life holding a bouquet of calla lilies, miniature carnations and baby's breath.

"Hi yourself." It was amazing that he could hear anything over the pounding of his own heart. "How was your day?"

"It was a great day." Andy pointed back toward the front door. "Katy will be in any minute. She forgot her phone." Realization dawned. She brushed her bangs out of her eyes. "She won't be right back, will she?"

Amusement glinted in his eyes as he shook his head. "No."

"What's going on here?" Tentative, now, Andy stepped closer to Tom and ran her finger along a petal on the closest calla lily, then brought her eyes up to meet his again.

"Dinner. Dancing. Romancing." Longing filled his voice. Heat rose up from the depths, consuming her.

The purr started in her chest and escaped her lips at the same slow, methodical speed with which she reached for him. "Where to start..."

With a grace born of practice, he answered, "I thought you'd never ask," as he took her hand and wrapped it around the stems of the bouquet, slid in slow motion down to one knee, and produced her engagement ring between index finger and thumb.

"Andrea Marie Parker, I have been in love with you for years. What do you say we run away to Vegas and elope?"

She sunk down and knelt facing him. "I love you, Tom Oliver, but no, I will not. There is no way we're eloping. We'll get married in the church like we planned to do the first time, with friends and family, and maybe even a limousine this time to bring me to meet you there. Elope? No way. Marry you? Absolutely."

As he slipped her ring onto her finger for the second time, he let out a whoop. "Yes, it's about time. I've waited long enough to make

you my wife. Let's call your mom and Katy, and tell them it's on."
Tom grinned from ear to ear.

"No." Andy's whispered word wiped the happy right off his
face.

"No?"

"We're not calling anyone. A few moments ago you promised
me dancing, wining and dining, if you'll recall." Her smile was slow
coming.

"You are absolutely right." He rose, pulling her up with him.
"Would you care to dance, Ms. Parker?"

"I thought you'd never ask."

Candlelight flickered across their faces. As they swayed to the
music, Andy looked up, into Tom's eyes.

"I have to wonder, Mr. Oliver, why my ring was too big when I
asked you to hold it, and now it fits perfectly. I haven't gained much
weight back yet. When did you have it resized?"

"I took it in a couple weeks ago. The jeweler said if it still didn't
fit, to bring it back, he would check your ring size and adjust it for
you."

"It's perfect."

"Good." They danced until the song ended. "Are you ready for
dinner? Please, have a seat. Allow me…"

CHAPTER THIRTY THREE

"Of *course* I'm happy for you. My brother is a great guy, and I always wanted you as my sister anyway. How much better can it get?"

"You have no idea how happy it makes me to know that you're on board with this. I am a believer in everything happening for a reason, and even though I don't know the reason behind your coma or my being hit by that car, there has to be one. Maybe everything happens in its own time, too."

The sun shone brightly through the dining room window, shining across stacks of bridal magazines that covered the table. Katy hopped up and headed toward the kitchen. "Need more iced tea?" she called over her shoulder.

"I'm good, thanks." Andy flipped page after page in her hunt for the perfect wedding dress. The one she'd been wearing when the car struck her had been cut off her at the hospital. Even if it hadn't been, it was ruined anyway; ripped and stained with dirt and blood...

...the veil floating down, down, down, draping over the wheel of the car. It looks so beautiful, floating on the wind that way. But really, what kind of artist would consider this a masterpiece? Certainly not Dr. Phillips, he'll see it when he gets out of his car. Dr. Phillips, I'm glad you came, I can't seem to move. Can you help me up? What? I can't hear you. Say that again? I still can't hear you. Why does your breath smell like alcohol...have you been drinking?

Dr. Phillips? Where are you going?

Where am I? Hello?

"Hello? Andy?" Katy snapped her fingers in an attempt to catch her attention.

Startled, she blinked several times in rapid succession and realized she'd been staring out the window at the back garden without seeing it at all.

"Holy crap," she muttered, turning her wide eyes to Katy.

"What's wrong? Are you okay? You look like you've seen a ghost."

"I know who hit me. The car, my wedding day, I know who was driving. I know who did it. The final missing piece just popped up."

Bridal magazines forgotten, Katy pulled her chair closer. "You remembered? Who was it?"

"Doctor Phillips."

"Who?"

"He was the psychiatrist I saw after the bast...after what happened to you that day after school. My parents sent me to talk to a professional. I was a mess. Anyway, in my flashback, I saw him getting out of the driver's side of the car that hit me. I remembered him getting back in and driving away, too."

"We have to call the police."

"We have to call Tom, too. But wait, that's not all. I know why."

"You do?"

"Yes. As his tires screeched around the corner, before he hit me, I looked back and saw his face right before the bumper sent me up and over the hood and roof of the car. Then, while I was lying in the road, he got out of his car and came over to me. I saw his shoes. They were the same shoes he'd been wearing when I went by to see him after I came back to town. They were these tacky, ugly, brown dress shoes. He squatted down and looked at me, and I looked him in the eye while he said...something. I saw his mouth move, but couldn't hear what he said. Then I smelled the alcohol on his breath.

He was hammered. The worst part, well, I guess it wasn't the worst part, but it was at the time because I couldn't feel anything yet...he left me there. Laying in the road, having hit me, stopped, saw I was still alive, he staggered back to his car and he drove away."

"Oh my God, that's awful," Katy hugged her friend. "We have to call the police now. They will arrest him for it and he'll go to prison."

Andy picked up her cell phone. "Wait, let me tell Tom first. This is so unreal. Ever since it happened I've wanted to know who it was, I wanted to remember. I definitely did *not* think in a million years it would be somebody I knew."

If karma is a well-thrown boomerang, I wonder what Dr. Phillips did that caused it to come back around. But if it was him, why was I in the way? Collateral damage, I guess. Like the girlfriend who was in the car when the mayor killed Jerome. I meant to keep tabs on her, see if she knew anything about what happened that she shouldn't have. I wonder what happened to her. Doesn't matter, I'd have heard by now if there was anything to be concerned about. Collateral damage makes sense. I haven't done anything to attract karma's attention to myself. Have I? What if it was me that karma had come for? In a convoluted way, could it be that karma thinks I am responsible for the deaths of those who hurt Katy? I didn't do it myself. Still...doesn't matter now. I'm alive, they're not. The program did its job, and it's destroyed. Karma's on its own now.

"Earth calling Andy," Katy patted her hand. "You've got to stop going away like that; you're starting to freak me out."

"Sorry. I was just thinking." The clock read four-thirty p.m. "Tom should be home in an hour anyway; let's not bother him at work. It's not going to hurt to wait another hour to tell everyone what I've remembered, since it's been weeks now anyway. I'll call my mom and ask her to come over, too."

"I guess you're right. It's going to be busy around here as soon as you tell everyone. We should clean up our mess."

"Ooh, wait, what do you think of this one?" Andy placed her index finger on the picture of a peach, off-the-shoulder semi-formal length dress. "I want you to wear something you'll look great in and still be able to wear again after the wedding."

"Gorgeous," Katy cooed.

"You think?"

"Absolutely. Are you sure you don't want me to wear some flamingo-looking taffeta with a big bow on the butt? That's what, oh, what's her name, that cheerleader we went to school with...you know the one, her photos were in the paper yes—"

"Cashmere?"

"—terday, right, Cashmere made her bridesmaids wear. That was hideous."

Both girls laughed. "No, I'm not so insecure that I would have you wear something like that. Besides, one day you'll get married, and I don't want paybacks."

It was almost ten o'clock p.m. by the time the police had all the information for their report and left. Katy excused herself shortly after, forcing herself to swallow a couple of aspirin—even though she disliked medication of any kind—to get rid of the pounding headache before she retired to her room and Denise headed home, as well. Tom sat on the couch next to Andy and held her hand.

"That was quite the excitement. How are you doing after all of that?"

"Tired, confused, and hungry."

"What are you confused about?" The worry lines across his forehead deepened.

"Karma. I'm just...you know how I feel about karma. Something this big, it makes me wonder what he could possibly have done for this kind of payback."

"There's no telling, honey. Though if it were his karma, wouldn't he be the one hurt?"

Andy cut her eyes sideways at him. "What do you mean by that?"

He pulled her closer. "All I mean is, why were *you* the one hurt if it was karma? I don't think karma had anything to do with the accident. I think being under the influence and unable to control the car was the reason. If it were karma, you were the one hurt. It would have been the boomerang coming back around to you, and you haven't done anything to create that kind of retribution on yourself. Have you?"

"Me? No. Maybe you're right."

They sat in silence, each lost in their own thoughts.

It couldn't have been the virus that brought karma back on each of those people. I only helped it tie up its own loose ends. I didn't create any more than already existed. Andy was convinced she wasn't to blame.

She couldn't have done anything even remotely worthy of what that accident did to her. That's ridiculous. Could she? No. Not a chance. Tom's mind circled around before dismissing the possibility.

"You said you were hungry. I think there's still pizza in the fridge we can heat up. What do you say?"

"Sounds good."

CHAPTER THIRTY FOUR

Andy woke to the smell of coffee. *Tom is up*, she thought, and smiled. Stretching, she luxuriated in the bed for another minute, making an imaginary snow angel while enjoying the ability to move her legs at will.

Finally, she threw back the covers and picked up Tom's t-shirt he'd worn to bed the night before, slipped it over her head and strolled down the hall.

"Good morning, sexy." The gleam in Tom's eye sent a tingle racing straight to Andy's center, warming her as it went.

"Hi there. Is there more coffee?"

"Sure is. Just finished brewing a couple minutes ago," he said as he blew across the top of his own mug. He watched her advance. As she neared him, he reached out and slipped an arm around her waist, and pulled her down on his lap.

"I love it when you do that," Andy murmured, resting her head on his shoulder.

"I love doing it. You look so sexy in my shirt, walking toward me, that bed head hair sticking up all crazy like that..."

She turned her face into his neck and couldn't help smiling before she planted a kiss at the crook, where his neck and shoulder met.

"Bed head. The real me." Her arm snaked around his shoulders as she scooted so she could see the newspaper, too. "What's happening in the huge metropolis of Aspen Grove today?"

"Not much, so far. I've only made it as far as the front page."

They perused the paper together, sharing the same cup of coffee. She would rather share his than to get up off his lap and get her own. From the feel of things, he was happy to let her.

Andy was caught up in an article about a new fashion boutique opening downtown when Tom pointed to the obituaries. "Honey, isn't this the psychiatrist you said was in your flashback?" Tom read it aloud to her. "*One found dead, apparent suicide. Christopher Phillips, 45, was found dead at 5:45 pm Sunday afternoon by detectives upon their arrival at his home. Dr. Phillips was a person of interest in an ongoing investigation. Cause of death was a self-inflicted gunshot wound to the head. Officers heard the shot through the closed door after identifying themselves, police sources say. There were no signs of foul play. The family has said that services will be held on Thursday at Scoffield's Funeral Home in Aspen Grove, followed by a graveside memorial.*"

Her heartbeat quickened. "Yes, that's him." She turned to look at him. "Do you think he killed himself because he hit me, or because he got caught?"

Tom saw the emotions as they scrolled behind her eyes: confusion, fear, realization, knowledge, and finally...was that pleasure? "Well, I would guess it was because he got caught. It's been weeks since he hit you, and he just now decided to off himself? That doesn't sound like a man who felt any remorse for his actions. Though if he is only now remembering what he did, and the full effect of his actions came down on him all at once, then it may be that what he did has caused him to commit suicide. We'll never know."

Sadness settled in behind her eyes. "No, you're right, we'll never know for sure. Whatever the cause, karma came full circle once again."

Karma. You are a cruel bitch, aren't you? Though it's not your fault, its people and their actions that put you in motion.

EPILOGUE

This has to mean something. Why would there be a stop here? The coding is brilliant. There has to be a reason. What information would be a variable and have to be inserted each time the program ran? What purpose would it serve?

Jerry paced the length of the unfinished basement. A corner underneath one of the windows was set up with all his computer equipment. This is where he worked when he tele-commuted to his job in the City two days each week, and where he played his online games on the weekends.

Red hair stuck up at odd angles all over his head where he'd run his fingers through it and tugged as he tried to decipher the meaning of the program. He hadn't been to sleep in two days, not since he'd heard that the flash drive had been important enough for someone to come looking for it.

He was working with the copy he'd made after his grandmother found it and tucked it in the abalone shell on the shelf with the rest of the miscellaneous flotsam she'd brought home from her walks: Seashells, even though Oklahoma was landlocked; plastic toys from kids' meals; a pair of reading glasses; even a disposable camera. That one had been in the bowl for two years or better.

If only he could figure out what was supposed to be keyed in when the prompt came up. He'd tried number combinations, addresses, even random words. Nothing made any difference. Jerry was almost to the point of posting a question on the forum to ask for ideas. Surely someone would know what else he could try.

"Jerald, dinner's ready," her voice carried down the stairs.

"I'll be right up, Grandma," he responded automatically.

The light bulb above his head clicked on.

A name.

He hadn't tried inserting a name. What if...

The chair squeaked in protest as he landed his full weight in it and advanced through the program to the prompt with a few short clicks.

Insert name...whose name.

The neighbor's yappy Chihuahua sounded off. Jerry typed in his neighbor's name. The program accepted his entry and scrolled quickly across the screen. Within seconds, his email program opened, with an attachment titled, "Boomerang.wmv." The cursor was blinking in the TO field, prompting him for another entry. Apparently he'd needed to insert a name. Okay. He cracked his knuckles, then hovered his fingertips above the keyboard. *Another name.* He thought for a second, then two, before his fingers flew across the keys. His own name appeared in the box.

Nothing happened.

Shit. Not a name.

The blank was filled in, the program had attached itself to an email, and now he needed to send the file somewhere. *It won't let me send it to myself. Why?*

Leaning back in the chair, he clasped his hands on top of his head and stared at the ceiling. *Maybe it knows this is my computer. There's no other reason. Won't send it to the address from which it's being sent. Stranger things have happened; I never would have thought to put a failsafe in like that, but that has to be what it is. So, if no one else knows I have a copy of whatever this is, who should I send it to? Who can I trust to tell me what it says, or what it does?*

"Jerry, get your ass up here, we can't eat until everyone's at the table."

"Coming, don't get your panties in a bunch."

The smile crossed his face wide and large. Terry. He entered the email and clicked send.

They were twins. They shared everything.

####

About the Author

Lindy Spencer currently lives in Oklahoma with Amazing Husband and Super Smart Dog. She has been killing people legally since 2012, and doesn't see it stopping any time soon. When she's not writing she's probably reading, riding motorcycles, or shooting things with a Canon.

Her other works can be found in print as well as e-book at most fine retailers, and include:

The Boomerang Effect

Between the Devil and the Darkness

There are more stories in the works, so stay tuned.

Lindy likes to keep in touch with her fans, and can be found on Facebook: www.facebook.com/LindySpencer.Author as well as Twitter: @_Lindy_Spencer ~ or feel free to send her an email: Lindy@LindySpencer.com. She would love to hear from you.

32144005R00144

Made in the USA
Charleston, SC
09 August 2014